Bunco Couture

The Slater Ibáñez Books

That First Heady Burn
True Vermilion
The Dark Shill
A Stack of Sawbucks
The Hillside Roble
The Peroxide Pomp
The Incidental Twin
Brawl in Bardo
The Window-Shade Job
The Convenient Patsy
The Artisanal Grifter
Shrink in the Shadows
Project Chartreuse
From a Desert Playa
The Tired Canary
A Desperate Frame-up
Trail of the Blue Agave
The Saucer-Heads
The Satin Squeeze Play
Chiseler in Jade
The Eagle and the Weasel
The Mojave Gimmick
The Hapless Gonif
Secondhand Inertia
Bunco Couture

Subscribe to the Slater
Ibáñez Books newsletter:

slaternews.dagmarmiura.com

Bunco Couture

Bunco Couture

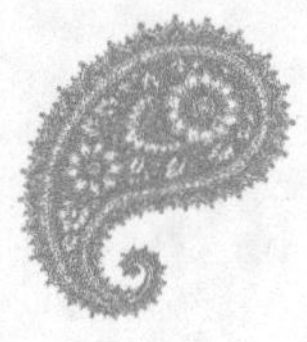

George Bixley

DAGMAR MIURA

LOS ANGELES

Published by Dagmar Miura
Los Angeles
www.dagmarmiura.com

Bunco Couture

First published 2026

ISBN: 979-8-89195-073-3

ONE

WHY WAS IT ALWAYS fricking night? It seemed to be dark whenever he was out here. Slater was walking a long block of retail stores, their graffiti-marred steel shutters uniformly rolled down, the neighborhood dead quiet. He'd been at a meeting at a late-night diner, in the Fashion District in Downtown LA, and he was headed back to his office.

The pavement was still damp from the rain, and he altered his gait to step over a puddle on the concrete. It would take a lot more water than this to get things anywhere close to clean, but at least the rain temporarily mellowed things out, took the edge off the acrid stench of the piss-stained sidewalks.

From behind him he heard the sound of paws moving fast on the concrete. As he turned he spotted the dog rapidly approaching. A gray pittie with a white chest. It jumped at him, nearly to chest height, deftly not making contact with him but coming awfully close, in the same moment emitting a high-pitched yelp. Slater flinched, but he knew it wasn't aggression. He knew this dog. This was a greeting.

"Rocky," he said, dropping to his knees. "How you doing, buddy?"

As Slater slapped his back and scratched his ears, Rocky waggled his whole body with delight. He briefly squatted, then jumped on Slater, who tumbled back on his butt. He had to laugh as Rocky licked his face. The pup was heavy, a solid mass of muscle.

He quickly stepped off him again. Back on his knees, he scratched Rocky's head, then batted him around. In the periphery he saw someone step toward them. A burly guy in a dark suit. Built thick, he looked like the guys who worked security at nightclubs. His demeanor was mostly indifferent, with the sleaze showing through the thin veneer of the suit, even in the dim illumination of the streetlights.

"Step away from the dog, amigo."

Slater heard it all the time, the assumption that he was an immigrant, a newcomer, because he had his father's dark Latin coloring, his black hair.

"I'm not your amigo, fool. And don't tell me what to do." Still slap-petting Rocky, he glanced up at the guy. "Why are you wearing sunglasses? It's fricking nighttime."

Leaning in, the guy put a hand under his arm and hauled him to his feet. Slater hadn't expected that, but he reacted fast, and managed to throw a right and punch the guy in the flank. With the impact of the blow Pike's chunky class ring bit into his finger. The guy was strong, and twisted Slater's arm, making him swivel away. They scuffled for a second, but the guy managed to overpower him, and grab his other arm, and held them both firmly behind his back.

Slater was breathing hard, and considered trying to flip

the guy, backing into him fast and throwing him over his head. But he was heavy, so that was risky. He could easily dislocate his own shoulder.

A woman's sharp voice came from behind them: "Knock it off."

The guy instantly shoved him away and stepped back. Slater turned and glared at him, and rolled his shoulders, then looked toward the voice. The woman was stepping toward them. Somebody else was with her, hanging back a few paces. The one who spoke had gravity, her presence demanding attention. He knew this woman. Not personally, but everyone knew her, whether they wanted to or not. She was a major pop star. This was Artémise.

Her look tonight was distinctive, as it always was, whenever he'd seen images of her—her hair in a tidy Afro, pink-tinted glasses, and a dark-blue suede suit. The jacket's fur collar was blue too, and looked bulky and loose, like a boa.

"Why is my dog so interested in you?" Artémise said.

Slater massaged his finger where the ring had bit him. At least it hadn't broken the skin. He needed to remember to turn it around when he had to throw hands.

"Why is your stumblebum bodyguard trying to manhandle me?"

Artémise made a languorous wave, and the guard growled and stepped away, a few yards up the block, toward a white SUV with dark tinted windows that was parked at the curb. He folded his hands over his crotch and stood there. He was probably scowling at him, but Slater couldn't see his eyes behind the sunglasses.

"I asked you a question," Artémise said.

Slater reached down to scratch the dog's head. "Rocky and I have met before. I took him to that lesbian dog rescue outfit."

"Seriously? No one there knew anything about his history. You and I need to talk."

"I'm sure you're used to people just dropping everything to do your bidding, but I've got stuff to do."

"So do I. Can I call you? We can talk when you have some free time."

He took a breath. She wasn't actually being unreasonable. That alone was disorienting.

"Why not?" He dug in his hip pocket and handed over his business card.

Not looking at it, she held it out to the side. The person who'd been hanging back took a step and grabbed it. A woman, Slater decided, with short hair, a little pudgy, wearing a dark jacket. She was half a head shorter than Artémise.

"What's your name?" Artémise said.

"Slater. The rest of it is on the card."

"Good night, Slater." She turned and walked toward the SUV, her assistant close at her side.

It was another couple of blocks to his office building. He didn't need to go in, and instead crossed the street to the surface lot. It seemed odd this late at night to see other cars here besides his beautiful 1970s Continental, but people lived around here now, in loft conversions, and there were theaters and nightclubs. His ride was never hard to find, as it was bigger than all the others, bigger than most vehicles on the road. Parked along the fence, it waited patiently for him, soft cloudy blue in the muted streetlights, the landau roof and the distinctive semicircle of the trunk glistening with myriad water droplets.

On the drive to his house it showered again, and he turned on the wipers. It never rained in summer, but here it was, falling out of the sky, the Southwest monsoon or maybe the remnants of tropical storms in the Pacific.

He pulled up to his house and waited for the garage door to roll up. It was an obnoxious modern box in an old neighborhood, built by some idiot gentrifiers. The garage and an ADU were at street level, with bedrooms on the floor above, and on the top floor a kitchen and lounge space and a deck.

His little black '99 Frontier was parked on the street, and he looked over at it as he pulled up, making sure it hadn't been molested. That had been a recent acquisition, and it was handy for hauling stuff around, but he didn't really need two cars. It had to sit out here as there was no room for it in the garage. Once the door rolled up, he nosed inside, next to Pike's bulky old SUV. It made his heart pound just to see his vehicle, just to think about the guy.

The house was quiet, and upstairs he saw Pike was in bed, the room dark. The guy had been out of town over the weekend. He worked for the feds, and was always tight-lipped about the details. The most he would say was that the trip had been to do interviews, but most likely he was out there knocking heads together.

Upstairs in the kitchen he pulled the fifth of bourbon from the cupboard, and poured his ration into a tumbler, then walked over to the French doors, looking out at the glittering city. At this hour and at this distance, glistening wet right after a shower, it actually looked halfway decent.

Slurping at the heady elixir, he relished the vapor in his nose, the burn in his throat. Thinking about Rocky, he had to chuckle. That dog had been so happy to see him.

He slammed the contents of the glass and headed downstairs, and got undressed in the dark, then climbed into bed. Pike turned over, and embraced him, and kissed his neck.

"You smell like bourbon."

"That's weird. I'm not really a big drinker."

Pike chuckled and squeezed his cock. "Are you sober enough for this?"

"Always. Are you awake enough for this?"

"It's been days."

Slater met his mouth, and got lost in it. He reached between Pike's legs, and pressed a thumb into him, then grabbed the lube. Shifting closer, grasping his hot skin, he penetrated him, leaning in to mouth his jaw and his ears, pressing his nose into Pike's hair. Pounding him for a minute, he came, straining into him, then pulled back.

In the low light he found Pike's cock, already hard, and went down on him. Pike moaned and thrust into him and quickly climaxed.

Slater flopped onto his back, and Pike shoved an arm under his neck, still breathing hard.

"Full service," Pike said.

"You're full service," he mumbled, already sinking toward sleep. "You're everything. Look in the damn mirror."

TWO

SUNLIGHT WAS IN THE windows when Slater woke. It was a workday, and Pike was already gone. He lay there for a while, gradually coming up to consciousness. Hopefully there'd be coffee. He knew how to work the machine, but Pike was better at that kind of thing, and he usually left some in the pot for him.

Maybe it was about morning. He needed the java to get rolling, but he couldn't bring himself to make the java before he got rolling. He should probably face up to the fact that he was never going to be a morning person.

On the bedside table his phone buzzed, and he grabbed it. There was a number displayed but no name with it. Picking up, he said, "Ibáñez."

"Iphigenia Stone. She or they."

"What?" Slater said. "Is that your name?"

"I'm Artémise's assistant. People call me Gene. Can you come to the house this morning?"

"Right." He rubbed his eyes. "That depends. Where's the house?"

"Does that matter? I'm calling for Artémise." She said the name slowly, like he might have missed the significance of it. "She wants to meet with you personally. I don't understand what the problem is."

"You don't have to feel bad. Lots of people are stupid."

"Do you not have a car?" she demanded.

"I'm not driving two hours out to Thousand-fucking-Oaks for a meeting when I know she comes into the city."

"The house is in town. In the hills above Sunset Plaza."

"That's not really in town," he said, "but I guess it's not too obnoxious. Text me the address."

Once he'd ended the call, he forced himself out of bed, and washed up, and pulled on a clean pair of jeans. He'd been rolling around on the grimy wet sidewalk with Rocky in the ones he'd been wearing yesterday.

Upstairs he found coffee in the pot. The heating element had timed out, but he was happy to have it, even tepid. It was better than the powdered cowboy coffee he used to make in the BP time, the era before Pike.

Trotting down the stairs to the garage, he climbed in the Continental and backed into the street. The Frontier was still parked out front. So far it hadn't been jacked or vandalized. It was scratched and dented and old enough that it didn't really look valuable enough to mess with.

Across the street he saw one of the neighbors, Tilly, standing in her yard. She waved at him, and stood there like she thought he might stop and chat. Shifting into Drive, he raised a hand to wave at her as he rolled down the block. Talking to her seemed beyond pointless. Neighbors were Pike's department anyway.

The freeway was sluggish on the way to Hollywood, and once he exited he headed west, a long slog through crowded neighborhoods. Eventually he turned off the boulevard onto the winding hillside streets, and soon pulled up to the gate at the address Gene had sent him. He'd barely stopped when the gate cracked open and swung inward. Gene had asked for his plate number, but there was no guardhouse in sight. Maybe somebody was watching the gate camera remotely. More likely it was all automated, and a plate reader had recognized his tag.

Rolling up the driveway, he saw that the house looked big even for the hills. It was an old neighborhood but this was a modern slab, sleek and white. They hadn't been building them this way for more than a decade or two.

At the side of the gravel courtyard several vehicles sat next to the boxy garage—an aging sedan with a dented door, a maroon pickup with a heavy gear box in back, a Prius with streaks from the rain in its coating of dust. These belonged to people with low incomes, the maids and drivers and gardeners, not the pop star.

Slater parked next to the pickup and climbed out. As he approached the front of the house, Gene stepped out the door, wearing a tweed jacket and jeans. He hadn't got a good look at her on the street last night, but her hair was short, and dark red, and slicked back, her pasty complexion a riot of freckles.

"You're Gene," Slater said.

She flashed a smile. "We almost met last night. I love that car."

"So do I. Is it she or they? You mentioned both."

"Most people find the traditional she more manageable. Come in."

Gene followed him inside, and paused to close the front door. The foyer was at least two stories high, and tiled in white, with a massive chandelier, lit up even though broad daylight streamed in the windows onto the courtyard. At one side was an open room, the carpet and sprawling sofas all in white. Inside was a kid with wild hair, kneeling on the carpet and working at a low table. There were more big windows here. The place got great light.

"Artémise has kids?" Slater said.

She frowned. "Do you live under a rock?"

The kid called to them. "Hey—come here."

Gene stepped into the room. "What is it, sweetheart?"

Following her, Slater saw that there were two of them, sitting adjacent at the table, its surface scattered with an array of felt-tip pens and wax crayons. They couldn't be older than six or eight.

"Where's Nadège?" Gene said.

"She said she had a phone call from nature," the younger kid said, then eyed Slater. "Are you the gardener?"

"Something like that."

He pointed to the other kid. "She says this is the wrong green."

The girl looked up. "It is wrong."

"What are you drawing?" Slater said.

"It's a palm tree." He pointed to it on the table.

As he stepped closer, Slater saw that they weren't using paper, instead drawing directly on the white tabletop.

"There's lots of kinds of palm trees," he said. "Usually the leaves are more yellow-green. Some plants are blue-green, but not palms."

The younger kid held up a big box of wax crayons. "We have all the colors."

"Hey, smoke 'em if you've got 'em," Slater said.

The boy shook the box at him. "Can you find it in here?"

Taking the box, he picked a couple of crayons. "These are pretty close." He handed them to the kid, then waggled a third one. "Use this one for evergreens."

"What are those?" he said.

"Trees that don't lose their leaves. Like Christmas trees."

The older kid eyed him. "We don't do Christmas."

Slater frowned. "Neither do I, but that doesn't mean it doesn't exist in this world."

"We should go," Gene said.

"Keep it real, kids," he said, and followed her into the foyer. "Does the nanny know they're not using paper? They're trashing that table."

Gene waved dismissively. "It's a borrowed house."

She led him through to the backyard, a big space with a pool and patio furniture. At one side was an expanse of grass bounded by a tall hedge and broken up by a couple of citrus trees. Perfectly uniform, the turf had no patches or distortions anywhere, no sign of weeds.

"Is that real grass?" he said.

"It's not plastic, if that's what you mean."

"The things you can do when you have money."

Rocky was out here, he saw, as the beast tore over to him, and greeted him with another leap. Slater chased him over onto the grass, and dropped to his knees. The sod felt damp, instantly soaking through the denim. It took a lot of water to make it this lush.

He slap-petted Rocky, then shoved him sideways. Rocky barked with joy, and jumped up on him. Slater let himself be pushed onto his back and laughed.

"You don't know your own strength, buddy."

Planting his paws on Slater's chest, Rocky loomed over him, tongue lolling.

"Oh, so you're the boss now?" Slater said. "Are you the boss of me?"

Rocky jumped off, and sat for a moment, then spun in a circle.

From the house he saw Artémise was walking over, wearing threadbare jeans and a knitted top in colorful stripes. He got to his feet.

"You got your knees wet," Artémise said.

"It doesn't matter."

"You're good with him."

"I'm surprised he remembers me. I haven't seen him for a while." Slater waved at the yard. "Does he have regular access to this?"

"Whenever he wants."

"Dogs need the space and the greenery."

"He's got plenty of both."

Rocky sat nearby, watching them, happily panting.

"Watch this," Artémise said, and turned to Rocky. As she started to sing, Rocky jumped up, and barked several times, and zoomed to the end of the yard, paws tearing into the turf, then ran back to them.

> Oh, you beautiful dog
> You great big beautiful dog
> Let me put my arms around you
> I could never live without you.

Slater glanced at Rocky's antics but mostly watched her sing. This was it, the reason people paid thousands of dollars to sit in a stadium and watch her perform—her voice, the power and perfection in it. She made it look completely effortless, like she was idly talking about the traffic. He was being given a glimpse of something rare and pure, he realized. Her exceptional talent.

He didn't need to be a sycophant, and undoubtedly she got plenty of that, but when she finished, he couldn't help himself. "That voice."

Artémise chuckled. "Come and sit."

She walked over to the patio furniture, closer to the

pool, and sat at the table. Gene pointed him to one of the chairs on the opposite side. Did it really matter where he sat? Giving her the once-over, he wondered how much Gene got paid to micromanage things like this. As he dropped into the chair, Gene took the one between them.

Rocky had a hunk of something in his mouth now, maybe rawhide, and he flopped onto the concrete near Artémise's chair to chew on it.

"Try one of these." Artémise gestured to a quartet of tall narrow drink cans on the table. "They're new."

Picking one up, he studied the yellow label. It had Artémise's name on it, then a string of Chinese characters, and under that it said MOON CAKE.

"You're selling these?"

"It's part of my food services line."

"I've heard about the vegan stuff you do." Slater popped the tab, and took a sip. It was unsweetened soda water. At first it just tasted like soda, but then a subtle flavor emerged, weird and cloying, and lingered on his palate. He set the can down.

"What does it remind you of?" Artémise said.

Slater furrowed his brow. "Something you'd get at a Chinese restaurant. Not in Chinatown, but way out in San Gabriel somewhere. In a strip mall. The kind of place where the menu has pictures but it isn't translated. It tastes like something you pointed at on the back page, with the desserts. But you had no idea what to expect."

Artémise beamed. "I'm glad."

Grasping the can, he shifted in his seat. He hadn't meant it as a compliment, but he didn't need to point that out.

"So tell me what you know about Rocky."

Once he'd slurped more of the weird water, he got into it. The whole story was brief. He'd only hung out with the dog for a day. Artémise sat absorbing it all, and asked him some questions. Eventually she leaned back and gestured to Gene.

Rising, Gene walked into the house.

"Rocky definitely remembers that you helped him out," Artémise said.

"I'm glad he has grass here, and space to run around."

When Gene returned, she had a thin brown briefcase in hand, and sat again.

"We looked into you, and your business," Artémise said.

He frowned. "Why would you do that?"

"It's standard procedure," Gene said. "We need to know who we're dealing with."

"I'm not one of your vendors." Slater raised his voice. "You asked me to come here, remember?"

"There's no need to get upset." Artémise raised her eyebrows. "It's actually kismet. I know what you do, and I have a gig for you."

He took a breath. "What do you want me to do?"

"Something has been stolen from me."

"Before we talk about that," Gene said, "You have to sign an NDA." She pulled a thick sheaf of paper from her briefcase and slid it toward him. Colorful sticky tabs lined the left side.

"I can talk about work, but I'm not going to sign anything," Slater said.

Gene flashed a palm. "I'm actually a lawyer, so I can assure you this is just a standard nondisclosure."

"And I can assure you it's still a hard no. I'm not going to get into any kind of legal entanglements with rich folks."

"That makes me think you'd sell the story to the first journalist who approached you," Gene said.

"You can think whatever you want. Have you ever been

on the receiving end of the justice system? Your privilege makes you blind to how things work at the bottom end."

Gene frowned. "I'm not privileged."

He scoffed. "You need to hire one of those guys with an office in Beverly. The burly type. Shaved head, wears a black suit day and night. They'll sign your NDA." Rising, he lifted the can he'd been drinking from.

"You can't take that," Gene said. "It's not on the market yet."

"Fuck me dead," he muttered, and set it down, then walked into the house.

A tall woman with myriad dreads bundled around her head was with the kids now. The nanny. Nadège, he remembered. She met his gaze and nodded as he walked to the front door. Both kids were jumping on one of the sofas now, shouting unintelligibly, and she was just standing there.

It took him a minute to figure out the door handle. It had to be twisted upward instead of down. Why was rich-people stuff so damn complicated?

"Idiots," he muttered, and strode out to the courtyard, and climbed in the Continental.

THREE

⌐¬⌐¬⌐¬⌐¬⌐¬⌐¬⌐¬⌐¬⌐¬⌐¬

THE NAVIGATION APP TOLD Slater to go west. That felt counterintuitive, as Downtown was in the opposite direction, but the 405 must be faster than the slow crawl through Hollywood. Even on the freeways it took almost an hour to get to the Fashion District, and he finally nosed into the surface lot across from his office.

The century-old building was mostly clothing factories, with the exception of his office. When he walked into the lobby, the day laborers had cleared out, everybody already having secured their gigs for the day, leaving just a few solicitations on sticky notes on the wall.

Slater rode the elevator up, and walked around to his office, admiring their names on the door:

SLATER IBÁÑEZ

MAXIMILLIAN CONROY

INVESTIGATIONS

Twisting his key in the deadbolt, he pushed inside and flicked on the lights. They had three small offices, one for him and one for Max, and between them the front office with a desk for their operatives. As he stepped inside he greeted Rey Pascual, a little plaster statue that sat on the front desk, a skeleton holding a scythe and wearing a crown.

Slater poked his head into Max's office to make sure no one was here, then went over and sat at his desk, and stared at the stack of mail he needed to go through.

He could have used the work from the pop star. The meeting he'd been at last night was about a window-shade job, and he'd blown the guy off, told him to call Max. Slater hated those jobs, surveilling cheating spouses, but Max thrived on them.

Before he could steel himself to dig into the mail, he heard keys in the front door, and Etta's familiar voice called a greeting. An operative who worked for him and Max sometimes, she stepped into his office doorway. Curvy, her black hair was butched short, and today she was wearing a blue baseball shirt and jeans.

Slater sat back. "Why aren't you in school? It's a weekday."

"You know it's July, right? There's no school." She waved an arm. "Dude, you're on, like, three different celebrity sighting sites."

"The fuck are you talking about?"

"You seriously haven't seen it?" Etta pulled her phone out of her pants. "I'll text you a link."

Digging out his own phone, he looked at her text. It was a link to a site with a photo of him from last night, on the dark street, handing his business card to Artémise. Rocky and the bodyguard and the assistant had been cropped out.

"Rats," he muttered.

Etta stepped behind his shoulder and pointed to the

screen. "Your butt looks great in profile when you stand like that."

"There's not much I can do about it. I can't really switch it off." He zoomed in on his face.

"I'd call that expression dubious," Etta said.

"I was more than dubious. Her bodyguard basically assaulted me."

"I can't believe you were out there hustling Artémise. I also can't believe she was in this neighborhood."

"It was about Rocky. He came to say hello. Artémise followed him."

"And you gave her your card. How cool is that?"

"She asked me for it," Slater said. "She wanted the rundown on how I knew Rocky."

Etta gestured at the screen. "Swipe through. You're in a couple of others."

He growled and swiped at the screen. The next photo was of him on his knees on the wet concrete, the steel shutter of a shop in the background, embracing the dog. He had a stupid expression on his face, his mouth agape.

"Damn it. I look like a moron."

"It balances out the first photo. In that one you're serving up dick swagger. Here you just look happy to see Rocky. He looks very happy to see you."

He swiped to the next photo. This was a wider shot. Slater was standing up, looking past the dog. Rocky was looking up at him, tongue lolling, intently focused on Slater. At least there were no photos of the scuffle with the bodyguard.

"I hate pictures of myself."

Etta stepped back around the desk. "Rocky knows you saved him. I'm glad Artémise got to meet you."

"She wanted to hire me for a research gig, but we couldn't come to terms."

"That sucks." She frowned. "I love Artémise. I'd work for her for free."

She went out to the front office and sat at the desk. Nobody else really used it, and Etta liked to hang around the place. She was learning the trade from them both and helped Max with paperwork sometimes.

Slater was halfway through his mail when his phone buzzed. It was the same number from this morning—Gene.

"Artémise feels like we got off on the wrong foot," Gene said when he picked up. "Can we meet?"

"There's no point. I'm not signing an NDA."

"Are you at your office? I can be there in a few minutes. I'm already in Downtown."

"How do you know where my office is?"

"It's on your business card, genius."

"Fine," he said flatly. "I'm around."

A while later he heard a knock at the door, and the sound of Etta flipping the bolt and pulling it open.

"Can I help you?" she said.

Gene's voice replied. "Are you Slater's assistant?"

"In a way," Etta said. "I can be whatever you want me to be."

He had to suppress a grin as he stepped into the front office. Etta had game. She must think Gene was hot.

"Come in." He waved her into his office.

"I'm on my way out," Etta called, and he heard her bolt the door from outside as he sat behind his desk. Gene took the guest chair opposite and picked up the other office tchotchke from its post next to his computer monitor.

"Who's this?"

It was a statue of a naked guy standing with a horse, and before he could answer, she read the name engraved on the base.

"Pollux. It looks like a bookend. Where's the other one? There's another guy. His brother."

"Castor," Slater said. "He's on the boyfriend's desk."

"That's sweet." She set it down and gestured to the room. "I like the art deco vibe. It feels classic."

"That's all about Etta. She found the furniture and the light fixtures. You can ask her out if you're interested."

Gene frowned. "Good to know. Most of this building is sewing factories."

"I'm aware."

"We work with lots of people in the neighborhood. Artémise has a fashion line. It's very upscale."

"Of course it is. Like the moon pie water."

"It's sparkling water infused with the essence of moon cake."

"You think people are really going to buy that?"

"Artémise is huge in China."

"Of course she is." Slater gestured impatiently. "Why are you here?"

She shifted in the chair. "So, against my legal advice, Artémise wants to hire you without requiring an NDA."

"She's too busy to show up here herself? How long have you been stooging for her?"

"She'll connect with you at a later date. For now, she wants you to get started."

"Like I said this morning, one of those thug PI types from Beverly Hills might be a better fit."

"She wants you."

He threw up his hands. "Why me specifically?"

"I'm not exactly sure. Part of it might be because you can handle her. You don't seem blinded by her luminance."

"You mean I'm not a yes man." That was actually a good sign. Artémise was smart enough to see the value in not hiring a fan or a partisan.

"You also come recommended," Gene said.

"By who?"

"Artémise made some calls. I wasn't in on those conversations. I don't like to get caught up in the drama. I just follow the law."

"That's so quaint. And also far-fetched."

Gene frowned. "I was told you know how to keep your mouth shut, flat-heel."

Lifting her briefcase, she pulled out a stack of cash. Those were C-notes, and the dark-yellow currency band implied they were fresh from the bank. She set it on the desktop and slid it toward him.

Slater sat up and fanned through the rack. They were crisp new sequential bills.

"Did you make these yourself?"

"They're real. You know they are. Is that enough money to take the chip off your shoulder?"

He set the rack aside. "That works. I'll need the dope on what I'm supposed to be doing first. If I don't like it, you'll get this back."

"For now you're working for Artémise, day or night. Whatever she asks."

He tapped the rack with a finger. "You've got my attention for a week."

"We'll be in touch."

Gene rose and walked out. He heard her flip the deadbolt, and open the door, and close it again. Sitting up, he looked at the rack. That was a lot of scratch. It needed to go in the safe.

He swiveled to the squat black box in the corner behind his desk. As old as the building, it was bolted to the floor, and had faded gold-leaf lettering that said

MONTCLAIR SECURITY. Once he'd dialed in the combination, he twisted the handle and heaved open the door, then tossed the rack in.

Scrabbling around, he found the cash envelope. When he and Max started out it had held all the money they had between them. They still used it for accounting, even though it was getting tattered, with several new pages added over the years, cut to the size of the envelope and taped one on top of the next. He wrote the date on the top sheet, along with:

Slater +10G

He should take some of it, he realized, if he was about to get into a job, even though he didn't know what the hell it was about. It seemed sad to break the strap on the pristine rack Gene had given him, so he found a nonsequential bundle of cash in the safe, bound with a blue elastic band, and peeled off three grand, and added a withdrawal line to the accounting envelope.

Once he'd locked the safe again, he sat and thought it through. He could search for info on Artémise, but she was so well-known that everything out there would be marketing, and gossip, and bullshit. It wasn't even worth trying to pan out any rare nuggets of reality that might exist.

Sitting up, he pulled his keyboard close, and searched for "Oh, You Beautiful Dog." The search engine came back with, "Did you mean 'Oh, You Beautiful Doll'?" That was in fact what he meant, he saw, scanning the lyrics. This was what Artémise had been singing. She'd just altered it to be about Rocky.

The style was called ragtime, and the song was over a hundred years old, he soon learned. But Artémise had brought it to life, like a blossom that had just opened that morning, damp with dew. Like Aphrodite, born from sea foam on that scallop shell, a thing of beauty arising from nothing and stepping fully formed onto the beach in Crete.

He got lost reading more about ragtime, and was eventually pulled away from it when his phone buzzed. When he checked the screen the caller ID said REDDY KILOWATT. His heart started to pound.

"*Mi vida,*" he said as he picked up.

"So when exactly did you meet Artémise?" Pike said.

"Last night. I saw her again today. Why are you looking at trashy celebrity photos?"

"I wasn't—Brewster was. She showed me the images. At least they didn't use your name."

"I didn't actually know I was being photographed."

"Are you in Downtown? We could eat, and you could fill me in."

"I'm at my office," Slater said. "I can be done for the day."

"First I want to stop by the central library. Is there a place for grub near there?"

"That brewpub with the vegan food. I'll meet you there after your errand."

"It's not an errand," Pike said. "I want to show you something. Meet me at the Fifth Street entrance."

Once he'd ended the call he got up, and locked his computer, and went out to the front office.

"Good night, Rey," he said to the little statue as he flicked off the lights.

Across the street in the surface lot he climbed into the Continental and drove into the Financial District. The office drones were clearing out of the neighborhood for the evening, and he found a meter not far from the library.

Pike was standing on the sidewalk out front as he walked up. Dressed for the office in a collared shirt and chinos, he had his dark hair slicked back, and stood with his back to the wall, feet apart, absorbed in his phone. Such a beautiful man.

As he stepped up, Slater briefly grasped his head with both hands and kissed him. "You look like you're working security."

"If I were, I'd be watching the street, not staring at a screen."

"What are we doing here? I already know what books look like."

"I'll show you."

Pike beckoned him to follow, and once they were inside, led the way up a staircase. At the top he stopped and pointed out the statue that stood in a niche above the stairs. It was a woman, life-size, standing with a staff and holding a book, it's pages turned outward. On either side of her were two black art deco sphinxes, each holding a book in their paws.

"Have you seen this before?"

"I'm sure I have," Slater said. "I never really focused on it."

"It's Athena. The artist called it *Civilization*, but he modeled it on her."

"She does look familiar."

When he'd met Pike, the guy had been reading about Greek mythology, and they'd finished the book together. After that they'd moved on to other books on the same topic. He wasn't especially interested in the classics, but it had incidentally become their thing.

"It's a hundred years old," Pike said, and they stood looking it over.

"What does her book say?"

"I can't remember. You could look it up. I just wanted to see this because we've been reading about Athena."

Slater looked at Pike as he studied the statues. Even in profile he could see the light in his eyes. Stepping closer, he wrapped his arms around him for a moment and squeezed.

Pike laughed. "What's that for?"

"You make my life good," Slater said. "Showing me the value of stuff I've walked past a thousand times and never paid any attention to."

Heading down the stairs again, they walked a couple of blocks to the brewpub, and got a high-top table, and ordered smalls of draft and burgers. As the server stepped away, Pike met his gaze.

"So what happened last night?"

"That's how you interrogate your drug dealers and your gun runners," Slater said. "Open-ended questions and intent focus."

He laughed. "I guess it's a habit."

Slater got into it, telling him about meeting Rocky on the street.

"You said you saw Artémise again today?"

"She wanted to know how I knew her dog. After I told her about it, she offered me a job."

Pike paused as the server set down their beer glasses, and tapped his against Slater's. "What does she want you to do?"

"All I know is she said it was about a theft." He slurped at his beer. "I'm not sure I love the idea of helping the richest woman in the country keep more of her dough."

"It doesn't matter how wealthy she is. If someone stole from her, she has the same legal rights as anyone else. You went to her office?"

"Her house. In the hills just west of the Sunset Strip." Slater waved a hand. "It wasn't actually her house. Her assistant said it was borrowed. Her kids were trashing the furniture. The nanny was just standing there letting it happen."

"F. Scott Fitzgerald said the rich are different than you and me."

"This particular rich person is pretty self-involved. That's saying a lot, rolling around this town." Slater scoffed. "F. Scott Fitzgerald. Biggie Smalls said 'More money, more problems.'"

"Also pithy and germane," Pike said. "Just don't get moon-eyed. One way rich folks stay rich is paying for stuff with exposure."

"What does that mean?"

"Get the money up front. People assume she's rich so she'll be able to pay her bills later. But maybe she won't bother. People get star-struck and wind up comping stuff. Like how she said the house was borrowed, not rented."

"Etta said she'd work for her for free."

"Exactly my point," Pike said. "That's not right."

"Her lawyer already paid me a rack to come on board, even though I refused to sign an NDA."

His eyebrows shot up, and he sat back. "In cash? It sounds like you've already got it figured out. You don't need my advice."

"You're wrong." Slater leaned toward him, his tone intent. "I always want your input."

"I feel like I'm telling you stuff you already know."

"That doesn't matter." He threw up his hands. "I want to hear it because it's you. Everything you say is important. Anyone else I'd just punch in the face."

"That has the ring of truth." Pike watched him for a moment. "She gave you ten grand before she even laid out the job? What is it with you and money? It pools around you like water."

"I'm pretty sure I'm going to have to bust my ass for it."

They'd just started into their burgers when his phone buzzed. Checking the screen, he saw that it was Gene. He picked up.

"Can you meet this evening to discuss the work?" Gene said.

"I've got ten thousand reasons to say yes."

"Are you still at your office? We can be there in half an hour. We'd like to pick you up in Artémise's car."

"Dealer's choice," Slater said. "I'm not far from there. I'll send you a pin. What are you driving?"

"A white SUV with tinted windows."

"Of course you are." He ended the call, and tapped at the phone to send her his location.

Pike gestured with his half-eaten burger. "It sounds like Artémise isn't really a nine-to-six type."

FOUR

AFTER THEY'D EATEN, OUT front on the sidewalk, Pike put his hands on his neck and leaned in to kiss him. As he pulled back, Slater looked behind him, up into the tree planted along the sidewalk.

"Something interesting up there?" Pike said.

"It's just a brush box tree. Not as unique as Athena and the sphinxes. But you don't see a lot of those around."

"It looks healthy."

"It's a scrappy little Aussie. They do well with air pollution, and they can fight off pests."

"I love that you love trees."

Slater squeezed his shoulders. "I love you, you big mook."

He cracked a smile. "Forever."

He watched him walk away, up the block, back toward where he'd parked. It wasn't swagger, exactly, but Pike was confident in the way he moved. Everything about him was pure gravy.

Slater didn't have to wait long. A white SUV slid up in the red zone, and the rear passenger door swung open as he approached. In the back, two rows of seats faced each other, like a club car on the train. Handling the door was the burly bodyguard, still wearing sunglasses. Sitting opposite were Gene, like the bodyguard dressed in black, and Artémise. She was wearing an olive-green outfit with an array of pockets, almost like coveralls but tighter fitting, and the pink-tinted glasses.

Slater climbed in and sat next to him, facing Gene, and once the guy closed the door, the vehicle pulled into the street.

"You always have people around you," Slater said, eyeing Artémise. "Doesn't that get tedious?"

She raised her eyebrows behind the pink lenses. "I don't really know any other way to do things."

The bodyguard folded his arms, his brow furrowed. Slater eyed him sidelong.

"Are you still upset that I rinsed you?"

He scoffed. "That never happened."

"I could make it up to you, toots, but you'd have to ditch that suit."

"Are you hitting on him?" Gene demanded.

"I thought that was obvious." He gestured to the guy. "I'm not getting any warmth here. If you need to keep the suit on, I guess I could smoke you."

The bodyguard turned to face him. "That's not going to happen."

"When a man is tired of blow jobs," Slater said, "He's tired of life."

"What is wrong with you?" Gene demanded.

Her implication was that he'd crossed some line, or offended the boss, but Artémise just laughed and looked out the window.

The vehicle soon turned onto a street in the Fashion

District, just a few blocks from his office, and pulled to the curb in front of a couple of stores. The one with the sign that said FRANCESCA'S FASTENERS had its solid steel shutter firmly closed, and the one next to it, the one they'd parked in front of, had a grid shutter, with chrome bars you could see through. Above it the sign was printed in a curling script, like a wedding invitation:

A Touch of Class Textiles

In the window was a length of fabric, draped to hang vertically over an easel. Artémise leaned toward the side door.

"Can you see what's in the display window?"

"Not really." Slater reached over and popped the handle.

"Hold on," the bodyguard said, but Slater ignored him, and climbed out, and stood on the sidewalk. It wasn't raining but the concrete was wet from another fleeting shower.

From the vehicle the guard got out, and looked around, then held the door, leaning in to speak to Artémise. "The street is clear."

She joined Slater on the sidewalk, looking at the display window through the steel grid. It was less obnoxious than a solid steel shutter but looked just as secure. There were several fabrics in the window, all of them partially unrolled bolts, he saw now, artfully draped and dramatically spotlighted. The one in the middle, a paisley in muted browns and purples, was more prominent, placed in front of the others.

"That's my print," Artémise said, standing next to him. "The paisley. I designed it."

"I like that the pattern is kind of nonregular."

"It's not supposed to exist in the real world," she said, raising her voice. "Not yet. It's not supposed to be here."

She waved at it. "This was stolen from me. It hasn't been licensed to anyone, and suddenly here it is."

Slater pointed to the sign above. "A touch of piracy along with that touch of class. How long has it been in the window?"

"One of my design staff noticed it last week."

"It's on full display. They're being pretty tits-out about it."

Farther up the block someone was walking toward them. Artémise gestured to the limo.

"I can't deal with fans right now."

It didn't look like a fan, he thought. More like a fentanyl zombie, stooped over and with that characteristic uneven gait. The guy was so high he wouldn't recognize his own mother. But Slater followed her to the vehicle and climbed in, leaning ahead to see the display window. The fabric was actually beautiful.

"It's not designed with your initials or anything," he said.

Artémise frowned. "Why would it be?"

"You people are usually a lot more literal."

"What people?"

He gestured vaguely. "Show people. Celebrities."

"A lot of work went into that design," Gene said. "They can't just copy it."

Slater glanced at the pedestrian shuffling by. He was wearing a bulky backpack and holding a ratty umbrella over his head even though it had stopped raining.

"You have no idea who stole it from you?" he said.

"One of my people did a look book and sent it around," Artémise said. "It was digital, so there's no telling how many copies went out."

"Explain what a look book is."

"It's like a catalog of what the collection is going to look like. A few pages with drawings of garments and fabric swatches."

"That's not a solid explanation, though," Gene said. "The swatch was only a small part of the pattern, and that roll of fabric has the entire design."

He gestured to the window. "Did you talk to anybody in here?"

"I sent a lawyer to talk to the shop owner, and deliver a cease-and-desist," Artémise said. "He clammed up and won't tell me who's wholesaling it."

"He obviously wasn't intimidated by that, if the fabric is still on display."

"He knows it's not really worth a lawsuit. The toothpaste is out of the tube. It just pisses me off that I did all that work and someone can just take it."

"What do you want me to do?" Slater said.

"I want to know who did this," she said, "so that maybe I can spank them. Do you think you could learn anything that a lawyer can't?"

Slater nodded. "I know how to buttonhole the saps and make them squeal."

"I don't need the unsavory details. But let's see how it goes."

"I'll need access to your design people."

"I have a studio near here. You'll have full run of the place."

They dropped him back at the library, and Slater climbed in the Continental and drove to his house. Upstairs he walked through the kitchen and the big empty room toward the French doors and the lounge furniture. Pike was sprawled on the sofa with a book, and when Slater appeared, he set it on the coffee table.

"So what was she wearing?"

Furrowing his brow, he thought about it. "It was dark green. Like military green. Lots of pockets. It looked like a flight suit." He waved an arm. "What are you wearing?"

Pike chuckled and sat up. "Not couture."

Dropping onto the sofa, Slater pulled off his boots, setting them on the lush faux grass. Instead of a rug Pike had put a swatch of turf on the floor under the coffee table. It didn't have the cool dampness of living grass, but apart from that it looked and felt real underfoot. He leaned back against Pike, and Pike wrapped his arms around him.

"What was her ask?"

Slater told him about the limo ride, and Gene and the bodyguard, and the fabric in the shop window.

"Is the place near your office?"

"Just a couple blocks." He reached for the other book on the coffee table, the one they'd been reading together. "You should read to me. All about Athena."

"We finished the part about her." Pike took the book and found the page. "Next is Hades."

"Who's that idiot?"

"He's no idiot. He's the god of the dead. Remember when they overthrew the Titans? Zeus took charge of the sky, Poseidon got the oceans, and Hades got the underworld."

"And who got the land?"

"I think they agreed to share it." Pike read from the book: "Worshipers of Hades brought offerings that were completely burned, and always at night. Offerings to Zeus and the Olympian gods were food and drink, meant to share in a festive atmosphere, but offerings to the underworld gods were smoke and ash. By destroying the offerings, people were acknowledging the gap between mortal life and the underworld. They didn't want companionship with Hades. Instead they were asking for release from his anger."

Slater would need to take his snort later, and he knew the bourbon was waiting patiently for him in the kitchen cabinet. But for now this felt good, this comfort, the warmth of Pike's body, being lulled by his words. Listening to his rich voice, he started to drift off.

FIVE

S LATER WOKE TO SUNLIGHT streaming in the sheers. It looked hot out. The monsoon rain must have moved back to Arizona where it belonged. Upstairs he found lukewarm coffee in the pot, and he slammed a mugful of it, and ate some fruit, and half a bagel.

When he got down to the Continental, Pike's rig was gone. He looked over the Frontier, still parked on the street, as he waited for the garage door to roll down, then drove to Downtown and parked across from his office. Instead of heading upstairs, he walked a couple of blocks to an office building similar to his, full of clothing factories. This one was bigger, though, and a little newer, and a little cleaner. He rode up to the floor where Kawada Couture was.

The place hadn't changed, he saw, walking in. A guy with gray hair stood at the long cutting table, working a pair of scissors on pieces of fabric. He briefly glanced up as Slater went past and walked around to where the desks were.

Steve swiveled his chair toward him as he approached. He cracked a smile and leaned back. "Slater Ibáñez."

"Steve Kawada."

The guy was lanky, his hair in a sharp cut, with maybe a little more gray at the sides than the last time he'd seen him. He'd forgotten how handsome he was.

"It's been a minute."

"Where's Carolina?" Slater said, pronouncing it the Spanish way, "kar-oh-*lee*-na."

"In New York, wrangling some clients." Steve grinned. "We're together now. Romantically, I mean."

"I told you she was the one for you."

"You actually said that?"

"You're welcome. I'm just glad you never went back to that grifter in true vermilion."

His expression sobered. "You helped me a lot back then. It seems like a bad dream now." He gestured to Slater's left hand. "You got married?"

"Not quite." He rubbed the gold band with the tip of his thumb. "I got embroiled in a multidimensional narrative complex."

Steve laughed. "What does that mean, exactly?"

"It's like a romance, but it's more than that. Happening on more levels." He swiveled his index finger around. "Extending in directions you can't point."

"That sounds intense. What's he like?"

"He's all gravy. He knows how to dance, and he cooks sometimes, and he reads books. He took me to the library. I do stupid things, and he's well aware that I'm no damn good, but he sticks around anyway." Slater threw up his hands. "He makes me a better man."

"That's what it's all about."

"Is it? I was thinking it was freaking weird." He shifted on his feet. "Do you have a minute to talk? I want to get some background on your industry."

He gestured to the chair at the adjacent desk. "Sit down."

This was Carolina's, he remembered, as he spun it around and sat.

"I thought fashion couldn't be copyrighted. Am I wrong?"

Steve nodded. "Lots of stuff can't be copyrighted. The cut and the look of a garment. But it's not considered a problem. Designers borrow heavily from each other. No one resents it because it's expected, and everyone benefits."

"How does that benefit anyone?"

"Well, a designer will make small changes to someone else's design, like playing a riff on it. So different iterations of new ideas appear. It makes fashion dynamic, not monolithic and static like industries that have solid copyrights."

"What industries?"

"That cartoon mouse hasn't changed for a hundred years," Steve said. "It's so valuable that they keep getting the feds to extend the copyright law just for that specific rodent. They plan to milk it for all eternity."

"What about fabric designs?"

"You mean prints. Those can be copyrighted, the same way a drawing or a photograph can. Some designers use them like signatures, and put them on everything."

"Like the ones with the initials."

"There you go."

"How do you source fabrics?" Slater said.

"You've seen fabric stores in the neighborhood. Lots of those are wholesalers. There's a dozen or more nearby."

"What if you designed your own print?"

"You'd hire a manufacturer. Most fabrics are produced in East Asia and Southeast Asia."

"The manufacturers have offices here?"

"Right. They market to businesses like mine. There's actually a fabric trade show coming up this weekend."

"That's good intel," Slater said, and stood up.

Steve rose with him. "How is that T-bird running?"

"Sadly the Thunderbird has left this world. I wrecked it."

His brow furrowed. "I'm sorry to hear that. It was fun to drive. What are you driving now?"

"A '73 Continental. They were built on the same chassis as the Thunderbird."

"Nice."

On the ride down to the lobby, Slater dug out his phone and checked the address Gene had sent for Artémise's design office. She'd said it was in this neighborhood, and when he looked at the map, he saw that he could walk there faster than looking for parking.

When he came up to the design office, the sign above the door read CONSOLIDATED in sleek chrome-plated letters. Had some junkie pulled down the rest of the name to sell it for scrap metal, or was it intended to be deliberately obtuse? A smaller sign next to the door said RING BELL.

When he pressed the button, the door buzzed open, and he pulled on it and stepped inside. It was a big space, with a high ceiling, redbrick walls, and a cutting table farther back. Beyond it were some desks, and small offices lined both sides. A guy dressed in black stepped in front of him. Half a head taller and built thick, he had a shield screen-printed in white on his polo shirt.

"Slow down," he said.

Slater scowled at him. "I have a meeting, Stretch."

"That's not how it works."

"Step aside."

As he moved to walk around him, the guard put a hand on his shoulder. Slater shoved the guy off, then threw a punch, landing it squarely on his chest. The guard didn't even blink as he grabbed Slater's wrist. He tried to twist out of his grip, and threw his other fist, connecting with his jaw. The guy yelped and shoved him away. Slater stumbled a few steps but managed to keep his balance.

"Idiot," he said through his teeth, glaring at the guy.

A woman was here now, he saw, curvy and wearing a dark skirt, a pile of dreads tied at the back of her head.

"Is your name Ibáñez?" she said.

"Might be."

She eyed the guard. "He's expected."

The guy turned away, ignoring the murder in Slater's eyes.

The woman waved for him to follow, and led him to the side of the space. Like the other offices, hers had a glass wall facing the main room, its vertical blinds open. She left the door ajar and waved him to a chair, then went behind the desk. Slater sat opposite and massaged his wrist where the goon had grabbed him.

"Why are men like that?" she said.

"It's nothing to do with me. Your ape is the one out there selling wolf tickets."

She sighed. "I'm Athena. I'm head of production for the clothing line."

Slater narrowed his eyes. "You're the third person in Artémise's orbit named after a classical Greek."

"Is that meaningful?"

"That's the point. I'm not sure."

It was definitely a coincidence that he and Pike had just been looking at Athena in the library. A while back, Doris's loopy friend Hugo had talked up meaningful coincidences. He'd called them synchronicities, and as much as Slater had wanted to dismiss it as the ravings of a burnout, paying attention to the idea had led him to actionable real-world information in the past.

"Who are the others?" Athena said.

"Artémise is obviously a version of Artemis, and her lawyer-gofer introduced herself as Iphigenia."

"You mean Gene."

"Gene is the short form. I'm not sure who Iphigenia was. Not a headliner like Artemis and Athena. But she comes up in antiquity."

"I'd say it's just a coincidence." Athena raised her eyebrows. "I've had this handle since I was born. Long before I met Artémise."

"Artemis was the hunter," Slater said, "but Athena took care of the city."

"That's not quite as important as the hunter."

"Athena was a badass. Skilled at strategic thinking, and she knew how to fight. Unlike the blockhead on your front door."

"Moving on." She waved a hand. "I usually ask people coming on board if they remember the first time they heard Artémise's music."

"I'm not really coming on board. I'm more like an outside contractor."

"The question stands."

He held her gaze. "I'm not sure I've ever heard her music."

Her brow furrowed, and she shifted in her chair. Of course he'd heard it. Everyone had, whether they wanted to or not. But he wanted to gauge her reaction. At first blush this whole thing had sounded like an inside job, and Athena was right here on the inside.

"You're looking into the paisley," she said.

"Tell me what happened with it."

"The design was created here, in house."

"Did you have it manufactured?"

"It's only ever been digital."

"Who had access to it?"

"Anyone in this building," she said. "There are nine of us with server access. Malcolm created the design file. I can introduce you to him."

"There was a look book."

"That came out six weeks ago. We spotted the pirated fabric last week. That would be a very tight turnaround for fabric production."

"So you don't think the look book was the source?"

"The look book contained a swatch that had only part of the design. The fabric in the window has the whole design."

"Is it possible some AI software could have expanded the swatch to replicate the whole thing?"

She smiled. "I'm the wrong person to ask about that."

"Who put the look book together?"

"Lenore." She sat up. "She's here today if you want to talk to her."

It felt like Athena was eager to pass the buck, but Slater stood up anyway. "Lead on."

Outside her office, they walked past the cutting table. It was like the one in Steve Kawada's factory, and like the ones he'd seen in other clothing factories, but something was off. This one was pristine, he realized, looking it over. Nothing was piled on it, there were no scratches from blades, no pencil marks, no scuffs or dents. Nothing was taped to the walls or hanging on racks either, like he'd seen in clothing factories. The whole place looked upscale, the furniture and the carpet, more a showplace than a factory. The cutting table was part of that—a prop, not something for actual production.

He followed Athena to Lenore's desk, in the middle

of the open room, near a couple of other desks. Lenore sat back as Athena introduced them. She was slight, with heavy blue eyeshadow, and wore her hair in an Afro, like Artémise. But it looked wilder than the pop star's, like she spent less time on it.

Athena tapped the back of the chair next to Lenore's desk. "Have a seat," she said, and walked away.

Lenore waited until he sat down. "You're looking into the bolt of fabric in that window."

"Did you get a look at it?"

"Just through the glass. It's terrible."

"The quality of it?"

"The colors are all washed out. It looks cheap." She huffed. "The weird thing is that the pattern is really good. Technically it's very close to the original."

"Is it identical? Could someone have extrapolated the larger pattern from what was in the look book?"

"I want to say no." Lenore bit her lip. "But generative software is evolving fast. I can't say that's impossible."

"You assembled the look book."

"That's right."

"Who did you send it to?"

"It wasn't printed. Only digital. We have email lists of buyers."

"How many people are on those lists?"

"Maybe two hundred," she said, "but the document wasn't copy-protected, so there's no reason a recipient couldn't forward it to someone else."

"Did you ask them not to?"

"We don't do that. Setting it free helps build our marketing. If journalists get hold of it, they treat it like a 'leak.'" She waggled her fingers to put air quotes around the word. "I know people beyond our list have seen it because I've had media queries about some of the designs."

"From journalists?"

"A couple of the fashion magazines, and from some influencers. Once the look book is out in the world, there's no way to know how far it will spread."

"Can I see it?"

Lenore swiveled to her computer, and Slater dug a business card out of his hip pocket, and set it on her desk. Glancing at it, she tapped at her keyboard, and a moment later he felt his phone buzz. He dug it out to scroll through the document.

Each page had a sketch of a garment with a fabric swatch or two, along with a brief description. He zoomed in on the text. It had prices listed. The tops were four and five hundred, the dresses six to eight.

"Are these retail prices?" Slater said.

"Wholesale. Full retail is usually two hundred twenty percent of those numbers."

He looked up at her. "People are going to pay fifteen hundred clams for a minidress?"

"Not lots of people. But there's definitely a market."

Slater held her gaze. "How do you think the design got from this room to that bolt of fabric in the window?"

"All I can say is I'm almost certain it wasn't from the look book."

"You need to send me the list of your recipients. You've got my email."

"I'll check with Athena," she said, and glanced at his card on the desk.

"Do whatever you need to do, but if I don't see that list, we're going to have a problem." He stood up. "Where's Malcolm?"

Lenore frowned and pointed to an office at the side of

the space. Slater walked over and stepped inside. Malcolm was parked behind his desk, and swiveled toward him as he walked in.

Slight, he had short dark hair, and a pencil mustache. It was too sparse to really butch him up, if that was the intent. But the guy was basically fuckable. Malcolm's eyes flicked over him, and he furrowed his brow.

"You're Rocky's friend."

Slater scoffed. "The boss hired me to find out how that fabric design got out of this building."

"Sit down." As he took the chair in front of his desk, Malcolm said, "You're talking about the paisley."

"You created the design?"

"All of the Artémise collection is the vision of Artémise."

"You can spare me the bullshit, babe."

He frowned. "What?"

"That's marketing talk," Slater said. "I'm working for her, same as you, with full confidentiality. Tell me the damn truth."

Malcolm nodded. "I created the paisley design."

"All of it? The shapes, the colors?"

"It's all mine."

"You draw by hand, or on a computer?"

"I use a drafting program. It's not really drawing. It's done in vectors, so it's scalable and repeatable."

"Have you seen the knockoff?"

"We've all walked over to look in that display window," Malcolm said.

"How close is it to what you created?"

"The colors are off, but the pattern is pretty close."

"Could some generative AI have filled in the rest of it from the swatch in the look book?"

"I don't know that much about AI. The images the

software generates are based on all the images that have been fed into it, so I want to say no, my work is so original that nothing like it has ever existed before. But I guess it's possible."

"Was it ever in physical form?" Slater said. "Printouts or fabric samples?"

"Nobody did anything like that. It's just a digital image."

"So how did it get from here into that display window?"

He spread his palms. "Search me. Maybe the generative thing you said. I hadn't even thought of that."

Watching him talk, Slater couldn't decide whether he was obfuscating or just not very bright. "Can you share an image of the pattern? Whatever will show up on my phone."

Malcolm turned to his computer, and tapped at the keyboard. "I'll send a vector file. It should render on your device. It's the best way to maintain the correct colors."

He could see the paisley pattern on Malcolm's screen, darker and richer than the bolt in the window. "Paisley's fun."

"It is fun," he said, still focused on the monitor. "I was reading about it. It's an ancient design. Based on almonds. One of the colors I used is almond. It's a warm creamy shade. With the royal purple and the brown-black, it looks like a Cabernet Chew. Remember those?"

"That's some fashion thing?"

Malcolm turned toward him. "There was a candy bar called a Cabernet Chew. It had grape fruit leather and almonds and dark chocolate. I wanted to use that name for the pattern, but one of the lawyers said somebody else owns it as a trademark, even though you can't buy a Cabernet Chew anymore. Somebody's just sitting on the name. I guess corporate America thinks it might be able to squeeze some more cash out of it one day."

"Artémise wasn't willing to buy the name?"

"Not for something like this. She also said candy would cheapen her brand. You know she does the gourmet vegan catering. It's not the kind of thing you can buy from the snack rack at the liquor store." Malcolm raised his eyebrows. "What's your number?"

He dug out a business card and handed it over. Glancing at it, Malcolm pecked at his keyboard. Slater's phone buzzed in his pants, and he pulled it out, and tapped at the screen.

"That worked," he said, studying the image.

"Show me."

Rising, he held the phone toward Malcolm.

"That's an accurate color rendition."

"Do you have a card?"

Malcolm rolled open a desk drawer and handed it across the desk.

Sliding it into his pocket with his phone, Slater walked out.

At the front door, the guard was sitting at his desk, glaring at him from under his heavy furrowed brow, his lip curled in disgust.

"Spread out," Slater said through his teeth, and jabbed a finger at him as he pushed out the door.

A S SLATER WALKED BACK toward his office, he pulled out his phone and texted Andy:

I'm on my way over.

When he got to the surface lot across from his building, he climbed into the Continental, and saw Andy's reply:

I'm not home. At that burger bar on Sixth.

Slater knew the place, not far away, and drove over, pulling in at a meter on the same block. When he walked into the place it felt quiet, with just a couple of people at the bar. Parked at a table, Andy sat with his back to the wall. His tousled brown hair was a perfect mess, and he always wore a few days' stubble, today with a black T-shirt. He had a half-eaten burger in hand.

His sticks were propped next to him against the wall. Sometimes Andy rode his mobility scooter, but this place was walkable, only a couple of blocks from his loft. As Slater sat across from him, he set his burger down and flashed a smile. Bright orange sauce was smeared across his mug. His lack of fine motor control meant eating looked like pure chaos, but he managed to get himself fed. Andy mopped his face with a napkin as he finished his mouthful.

"Great photos of you and Artémise's dog."

Slater folded his arms. "Why does everybody look at trashy photos of celebrities? It makes no sense."

"Kyle noticed them."

"Of course he did, that little toothache."

"Kyle said, 'If Ibáñez dealt with … people the way he's connecting with that dog, he could … almost pass for human.'"

"Just what I need: psychoanalysis from that affluent zombie."

The server came over, and Slater met her gaze. "Just a soda water."

"She can slip some bourbon into it," Andy said as she stepped away. "You don't have to … behave on my account."

"Where is Kyle, anyway? Is his eye already wandering? Staying late at work? Unexplained charges on his credit cards?"

He picked up his burger. "Man, knock it off."

"That's not what you said when you had your dick down my throat," Slater said. "Just say the word and his luck can run out. His Bentley could have a little mechanical malfunction. I'll make sure it looks like an accident."

His soda water arrived, in a highball glass with a lime wedge on the rim.

"Why would you think he … drives a Bentley?" Andy said, his mouth half full.

"Doesn't he? He seems like the type."

"What do you need, Ibáñez?"

"It's work. That's all I fricking do."

"At least you get to bone that … primo snack you've got at home."

"I have to bone somebody, since you and that gunsel cut off my sex supply."

"What do you need me to do?"

Slater pulled out Malcolm's business card and slid it toward him. "Look into this guy. I also need you to look into a retail outfit in the neighborhood. It's called A Touch of Class."

"Text me all the names."

Pulling the card back, he snapped a photo of it, and texted it to him. In a second message he thumb-typed the name of the shop and the street it was on.

Andy waved at the server, and when she stepped over, handed her a credit card. "I'll get his drink too, unless you want to … comp it. He's my designated driver."

"You've got chutzpah, I'll give you that," Slater said, once she'd walked away. "You're not even drinking."

"What's the ask on these targets?"

"I just need to know if they're crooks or civilians. Plus whatever else you can figure out."

"I'll see what I can do," he said. "Do you want to give me a lift?"

Once Andy had his card back, they got up, and he took a minute to get his arms into the cuffs of his walking sticks. Like a lot of what he did, superficially it looked chaotic, but eventually he had them attached, with a solid grip on the handles. They made their way to the door, and Slater held it open for him.

As he stepped out, Andy eyed him. "Try to keep up."

He had to chuckle. The guy had no trouble with the smack talk.

Once he'd dropped Andy, he parked at his office, and hustled across the street in a break in the traffic. Upstairs he flicked on the lights and double-clicked his tongue to greet Rey Pascual. Etta turned him to face the front door when she wasn't here, so Rey could surveil the comings and goings with his empty eye sockets.

There was someone else he could talk to, he remembered, before he even sat down, and stepped out again, and locked the door, and walked down the hall.

Cassidy's door was propped open, revealing a much larger suite than his. Inside were a couple of desks, rolling racks hung with garments, bolts of fabric propped in a corner, and a long cutting table. A couple of sewing mannequins mounted on stands stood by the windows. They were in the shape of female bodies, in different sizes, made of coarse material the color of sisal.

This was a manufacturing space, a lot smaller than Artémise's studio, but it wasn't for show. The cutting table was scuffed and scratched and marked up like work actually happened on it. Manila cardstock clothing patterns were clipped in bundles and hung on hooks, and farther along drawings on onionskin were taped to the wallboard.

The place got great light from the big multipane windows along one wall, unlike the lone window in his own office, behind Max's desk, with a meager view of the adjoining building. Cassidy had the bottom row propped open for the cross-breeze. It actually felt good, despite the constant rumble of the streets and the crummy air quality in Downtown.

Standing behind her desk, Cassidy was Westside thin, probably still in her thirties, her coiffed blond hair to her shoulders. Today she was wearing dark pants and an olive-green shirt open a few buttons. As she pulled her bag onto her shoulder, she smiled in recognition and greeted him.

"You're leaving," Slater said.

"I'm going to an art show. For my side hustle as an interior decorator. I'm acquiring art for a client."

"I won't hold you up. When you get a minute I want to ask some questions about the industry."

"Come with me," she said. "I won't be there long. We can get a drink after."

Slater put his hands on his hips. "I'm on dick, sister."

Her eyes narrowed. "I'm aware. I'm not hitting on you. Not everything is about sex."

About that, she was misinformed. But he didn't need to point it out. "Want me to drive?"

"It's walking distance."

They went down to the street, and Cassidy pointed the way.

"So do you wear those vintage suits?" she said, walking abreast.

A while back she'd taken him and Max upstairs to a cache of menswear dead stock that she'd found. It all dated from the 1970s and was mostly in mint condition. They'd both bought a lot of clothes that day.

"More often than I thought I would," he said. "They kind of amplify my presence. That's useful in some situations. Max wears the shirts all the time."

She laughed. "I'm glad."

The gallery was a storefront at street level. It felt like this was the fringes of the Fashion District, but not quite the Arts District, with a fabric store on one side and an unsigned graffiti-marked building on the other. The front of the gallery had full glass windows, like a retailer, and he could see there were a lot of people inside. The door was propped open, and they stepped in.

"There's an open bar," Cassidy said. "That always pulls a crowd."

"I'll hit the bar. You can do your art thing. What do you want to drink?"

"Whatever they're serving. There won't be a choice."

As he joined the end of the bar line, he looked around at the walls. There were dozens of paintings of clowns, large and small, mounted close together. They were in different styles, some with bright and vibrant colors, some dark and moody. Some looked old, with ornate frames, and others were simple unframed mounted canvas.

Cassidy was talking to a guy in a sport jacket, he saw, her body language animated, punctuating her words. By the time he got to the bar he'd lost sight of her.

"Just the red wine?" Slater said.

The bartender nodded. "Or bottled water."

"Two of the red."

Once the guy had poured, Slater carried the plastic cups deeper into the gallery, navigating among the bodies. Most people were focused on conversations rather than the clowns on the walls. Cassidy was on her own now, studying a painting, her head cocked. Slater handed her a glass and tapped it with his own.

"Some of these are so simple I could pound them out in my garage in half an hour," he said.

"But you didn't," she said. "That's the key."

Slater slurped at the wine. It was acrid and acidic. "How is that the key?"

"Execution doesn't matter anymore. Only the idea."

He glanced around the gallery. "That fits with what I'm seeing here. It's quantity over anything else."

"Hey," Cassidy called. She was looking past him. "I know her," she said, and stepped away.

Slater watched her approach the woman, and greet her, and chat. Slurping the rotgut, he turned to study another piece. It looked like an oil, a sad clown with faux teardrops painted on his cheeks, a downturned mouth, giving the viewer the side-eye.

A guy stepped up beside him, looking at the painting. "It's intense, isn't it?"

He had great Latin hair, Slater saw, looking him over. Wearing a dress shirt and dark pants, he was a bit paunchy, and had a great butt. Totally fuckable, he decided.

"I don't think I understand it," Slater said.

"You mean the artist's intention?"

"I mean, why would anyone want this on their wall?"

He chuckled. "It's not my taste either. You'd have to pay me to take this. Even then, I'd take it straight to the dumpster."

Slater sipped at his glass. "When you make an offering to the god of the underworld, you burn stuff. So the actual offering is smoke and ash. Have you got a lighter on you?"

"I wish. You might have to buy it first. Who's the god of the underworld?"

"In classical Greece his name is Hades."

Cassidy stepped up to them and greeted the guy by name. "It seems like Slater is entertaining you."

"I shouldn't be laughing," he said. "It's serious business. We were plotting an offering to Hades."

"I won't ask."

As they chatted for a minute, Slater looked over the crowd. The conversations seemed to be getting louder, probably fueled by the wine. Eventually the guy stepped back, and nodded to him, and walked away.

"We can go," Cassidy said.

Slater slammed the rest of his wine. "You're not buying any clowns?"

"They make my retinas ache." As they walked toward the door, She leaned in and lowered her voice. "I'll buy up the leftovers once the show closes. They'll be in a negotiating mood then."

He set his empty glass on the front desk and followed her out onto the street. Cassidy pushed her hair back and took a breath.

"There's a bar up here a ways. I feel like I need a real drink after that."

"You seem to know people in the art world," Slater said.

"It's mostly people from the neighborhood."

Walking into the place, they sat at the bar. When the bartender stepped over, Cassidy leaned toward him.

"A small of whatever light ale you've got on tap."

"Same for me," Slater said, and set a twenty on the bar. He eyed Cassidy. "Why are you working as a decorator? The clothing line doesn't take all your time?"

"It's not as lucrative since fashion has sped up."

"What sped up?"

"The cycles of trends. It's because everyone can see anything anywhere on their screens in real time. Some legacy lines still do seasonal collections, but I can't do that anymore. Trends come and go so quickly that it's impossible for any one thing to really catch on and become ubiquitous."

"Is that a positive development?" Slater said. "It sounds like fashion has been liberated from trends."

She waited as the bartender set down their glasses and whisked away the twenty. Tapping her glass on Slater's, she took a sip.

"It's also been liberated from profitability. Magazines aren't the arbiters anymore, so we have to try to get attention online. Usually that means buying advertising. I thought about doing couture, but I'm not ready to deal with rich idiots."

"Couture means expensive clothes?" Slater said.

"In the industry couture means anything that's made to measure. So you have to deal with the person who's going to wear it. Measuring them, and multiple return visits, and uh-oh, they put on five pounds between fittings, and that's my fault because the clothes fit wrong. Nope, nope, nope."

"People are idiots."

"Not all of them," Cassidy said, "but rich people are usually entitled."

"What's your line if it's not couture?"

"It's called ready-to-wear, or prêt-à-porter, which is just French for the same thing. Consumers usually call it off-the-rack clothing."

Slater slurped at his beer. "Have you ever run into a vendor called A Touch of Class Textiles?"

"I know who they are. An acquaintance of mine was going to sue them. I'm not sure if he ever did."

"What acquaintance?"

"The designer Irving Irving."

"You say that like I'd know who that is."

She chuckled. "You should know who that is. Men's underwear and swimwear. It's extremely glamorous stuff."

"Why was he going to sue them?"

"A Touch of Class was selling swimwear with nearly identical designs."

"I thought designs couldn't be copyrighted."

"It was about the timing. Usually a knockoff takes time to produce, so it's a while before it can detract from the original. These came out at almost the same time. It was odd."

"Irving thought they'd stolen it?"

"There was no other explanation," Cassidy said. "No way was it a coincidence. They had versions of half a dozen of his new designs in shoddy cheap fabrics. He wanted to file the lawsuit to uncover their sources, not to get compensation. The lawyers would have cost more than any damage award. I never heard if he pursued it."

After they'd finished the beer, they walked back to their office building, and Cassidy paused at the entrance.

"I'm going back upstairs."

"You really are grinding."

"Gotta pay the rent."

He waved, and crossed to the parking lot, and climbed into the Continental. At his house he nosed into the garage. Pike's ride was parked inside, but when he got upstairs there was no sign of him.

Slater pulled the bourbon bottle out of the cupboard and poured his ration into a tumbler. He took a satisfying slurp, then slammed the rest, eyeballing the empty glass, resentful that it was so quickly gone. Setting it in the sink, he walked over to the sofa, and sprawled out, and put on the radio, savoring the golden warmth spreading from his belly.

Sometime later Slater woke to find Pike next to him on the sofa. That beautiful smile. Pike climbed on top of him and mouthed his neck.

"I saw your rig," Slater murmured.

"I took a rideshare so I could drink. What is this music?"

"Public radio at night."

"It's giving me a flashback. Riding in the back of a taxi in Taipei. The drivers listened to stuff like this."

"What were you doing in Taipei?"

"That was my life before you crashed into it." Pike undid a couple of buttons on his shirt and mouthed his chest.

"Has the taxi music got you wound up?"

He pulled back and grabbed Slater's belt buckle. "Let me smoke you."

"Who's ever going to say no to that?"

He shifted position as Pike pulled out his junk and went down on him. As he worked him he quickly got hard. It didn't take long for him to climax, groaning and straining into him.

Breathing hard now, Slater pushed himself up off the sofa, and knelt in front of him, and shoved Pike's knees apart. He unzipped his fly and took him into his mouth. It took Pike a minute, but he came with a grunt, twitching, and ran a hand into his hair.

"I've been thinking about that all day," Pike said.

Slater moved back onto the sofa. "You went out with your colleagues?"

"Just a couple of them."

Pike squeezed the back of his neck, and Slater dipped his chin to savor the massage.

"I'm glad you came to me instead of fucking that deadbeat Davis."

"He's not that guy. Neither am I."

"Davis wants you so bad. He looks at you like you were a fresh burrito and he hadn't eaten in days."

"Shifting focus to reality," Pike said, sitting back, "What's up on the Artémise front?"

"I think I might have to go undercover in the schmatte trade."

"At least it's not bikers, or robbing trains. Do you know enough about it to fit in?"

"Not yet." Looking him over, he saw that Pike's eyes looked heavy. "You're going to fall asleep."

"Beer and Taiwanese folk music and a blow job. My evening is complete. It's time." Pike stood up. "Are you coming?"

Slater got to his feet. "I'm right behind you."

He followed him into the kitchen, and as Pike descended the stairs, he poured more bourbon, then walked out to the deck. The night air felt cool, and he stood looking out at the city, and slurped at the tumbler, savoring the heady burn.

Pike was right. He didn't know enough about the rag trade. Steve and Cassidy had given him glimpses into it, but he needed to get up to speed.

SEVEN

<hr>

"**N**O WIRE HANGERS! WHAT'S *wire hangers doing in this closet when I told you no wire hangers—ever!*"

Daylight streamed in the windows, and his head hurt. It was his phone, Slater realized, swimming up to full consciousness. The most annoying ringtone of them all. He scrabbled for it on the bedside table and picked up.

"What do you need, Doris?"

"One of my friends thought she recognized my handsome son in a paparazzi photo with Artémise. I told her that was definitely you."

"I was minding my own business. Her dog recognized me."

"How do you know Rocky?"

"How do you know the name of Artémise's dog?"

"It's common knowledge," she said.

"You're too smart to be following celebrities."

"Answer the question."

He sighed as audibly as he could. "I was in a boat, coming back from one of the Channel Islands, and I spotted this dog. He was just hanging out on this rock in the ocean. All alone. There was nobody around, no boats in sight, no debris. So I grabbed him and brought him to shore. I got Etta to take him to a lesbian dog rescue. Etta's the one who named him. Because I found him on the rocks. And he wound up with Artémise."

"What kind of boat?"

"A little runabout. I was on my own."

"That's such a strange story."

"It sounds like you don't believe me. Why would I make that up?"

"Of course I believe you," Doris said. "There's photographic evidence. The shot of Rocky looking at you with adoration."

"So you believe the dog, but not me? Stop reading celebrity gossip."

"When you're embroiled in it, sweetie, I have to."

Slater huffed. "I'm hanging up now."

"See you this evening."

"Why?"

"Pho. Pike and I set it up. Did he not tell you?"

"Nobody tells me anything. I don't know what you two are up to, but know that I am very suspicious."

"It's not always about you. It's about pho."

"Love you, mean it," he said, and ended the call.

His head was killing him, and he took deep breaths as he sat up. He'd overdone it on his second chapter last night. At least the room wasn't spinning.

He pushed himself out of bed and padded into the bathroom. Shaking some ibuprofen out of the bottle, he held them in his teeth, then stepped into the shower, and washed them down with hot water from the showerhead. His body shuddered with nausea. He wasn't sure if it was the drug hitting his belly, or gulping the tepid water, or just the katzenjammer.

Upstairs he found Pike out on the deck with his laptop, stretched out on a lounger.

"You're working remote today?"

Pike looked up. "You look a little haggard."

"You can just say rum-dumb. Kyle calls me the booze hag."

"Is it time for a twelve-step meeting? I'm sure we could find one today."

Slater scoffed. "You don't kick a man when he's down. Did you know Doris somehow shanghaied us into having dinner with her?"

"I mentioned it to you a few days ago."

"And I didn't say no?"

"I think your exact words were"—Pike waggled his finger to put it in air quotes—"'if we must.' I put it in the shared calendar. I thought you'd see it."

Frowning, he dug out his phone, and opened the calendar. "It's there. Dinner with Doris."

Pike laughed. "So are you convinced I'm not lying to you?"

"It's OK to keep your distance from her," he said, and tucked the phone away.

"I know. It's also OK to have dinner with your mother once in a while."

Slater knelt next to him, and leaned in, and savaged his neck. Tilting his head back, Pike ran a hand into his hair.

"I'm supposed to be working," he murmured.

"So am I. So quit assaulting me." Slater leaned closer, and squeezed his biceps, and mouthed his ear. "I'm going to fuck you up so bad."

When he pulled back, Pike was red-faced and grinning.

"I can't wait." As Slater walked inside, he called after him, "Drink water."

In the kitchen he ate a bagel and an apple, and slammed some java. It felt like he was moving in slow motion. His head was throbbing now. Why did he do this to himself?

Once he had some food in his belly he went down to his car and grabbed the parking pass for the lot at his office. He took it out to the street and climbed in the Frontier. It needed to be driven once in a while, and when his head hurt like this, a smaller vehicle felt easier to handle. Like it would fit better between the lines on the road.

It was hot out, even this early in the day, and he cranked up the fan. Firing up the engine, he listened to it run as it warmed up. He loved the peppy high-revving sound. Once he'd run the wipers over the grimy windshield, he shifted into gear, and drove to his office.

As he was crossing the street to his building, he spotted a guy on the sidewalk, dressed in jeans and a black shirt, a camera with a heavy lens slung around his neck. Lifting it, he aimed it at Slater. As he approached he could hear the shutter fluttering.

"What the fuck, man?" he demanded.

"I know you must have security inside," the guy said, lowering the camera. "The lighting is better on the street anyway."

Stepping up to him, Slater slapped him, hard and fast, a solid kovac. "Why do you make me do this to you?"

The paparazzo hadn't expected that, and stumbled back. "Knock it off."

"You want me to break you in half?" Slater demanded. "Is that what you want? Why do you make me hurt you?"

He trotted backward, quickly moving out of reach. The guy was nimble. It was probably an advantage in that job.

"That isn't how things work. If you want to be famous, you have to play the game."

"If I see you pointing that camera at me again," Slater said, "I'll break your fucking nose."

He wasn't looking through the viewfinder, holding the camera at his belly, but the lens was still aimed at him, and Slater could hear the shutter. Before he could go after him, the guy turned and quickly strode away.

The ibuprofen and the breakfast carbs were starting to take the edge off his headache, he decided, as he stepped into his office and flipped on the lights. Maybe they'd compensate for some of the damage he'd done with the bourbon.

At his desk he pulled his keyboard over and looked up Irving Irving, the designer Cassidy had talked about. His stuff was colorful, an array of briefs and boxers and swim trunks, and he had an office in the neighborhood. Next he looked up the fabric trade show Steve had mentioned. It looked big, with talks and seminars, and a long list of companies that were putting up displays. Scanning the list, the name of one of the exhibitors jumped out at him: A Touch of Class.

Eventually he got up, and locked the front door, and walked down to Cassidy's studio. Knocking on the open door, he stepped inside.

"Did I ever tell you I envy your windows?"

Cassidy was sitting at her desk. "You need natural light in this business."

He gestured to the sewing mannequins. "Do you only make two sizes?"

"Those are adjustable. I also try the smaller sizes on myself." Her brow furrowed. "You look a little rough."

"I might have a touch of the flu."

"You looked fine last night. What were you drinking?"

He gestured helplessly. "Just applejack."

"I didn't know that about you. Do you think you have a drinking problem?"

"I've got a people problem. I drink to make people bearable."

She sat back. "So what's up?"

"I feel like I'm taking a lot of your time," Slater said. "I can pay you."

"It depends on what you need."

"A primer on all this." He gestured to the tables and the racks.

She laughed. "Sit down. Why?"

He sank into the chair across the desk from her. "My job. I need to pose as a designer, or a fabric buyer, or something like that."

"You probably know lots about the industry just from being in the neighborhood."

Cassidy spent a minute explaining the basic structures of the business. She was right, that he knew a lot of it already—lots of the terminology, and what the jobs were in the factories and the showrooms.

"So the blue-collar types running the sewing machines and hauling garments seem like ordinary people," Slater said, "but lots of the white-collar types dress weird and have an attitude problem."

"They're trying to dress avant-garde, or at least fashionably. And it's not attitude. It's fear."

He frowned. "I never punched any of them."

"It's not about you. It's fear of not being up-to-date. Fear of not knowing what's trendy, and how things are changing. Did you go to school?"

"You mean after high school? I studied horticulture at community college."

"So you know about plants and landscaping," Cassidy said. "I'm thinking that doesn't really change. You can be confident that your knowledge will still be valid six months from now. But fashion is always in flux. If you're not paying attention, you could suddenly be on the outside. Uninformed and clueless."

"That actually presents a great tool."

"Right?" she said intently. "You can connect with people over evolving trends, and share the new knowledge."

He'd actually seen the opportunity to leverage the fear. If he could imply he knew something they didn't, he could use it to manipulate the saps, not connect with them. But he didn't need to tell her that.

"Have you worked with celebrities?" Slater said.

"A few. They expect free stuff. Their pitch is, 'I'll wear your top to a high-end restaurant, and your sales will jump.'"

"Does it really drive sales?"

"It's hard to say. It only works if there's a paparazzi photo and someone identifies the garment online. I've had better luck giving freebies to influencers, as long as they have a lot of followers. That's changing though. Lately they want free stuff plus cash, like paid advertising. It feels like the influence industry might be starting to implode."

Slater folded his arms. "I can see how things work, but I don't know enough about the fashion world. The trends, the names of the players. I'm not sure I can look and sound like I know what I'm doing."

"Wear the 1970s dead stock we found upstairs."

"You're the one who found it."

"Oh, those beautiful suits." She closed her eyes for a moment. "Any of the shirts will go with your jeans. A retro look is fashionable in the industry."

"I usually only wear those at night."

"You'll stand out," Cassidy said, "but in a good way. You'll look like you know what you're doing."

"What if I need to talk about trends and styles and designers?"

"Trends are easy now because things change so quickly. If you're tight-lipped, people will just assume you're protecting your knowledge."

"That's a good insight," Slater said. "What about designers? Whose names do I need to know?"

"You can own any conversation with one name." Cassidy raised her eyebrows. "Just say, 'There's Yves Saint Laurent, and then there's everything else.'"

"She's a designer?"

"He's a he, and he's *the* designer. He's actually dead now but his legacy endures."

"Got it." Slater sat up. "Can I pay you a consulting fee?"

"Maybe you can do a small job for me."

"Like what?"

"I've been seeing this boy. His name is Frank. He seems a little shady. Like you and Max."

He narrowed his eyes. "What kind of shady?"

"The details change, depending on who he's talking to."

"What kind of details?"

"Like what he does for a living," Cassidy said, "and where he works, and where he's from."

"The truth doesn't drift. Frank is definitely lying to you."

"Can you look him up in some database, and tell me if he's bad news?"

"Text me his name and whatever details you have about this sap. A date of birth is useful if you know it's for real. A photo too. Full face is best."

She dug out her phone. "I definitely have photos of him."

"Max can find out if he's got a record, and where he's been living the last ten years or so. He should be able to tell if he's been arrested, even if he wasn't charged."

"That would be amazing," Cassidy said, tapping at her screen. "Why can't you do it?"

"Max has better access to resources because he's a licensed PI. I'm not."

She met his gaze. "I didn't know that. I know you're not doing horticulture. So what are you?"

Slater rose. "Trouble, toots, if you ask around."

EIGHT

SLATER WALKED BACK TO his office and unlocked the door. Max was here now, he saw, parked behind his desk. He was a burly guy, his gut hanging over his belt, with mousy brown hair. At least his girlfriend made him keep it trimmed. Wearing that fugly brown suit, he was peering at his computer screen, his thick fingers poised on the keyboard.

"Do you have a minute?" Slater said, standing in his office doorway.

Max sat back and gestured to the guest chairs. "Sure."

"I love that you always make time for me." He sat in front of his desk. "And I hate that suit."

"I'm aware. Wait a couple days and I'll wear a different one."

"So I picked up a gig. I got hired by this pop singer."

"Artémise," Max said. "Etta sent me the photos of you with her dog. They're hilarious."

He told Max a little about the case. "Cassidy down the hall helped me out with some industry intel. To return the favor she wants me to look into some guy who's sniffing around."

"I bet there's a few. She's beautiful."

"Is she?" Slater said. "I can't really detect hotness in women."

Max guffawed. "That is such a lie. She's a knockout and you know it."

"Can you do a cursory background check on the block-head?" Digging out his phone, he found Cassidy's texts. One was a photo, with her posing with a guy with a busted nose and buzzed hair. She was dressed up, with heavier makeup than she'd been wearing today, and he was in a suit. They were standing on the street at night. Maybe they'd been clubbing. He forwarded the image to Max along with the details Cassidy had sent.

Turning back to his screen, Max pulled the keyboard close and tapped at it.

"Did you know Cassidy works as a decorator too?" Slater said. "She calls it a side hustle."

"That's a euphemism for a part-time job. It means she's not killing it in fashion."

"She implied nobody is unless you're a transnational corporation."

"So Frank isn't a real person," Max said, peering at his screen, "unless he's eighty-six and living in South Florida."

"It must be an alias."

"This is a clear photo of him. I'm going to run it through a facial-recognition service."

"What does that cost? I'll pay you for it."

"The business can pay for it," Max said. "Operating expenses. It falls under PR. Good relations with the neighbors."

"How long will it take?"

"I'm not sure." He looked back to his screen. "I guess no time at all. It's done already." He twisted the screen toward Slater. "This looks like the guy."

Rising, Slater leaned in to study the grid of photos. In some of them the guy had less mileage on him, and in some he had longer hair, but it was all the same face.

"That looks like Cassidy's snapshot," he said, pointing to one. "And that one looks like a mug shot."

"That's exactly what it is." Max twisted the screen back and clicked around.

He sank back into the chair. "What's his legal name?"

"Edward Brinsley Cramp."

"Ouch."

Max's brow furrowed. "Did he mention that he was on a retreat upstate? Five years."

"What for?"

"Burglary, armed robbery, elder abuse." He scanned the screen. "Some of it got knocked down on appeal. The guy is a frequent flyer in the judicial system. He's still on parole."

"Cassidy doesn't know any of that."

"So add liar to the list. She can definitely do better. I'll send you these."

"Great. Can you send them to the printer too?"

"You want me to walk them over there?"

"I might need to query her expertise again. Plus if we wait a day or two, it'll look like it was more work. A bigger favor."

"That's smart." Max met his gaze. "It's always that way with you. Working the angles. Like an OG con artist."

He scoffed. "Can you send the facial-recognition results as well? Just a screen grab is enough."

"Can do." He tapped at the keyboard, then sat back.

Slater heard the printer hum to life, and then the sound

of the front door, and a woman's voice call out a greeting.

Max sat up. "It's the most beautiful woman in the world."

Vanessa stepped into the office doorway. Somehow she managed to look elegant and collected even in the summer heat, even in this gritty neighborhood. Her hair was bundled up, and she was wearing linen capris with sandals, and a print top, a gold necklace glowing warm against her dark skin. Both Max and Slater stood up. It seemed old-fashioned, but it felt like Vanessa's vibe warranted it.

She greeted Slater with an air kiss. "I saw the photos of you with Artémise."

"I didn't even know I was on camera."

"When Artémise is around, there's always going to be a camera. So what's she like?"

"Well, there's always people with her," Slater said. "A bodyguard and a PA and a nanny. It feels kind of chaotic. She definitely didn't high-hat me. She's wealthy but it's not like people with old money, or Wall Street jack, or the Frisco tech bros."

"She's entertainment industry wealthy," Vanessa said.

"That fits." He pursed his lips to think about it. "You don't have to tell her anything twice. Does that make sense?"

"You're saying that she's not dumb. What are you doing for her? Is it about her music?" Vanessa flashed a palm. "I know I shouldn't ask. I'm sure she had you sign an NDA."

"That was the first thing that came up."

She gestured to Max. "There's video footage of this one escorting Lindy G into a courthouse, pushing through a crowd of fans and journalists, but he won't breathe a word about her, even to me."

"Is she that rapper who shot her boyfriend?" Slater said.

"She shot her manager," Max said. "Allegedly." He waved a hand. "The court case is ongoing."

Vanessa eyed Slater. "He sounds like he's on her defense team."

"It was just a babysitting job," Max said. "I don't really know anything about her."

"Babysitting?" Vanessa raised her eyebrows.

"It's what we call acting as a bodyguard for civilians in unfamiliar situations," Max said.

"You mean naive civilians. I don't think Lindy G fits that paradigm." She looked to Slater. "Are you buying this? You can spare me the male solidarity."

Slater shrugged. "I haven't heard any more about it than what he just said."

"Lindy G is no Artémise," Vanessa said. "Is it about her clothes? I love her fashion line. Simple and elegant. I'd love to talk to her about her inspirations. Us Black girls have to stick together."

"Well," Slater said, "in fashion, there's Yves Saint Laurent, and then there's everything else."

She gestured helplessly. "I mean …"

Watching her, Slater thought she might be about to challenge him. But she just added an emphatic *yes*.

Max frowned at him. "You've been wearing a lot of haute couture lately, Ibáñez?"

"Gay guys just know these things," Vanessa said.

Slater eyed Max. "I thought you two met at an haute couture show. When you bought that suit."

"We met at a coffee place," Max said. "I made fun of her silly twelve-dollar drink order."

"I bet you were wearing that suit."

"He actually buys me that same silly drink a few times a week," Vanessa said.

"That sounds shrewd." He met her gaze. "You know you're too good for him, right?"

Vanessa laughed. "Max is very good to me."

"He's right, though," Max said. "I know I'm a lucky man."

Once he'd said good-bye, Slater stepped out, and rode down to the street. On his phone he checked the address for Irving Irving's office. It was close enough that it would be faster to walk than to drive, even though he'd work up a sweat in the heat of the day.

The building was a ground-floor space with no windows, cleaner than the others on the block and free of graffiti. Irving's name was in raised white letters high above the entrance. The door was locked when he pulled on the handle, and he stepped back to look for a bell. A moment later the lock buzzed open, and he stepped inside.

Cassidy had told him that buyers traditionally saw clothes at third-party showrooms, but Irving must use this as his own showroom, as there were samples on display, lining both sides of the room. The headless gray mannequins had ripped abs and massive pecs, wearing Irving's colorful high-cut underwear and sleek swim trunks. The wood paneling, the lighting, the marble tile—everything about it was more upscale than any place he'd been in this neighborhood, even more bougie than Artémise's studio.

"Can I help you?"

A woman was sitting at the desk beyond the mannequins, her dark hair piled up in a messy bundle, and wearing glasses.

"I got distracted by the merch." Slater walked toward her desk. "I wanted to talk to Irving."

"Do you have an appointment?"

"I don't." He dug out a business card and set it on the desk. "He'll want to talk to me. It's about copyright infringement."

She frowned but rose and stepped through a doorway behind her desk.

Slater wandered back toward the mannequins. Even headless they were easy to look at. Not many real men were that well built. Digging out his handkerchief, he mopped the sweat off his brow and the back of his neck as he looked them over.

The door swung open and a man strode out, followed by the clerk. Slater recognized Irving from the photos of him online, although he was shorter than he expected, and quite a bit older now than the portrait on his web-site. Irving's hair was bleached blond, but he could pull it off, as the roots were mostly gray. He was wearing glasses with thick black frames. That was a familiar tactic among performers and fashion types. When you hit a certain age, glasses made you look younger. A charcoal-gray turtleneck and black pants completed his look.

Irving smiled at him. "You're lucky to find me here. I was in New York last week, and I might have to go back in a few days."

"I know the industry's bicoastal." Slater gestured to one of the mannequins. "Your work here is making me chubby."

He laughed. "I'm glad. You're researching copyright?"

"I'm researching A Touch of Class Textiles."

His eyebrows shot up. "I've had issues with them."

"I heard." He glanced at the clerk, sitting at the desk again. She was ignoring them but well within earshot. "Can I buy you a coffee?"

Irving pointedly looked him up and down. "The way those jeans fit, you can buy me anything you want."

"There's a java joint on the next block."

"We'll go to the French restaurant on the corner."

He knew the place. He'd eaten there with Max. It wasn't exactly a rug joint, but it was upscale. Following him out the front door, Slater matched his confident pace as he walked up the block.

Irving eyed him sidelong. "I like the look you're working. It's essential. Rootsy."

"You can just say gardener."

"It's more than that. When you're not in streetwear, which designers do you wear?"

"Well, there's so much going on these days. Things change so quickly. But at the core I'd say there's Yves Saint Laurent, and then there's everything else."

"Truer words have never been spoken."

When they stepped into the restaurant's little courtyard, the host greeted Irving by name and flashed a big smile. She led them to a table next to a wall covered in English ivy. Even though it wasn't a native, it wasn't a bad choice to separate a patio from the street, as it was evergreen, and it sucked up air pollution. You had to respect a plant that ate benzene and formaldehyde for breakfast.

"She treated you like an old friend," Slater said as they sat down. "You must come here a lot."

"I don't, but I tip obscenely well." Irving whipped his napkin into his lap. "Your card says you're an insurance investigator. What does that have to do with those thieves at A Touch of Class?"

"It's not about insurance. I'm working for someone they ripped off. Why do you call them thieves?"

Leaning toward him, Irving spoke intently. "They ripped me off too. What happened to your client?"

The server stepped over, and Irving looked up. "A cappuccino."

"Espresso for me," Slater said. "Better make it a double."

Once she'd gone, he eyed Irving. "I can't discuss an ongoing case. Can you tell me about A Touch of Class?"

"So you're gathering intel. I'm happy to talk about it, although it makes my blood boil." Irving scoffed. "When you have to call yourself classy, you're not. Like gentlemen's clubs. Gentlemen don't leer at naked women. Degenerate straight guys do."

"So what happened?"

"I had a collection coming out. New designs. At the same time, A Touch of Class launched the same garments in the same colors. They copied my work." He waved a hand. "Of course clothing styles can't be copyrighted."

"I know that."

"Getting my drawings turned into clothing takes months. By the time the garments are completed, I'm already on to the next thing."

"The next season."

"We used to call them seasons. Things change too quickly now. We just call them collections."

"And A Touch of Class copied your work quickly," Slater said.

Irving paused as their coffees arrived, and took a delicate sip. "It wasn't quick. It was simultaneous. That's why I wanted to sue them."

"Why didn't you?"

"The only reason to do that would be to force them to reveal how they acquired my designs. Lawyers call it the discovery process. My lawyer said that was a long shot. Who's going to preserve evidence of their thievery? In terms of winning the case, there was no proof they'd taken anything from me. In a courtroom it could plausibly be called a coincidence. I would have spent a lot of money on lawyers without learning anything." He raised his eyebrows. "With that kind of company, if they'd lost the case, they'd just go bankrupt and start up again with a new name. Win or lose, I'd achieve nothing."

Slater sipped at his java, watching the guy talk. "You're still the name-brand designer. Their stuff is always going to be the knockoff."

"Knockoffs come later," Irving said. "Like an echo. The simultaneous timing destroys my advantage. Cheapens my product."

"Did you ever talk to anyone at A Touch of Class?"

"I had my lawyer send a cease-and-desist. That's as far as it went."

Sitting up, Slater drained his cup, then dug out his wad of cash.

"I'll pay," Irving said.

"I said I'd buy. A small compensation for your time."

He waved dismissively. "It's one of the privileges of age, my boy."

Irving dropped two twenties on the table, and set his cup on them, and got up. The place wasn't cheap, Slater knew, but that was still a heavy tip.

Once they were out on the sidewalk, Irving said, "Where are you parked?"

"My office is a couple blocks that way."

"Then come back to my office with me. I have something for you."

It wasn't far, so he didn't bother to ask, and walked with him. When they stepped into the lobby there was no sign of the woman who'd been on the front desk.

"Give me a second," Irving said, and walked into the back.

A moment later he returned with a swatch of royal-blue fabric in hand, and gave it to Slater. They were underpants, he saw, folding them open. The fabric was soft, and the size looked right.

"Would you wear them?"

"They might be a little tight in front."

Irving laughed. "That sounds like swagger, but I like it. The fabric will stretch to accommodate whatever you're packing."

"I appreciate this." He folded them up again.

"I wish I could see them on."

"Why do you think that's not an option?" Slater said. "You haven't flirted with me at all. It's like you're leaving money on the table."

His eyebrows shot up. "You're interested in a man like me?"

"I'll smoke you, Irving, if that's what you want."

"Would you model the briefs for me?"

He pursed his lips for a moment. "For your eyeballs, not for any camera."

"Deal," Irving said. "And I'm going to smoke you."

He led him through the doorway into a hall. This side was built to be functional, with a concrete floor and basic white drywall instead of the tile and wood paneling. There were doors on both sides, and he could see a row of sewing machines in a big room at the end. Irving pushed open a door, and stepped into a small office, and closed it behind them, flipping the bolt. Leaning on the desk, he folded his arms, and raised his eyebrows.

Slater squatted to untie his boots, then held Irving's gaze when he stood erect, and unbuckled his belt, then popped his fly, and pulled off his jeans.

"The shirt too. I need the full effect."

Once he'd pulled it off, and ditched his skivvies, Slater stepped into the blue underpants and adjusted the crotch.

These actually fit really well, like they were custom-made for him. Couture, Cassidy called it.

Irving swirled a finger in the air. "Do a little twirl."

He spun slowly around, and when he was facing him again, flashed his palms.

"They look amazing on you. A few weeks in the gym and you could model them professionally."

"No thanks."

Irving chuckled. "We have to hire two types of models. Torso models and underwear models. The boys with the great glutes are never the same ones as the boys with the great pecs and abs."

"You're saying there's no perfect man."

"Come here."

Slater stepped close to him, and held his arms away from his body as Irving slid his hands into the waistband of the blue underpants and shoved them down. Dropping to his knees, Irving started to smoke him, and he quickly got hard.

He was skilled at it, and intuitive. Despite the katzenjammer Slater got there fast, and put a hand on Irving's head to stop him as he came, a shudder running through his body. The guy's hair felt taut, like it had been sprayed into place, a blond helmet.

Slater took a breath. "What do we do about you?"

Red-faced, Irving got to his feet. "That doesn't really happen anymore."

"Are you sure about that? It might be worth investing the time."

"You're very sweet. But it's a mechanical issue."

"Can I kiss you, at least?"

Irving dropped his chin. "I'd like that."

They spent a minute with their mouths locked together.

The guy was good at this too, and mouthed his jaw, and his ear. Eventually Irving gently pushed him back.

"You have to stop."

"Thanks for the info," Slater said, as he pulled on his pants. "And for the blow job."

He laughed. "I need to get back to work."

NINE

W ALKING OUT THROUGH THE showroom, Slater headed to the building where Steve Kawada's factory was, and went up to his floor. A guy was at work on the cutting table with a big sheet of cardstock and a grease pencil. He walked around to the desks and found Steve on his desk phone. He smiled and held up a finger, a tacit *Wait a minute*.

Slater wandered toward the sewing machines set up under the big windows. Women sat working at three of them, running fabric through, the electric motors and staccato mechanism cycling on and off.

Eventually Steve ended his call, and got up, and called, "Ibáñez." As Slater walked over to his desk, he frowned. "What happened to your face?"

"What are you talking about?" Slater demanded.

"Around your mouth. It looks bruised."

He wiped at his cheek. It felt a little greasy, and when he looked at his finger, it was smeared with dark red. "It must be lipstick."

"You're not sure? What, you just make out with people on your lunch break? Is that part of your torrid love affair or whatever you called it?"

Slater groaned. "It's complicated." Pulling out his handkerchief, he wiped at his mug. "Are you going to that fabric trade show?"

"I wasn't planning on it. I'm too busy. But I know people who'll be there."

"I want to pose as a fabric buyer or a sales rep. I won't be able to get in without credentials."

"The credentials aren't difficult," Steve said, "but do you know enough about the industry to pull that off?"

Slater put his hands on his hips. "I know you've got an order due, since you've got three seamstresses working. I know you do couture, but from what's hanging on the racks, this order is definitely prêt-à-porter. I can also tell you I know that guy over at the cutting table is grading patterns. You're lucky to have him because that's a rare skill."

Steve's eyebrows shot up. "That's all accurate."

"Big picture, I can tell you there's Yves Saint Laurent, and then there's everything else."

"There's more to it, but you're not wrong about that either."

"So I know what I'm doing. Hook me up. Can I pose as your rep?"

"I was thinking about what you said. About Carolina. Was it really you who told me I should date her?"

Slater waved a hand. "I might have said it, brother, but it's not like it was my idea. Clearly it was in your mind already, and hers."

Steve nodded. "It would be a lot easier if you worked with someone who's already going to the show. My friend Helen is setting up a booth, and she owes me a favor. She's a fabric dealer. Let me talk to her."

"She does wholesale?"

"Retail too."

"If the show is this weekend," Slater said, "you need to make that call."

He laughed. "I remember this part. You have no manners."

"I get that a lot."

"You did drive across three states to get me out of a jam. I'll make it happen."

"Chop-chop," Slater said, and walked out.

On the way back toward his office, he checked the time on his phone. The summer sun was still high in the sky, but it was time to roll. He crossed the street to the surface lot and climbed in the Frontier. When he got to his house, he parked on the street out front.

Upstairs he found Pike in the front bedroom. He was getting dressed, in golf shorts and a fun shirt with short sleeves in a pink and blue plaid. Once he'd embraced him, Slater stepped back.

"So where is this pho place?"

"I think I put it in the calendar," Pike said. "Doris told me, 'It's near where that bowling alley used to be.' I haven't lived here all that long, but I'm flattered that she forgets that."

"I know where she means."

He pulled a clean shirt out of the closet, and once they were both dressed, they trooped down to the garage, and got in the Continental. The place wasn't far from Doris's neighborhood, and he pulled into the strip-mall parking lot, and nosed into the stall next to Doris's Buick.

"This looks a little rough," Pike said. "I can't believe she wanted to eat here."

"It's not a universal rule, but sometimes the grungier the strip mall, the better the food. One of her friends probably tipped her off."

Inside the place wasn't grubby, but it was basic and functional, with fluorescent lighting, and a generic drop ceiling, and a couple of plastic potted plants. Doris was at a table, looking at the menu. Petite, she had some gray in her dark hair, today wearing a wrinkly yellow shirt. They leaned in to kiss her hello in turn, then sat opposite.

"They have a vegan version for you," Doris said, eyeing Slater. "I checked in advance."

Pike leaned toward her. "That was very thoughtful."

"What happened to your shirt?" Slater said. "Did your iron break down? I might have one you could borrow."

"It's the style," Doris said. "Crinkle fabric. And when is the last time you used an iron?"

"Slater's actually becoming well versed in fashion," Pike said.

"It's for the case I'm on."

"With Artémise? I know she does clothing."

The server stepped over, and once they'd ordered, Doris handed her the menus, and eyed Slater.

"I saw the new photos," she said. "You look good."

Slater frowned. "What photos?"

She dug her phone out, and tapped at it, and handed it over. It was on one of the celebrity gossip sites. In the image he was standing with Cassidy at the art gallery. They were both holding plastic cups, facing the camera, and leaning toward each other. A couple of the clown paintings were visible behind them. It was actually a good photo, flattering of both of them, and made it look like something important was going down.

"That was last night. I didn't even see a camera."

"It looks like an art gallery," Doris said. "Were there windows? The photographer was probably on the street outside."

"Show me." Pike took the device, and studied the image, then met Slater's eye. "It looks like an intimate conversation."

"The subject matter required discretion. She was explaining the racket she's running on the gallery, and we were still there."

"Do I need to be jealous?"

Slater scoffed. "Her name is Cassidy. Her clothing factory is down the hall from my office. I asked her to educate me about the fashion industry."

"Did you read the caption?" Doris said.

Pike swiped at the screen and read it aloud: "'Rocky's dog walker steps out with blond gal pal.'"

"I'm not a dog walker. They don't even know my damn name."

"You're mistaking this for journalism," Doris said.

Pike handed her phone back. "What would you call it?"

"It's marketing. They'd print your name if your agent called them and offered payment."

"I don't want any part of this," Slater said intently.

"The photos with Rocky and Artémise were better," Pike said. "You looked engaged, and the dog looked happy, and Artémise looked radiant. In this one you just look gossipy."

"My son, the macher," Doris said. "Rubbing elbows with celebrities."

"Not by choice. Rocky just wanted to say hello, and Artémise basically jumped me on the street."

Doris waved a hand. "I do think those people underestimate the value of anonymity. It's like breaking a wineglass. Once you lose it, it can never be restored."

"I need my anonymity for my work. It's already slipping away with all the facial recognition and the plate readers."

"So be grateful they're not using your name," she said. "Just don't do anything gauche, like those truculent house-wives, or one of those dance competitions."

The server brought their bowls over, and they dug into the noodles.

"Where is that gallery?" Doris said.

"Kind of in the Arts District, kind of in the Fashion District. In the liminal space between them."

"Listen to you, with the ten-dollar words." Doris leaned toward him. "I love that you have that kind of vocabulary."

"That's all about this guy." Slater nodded toward Pike.

"We've been reading about the Greek gods," Pike said. "That word comes up with Hermes. He's the god of bound-aries and liminal places."

"I thought he was the god of creativity."

"If you think about it, they're related. Liminal zones aren't predictable or routine, so you need to be thoughtful to navigate them. Meanings shift, so things get reassem-bled in new ways. That's the definition of creativity."

"Those five thousand years of scholarship in your veins," Doris said. "It shows."

"Don't tell his mother that," Slater said. "She already thinks he's too good for me."

"She's warming up to you." Pike eyed Doris. "Where's Albert this evening?"

"His step-brother died," she said, "and the family is gathering in Sonoma for the reading of the will."

Slater gestured with his chopsticks. "That is the most goyishe thing I've ever heard."

"It is a little Waspy."

"I'm sorry to hear about his step-brother," Pike said.

"They weren't close. There might be some money for Albert, although they're not plutocrats."

"Once he gets his inheritance maybe he'll stop schnorring off you," Slater said.

"He's never been that man. I actually spoke to him on my way here. He said it took him eight hours to get up there even without traffic."

"How did he manage that?" Slater demanded. "That stupid Boxster isn't meant to go slow. I bet he drives in lane one anyway. Pike says everybody driving half the speed limit in lane one is fighting a battle you know nothing about."

Pike laughed. "That's not exactly how I put it."

"Still, why does it have to be on the freeway? Go fight your battles somewhere else."

"He means you have to cut people some slack," Doris said.

"Lo, they can have all the slack they want, once they quit hogging up the road, and move into lane two. Tell Albert he needs to merge right."

After they'd eaten, they got up, and Doris went to wash her hands. As he stretched his back, Slater looked out the front window. There was a guy outside with a bulky black camera, its long lens aimed right at him.

He hustled out to the parking lot. This was a different guy than the one who'd been stalking him at his office. Scruffier, in ripped denim, with a ratty beard. As he approached, the guy took more photos, then lowered the camera and stood up straighter. He looked surprised that Slater was coming at him. Slater grabbed his wrist and twisted hard. With a yelp he spun around, the heavy camera bouncing against his belly, and Slater pushed his arm up his back.

"You pull this bullshit when my mother is right there?" Slater demanded.

"Let go of me." He yelped in pain. "Come on, man. This isn't how you play the game."

Reaching around for the camera lens, he twisted it onto the guy's back and then pulled hard, choking him with the strap.

"You want to make her watch me break you?" he shouted. "What is wrong with you?"

The photographer gurgled and clawed at his neck, tugging at the strap. It was no way to get out of the situation, but it was so predictable. Why were these birds always like this?

"Stay the fuck away from me," Slater growled in his ear, and finally shoved the guy off.

Not looking back, he stumbled toward a parked car, and then loped off, pulling the camera around from his back.

Pike was on the strip of sidewalk in front of the shops, watching him, arms folded. "If there had been two of them, the other one would have filmed that, and you'd be explaining it to a judge."

"He was alone."

"You're still taking a risk."

Slater threw up his hands. "Do you not get that it's infuriating?"

"I'm sure it is." He cracked a smile. "I don't get to see you mix it up very often. You move fast."

Doris pushed her way out the door of the restaurant and looked him over, her brow furrowing. "You look upset. What did I miss?"

"A paparazzo may have taken some photos of us when we were dining," Pike said.

"Is he still breathing?"

"He's fine," Slater said flatly.

They stepped over to their cars, and Doris kissed Pike, then embraced Slater.

"Love you," he said.

She grasped his forearms and held his gaze. "All this tsuris. Forget about the paparazzi. Unless you hang out with Artémise again, they're quickly going to lose interest in you."

AT HIS HOUSE, UP in the bedroom, Slater untied his boots and pulled off his shirt.

"This media bullshit is a distraction. I need to focus on the work."

Pike got undressed and stretched out on the bed. "You mean the fashion world. You said your neighbor was coaching you. Do you know enough about it to talk the talk?"

"Cassidy told me I can say, 'There's Yves Saint Laurent, and then there's everything else.'"

He laughed. "They say that about philosophy. 'There's Plato, and there's everything else.'"

"You would find a way to bring the ancient Greeks into it."

"They're the source of everything," Pike said. "The core of Western civilization."

Once he'd undressed, Slater climbed on top of him, massaging his biceps. "You're the core of Western civilization." He raised his voice. "You."

"What are you going to do about it?"

"I'm going to fuck you senseless," Slater said through his teeth.

"Bring it." Pike ran a hand into his hair, his eyes bright. "I'm so glad I found you. I think about that every day."

"I actually found you, big guy."

"So you're the one in charge."

"Always."

Leaning in, he mauled his mouth, and his neck, and squeezed his cock. Pike was soon hard enough, and he lowered himself onto him, wincing at the intensity of it. Pike grabbed his cock, pumping him as Slater rocked back and forth. Massaging his pecs, leaning in to meet his mouth, Slater soon came. With that, Pike strained into him, grimacing and red-faced.

After a moment Slater rolled off him, flopping onto his back, and lifted his head as Pike shoved his arm under his neck. He could feel the heat of his skin, and hear the rhythm of his breath gradually slowing. He'd have to go upstairs and slam his ration at some point. He couldn't really sleep without it. But for right now he was content to relish the warmth of his body, the golden feeling of satiety.

TEN

WHEN SLATER WOKE HIS head didn't hurt. He must have stuck to his ration last night. It was early, as Pike was still in bed, sitting up and looking at his phone.

"You're awake," Pike said.

He shifted to look at him. "I had this weird dream. It's fading but I can still see it. There's this curtain thing, made of batik." He gestured vaguely. "One of those fabrics from India. It was all complicated. Like those pillows with little mirrors sewn into them, you know?"

Pike chuckled and set his phone down. "Sure."

"But it's not just a curtain. It's kind of alive. It's snarling and yelling at me. Telling me to back off."

"That sounds intense."

"Then in the dream I figured out it's just a gimmick," Slater said. "Like a sentry. The real story is behind it. So I whip the curtain aside. Behind the curtain it's this ordinary place. Like a town square or something. You're there, and some other people. I said, 'Where were you?' and you said,

91

'Oh, you know, I've been around.' You were being vague, and indifferent. It was rude. You said, 'Well, you can hang around, since you're already here, but I've got stuff to do.'"

"I guess I was busy."

He scowled. "How could you do that, just blow me off?"

Pike leaned in to nuzzle his neck. "I would never do that, petal. I'd always find you a chair and a popsicle before I took off to do stuff."

"Dick."

Pike laughed. "That dream is just your insecurity about me. I'm not indifferent. The evidence is in my actions. I'm sleeping next to you, and pounding you with some regularity, and going halfsies on that giant tlayuda from the place on the corner. I'm here, and I'm with you."

"I just wish I knew what was so important back there. What you were up to."

"I can't really answer that," Pike said, "since I wasn't actually there, and it wasn't real."

He frowned. "If you say so."

Kissing his neck again, Pike got out of bed. Slater rearranged the covers and lay back. He'd get up soon too, but he wanted another minute in this warmth.

His phone buzzed, and he reached over to grab it from the bedside table. Gene. It had been a few days. She'd want an update.

"Things are progressing," Slater said when he picked up. "I've done some interviews, and I'm setting up a meeting with the fabric retailer this weekend."

"Good to know," she said. "I'm calling to invite you to a pool party at Artémise's house on Sunday."

That sounded like work. Specifically the kind that wouldn't generate any revenue or lead him anywhere. But this was the client, and he knew he had to play the game.

"I'll be there. Is there a dress code?"

"Not at all. Wear whatever you wear to hang out by the pool. It's just a small gathering."

"How small?"

"We're trying to keep it under two hundred," Gene said.

"Can I bring a plus-one?"

"Of course."

Once he'd ended the call, he pushed himself out of bed, and took a shower, and got dressed. Upstairs he found Pike in the kitchen making oatmeal.

"Want some of this?" Pike said. "There's plenty."

"Set me up. So are you free on Sunday? There's a pool party at Artémise's place."

"Whoa." Pike paused to look at him. "Why would I ever hide behind an angry batik curtain when you make stuff like this happen?"

Slater embraced him for a moment and mouthed his neck. "Ditch the batik, bucko," he murmured.

They sat together on the deck to eat, enjoying the morning sun.

Pike soon got up. "I have to get to work."

A while later, still on the deck and almost finished his java, Slater dug out his phone when it buzzed. It was Steve.

"Helen is willing to let you use her company to get into the fabric show," he said.

"Does that cost her anything?"

"I don't think so. She'll just get them to issue an extra exhibitor pass. She can meet you today to talk about it if it's brief. The show starts tomorrow, so you can imagine how busy she is."

When he ended the call, he checked the address Steve texted. Helen's company was in the Fashion District, near Steve's building, just a couple of blocks from his own.

Downstairs he dug in the closet for the seventies shirts Cassidy had found and pulled one out. It was polyester, with a brown and orange pattern of interlocking squares. That felt like a lot. The pattern was loud, he decided, but the colors weren't overly obnoxious, and he pulled it on.

Trotting down to the Continental, he drove to Downtown, and parked at his office, and walked to Helen's place. It was a storefront business in a low-rise building, with a retail vibe, big display windows flanking both sides of the entrance. The door was locked, and he rang the bell.

A woman stepped up and pulled open the door. Curvy, she was wearing gray pants and a loose white shirt, her black hair tied back.

"I'm a friend of Steve Kawada," Slater said. "The name is Ibáñez."

"Helen." She waved him in and looked him over. "That's a great shirt."

"It's 1970s dead stock."

"Steve said you weren't in the industry."

"I'm industry adjacent," Slater said. "My office is in the Del Rio Building. A neighbor found a cache of this stuff in a workshop upstairs."

"We can talk in the back," she said, and waved for him to follow.

The place was chockablock with bolts and folded piles of fabric, he saw, following her, with just enough room to walk between the tables.

"Do you specialize in sheer fabrics?"

"You're seeing the tulle and the organza," Helen said. "I sell a lot of that to consumers. My commercial clients buy a wider variety. I'll show you."

She led the way into the back room. Here the bolts were organized in deep box shelves, six or eight in each box, with others propped against the back wall, in an array of colors and textures. A couple of desks were wedged in among the clutter.

"It's so quiet," Slater said. "The acoustics in here are like a recording studio."

Helen chuckled. "I wish there was room to rent it out for that. So what exactly are you going to do at the show?"

"I need to meet a specific vendor. A company called A Touch of Class."

"I don't know that name. Meet them means talk to them?"

"People are more forthcoming when they think you're a colleague."

She raised her eyebrows. "So no *desmadre* with my name tied to it."

"Absolutely no *desmadre.*" Slater flashed his palms to demonstrate his innocence.

Helen said something else in Spanish.

"I don't actually speak the language," he said. "I know I look like I should."

"Well, I do, and I look like I shouldn't."

"I bet that gives you an advantage."

She chuckled. "At times."

"What should I wear to look like I belong at the trade show?"

"Business casual." She looked him up and down. "The shirt works, but ditch the vaquero jeans. The show is at the convention center. I'll let you know where we can connect. Can you give me your number?"

He dug a business card out of his hip pocket and handed it over.

"I'll text you mine," she said, and glanced at the card as she tapped at her phone.

"I know you're busy. I'll get out of your hair," he said, and walked back through the shop, and out to the street.

His phone had buzzed in his pants a while ago, and he checked it as he walked. Helen had texted her name, and before that was a message from Andy:

Info for you. Drop by.

There was a print shop in the neighborhood, and he'd done some work for the owner, Monta. It was on the way to his office, and he went inside, setting off the electronic chime over the door.

Monta came out of the back and greeted him as she stepped up to the counter. In her thirties, she wore glasses and had her dark hair bundled back.

"What are you doing here?"

"Did you not do a star chart this morning?" Slater said. "It should have told you I was headed over."

Monta chuckled. "That's not how astrology works."

"I need some business cards printed up. Can I write down the name?"

She handed him a little yellow pad and a pen, and he wrote:

John Slade
Slade Wholesale Women's Wear
Del Rio Building

Below that, he added his phone number, then turned the pad around to face her.

"I only need a dozen or so."

"John Slade is an alias?" Monta said. "Are you going undercover?"

"Max and I come here because you're discreet," Slater said. "Because you don't ask questions like that."

"You've worked for me," she said. "I'd think you know me well enough to know I'm no gossip."

She'd also lied to his face when he'd worked for her, but he didn't need to point that out.

"No email, no suite number on the address?" Monta said.

"It needs to be vague. If they check my horoscope, it should tell them what floor I'm on."

"Funny. I'll have these for you later today."

Walking out, he went back to his office to retrieve the Continental, then drove to Andy's building on Broadway, and parked in the lot behind it. Upstairs he knocked on his door, and waited for him to answer.

When he pulled it open, Andy was wearing his usual tank top and boxers, and flashed that beautiful smile. Slater followed him inside. It was mostly one room, with big windows over the square. The original glass panes and the board floor under a layer of hard acrylic were a hundred years old, from when the building had been a textile warehouse.

Andy sat at his desk, in front of his array of screens, and Slater stood nearby.

"You seem upbeat," Slater said. "Is Kyle out of town?"

He laughed. "You think he brings me down?"

"You ought to know whether he does or not." He raised his eyebrows. "You married him. I'm just the second-best man."

"That, I did, and that, you are. You could have been … number one, and had your shot at all this." Andy gestured to his torso.

"You would have dumped me already. Thrown my stuff out on the sidewalk and changed the locks. And you still would have wound up with that twinky toothache."

"It might have been nice to work through that myself."

Slater put his hands on his hips. "Have you worked through that little gunsel yet? If you need me to dump him for you, I can do it. If he chooses his words carefully, it might not even require giving him a tune-up. I have a locksmith who can swap out your deadbolt. Just tell me what's his and I can haul it down to the dumpster."

"Stop talking smack about my husband. I got some … background on Malcolm. He went to Fashion Institute."

"The fuck is that?"

"A college where you learn about the industry. It's in … Downtown. The guy is pretty low-key. He posts a lot online about … R&B music and the performers. He has a couple of different … accounts."

"Is he a hater or a troll? Trash-talking his boss?"

"The opposite," Andy said. "He's stanning her. But there's nothing private and … personal. I get the sense he works for her but doesn't … see her very often. He also posts a lot on … a Tagalog message board. I did a machine … translation, so I could only get an imperfect understanding, but it's … mostly about food."

"So he's Filipino."

"That's a reasonable deduction."

"There's nothing to imply that he's a crook? No rap sheet, no warrants?"

"Not that I found. He looks like … a civilian."

"What's the dope on the fabric shop?"

"A Touch of Class. I think the owner's name is … Boyd. That's an inference, based on what other … people have said about the company, about working with … somebody named Boyd."

"It's not registered in his name?"

"The ownership is obscured," Andy said. "That makes it feel hinky. There's … three different companies linked to that address, all of them … with the ownership buried in LLCs. That's usually either corporate America … trying to disguise a monopoly, or small-time crooks."

"What are the other businesses?"

"I'll send you the names. It's possible they're … former tenants, because A Touch of Class has been there … just a couple years. It's also odd that A Touch of Class isn't … specialized."

"Meaning what?" Slater said.

"In that industry most companies sell fabric, or sew … garments, or sell stuff wholesale. A Touch of Class does … retail but also runs a fashion line. On a business … networking site they offer consulting services, whatever that means."

"What's the fashion line?"

"It's also called A Touch of Class. Women's clothes. It's in a … show that's happening tonight. And that's … all I got."

"Send me dude's name, and the details on that event." Slater shifted on his feet. "Let me know if Kyle becomes any more of a problem. Day or night. I can take care of things."

Andy waved an arm. "Get out of my place."

"Bye, beautiful."

ELEVEN

S LATER WALKED OUT AND drove back to his building. Upstairs the office was dark. He flicked on the lights, and sat at his desk, and stared absently at the plaster statue of Pollux with his horse. That guy had amazing hair.

A Touch of Class had Artémise's fabric on prime display in their window. If they did a clothing line, maybe they were using it for those clothes. He needed to go to that show. Pulling his keyboard close, he checked the stuff that Andy had sent. There was a link to a listing for the event, and he briefly scanned it.

Digging out his phone, he called Etta, glad that she picked up.

"Can you dress like a fashion victim?" he said.

"What does that mean?"

"I have no idea. You need to look like you work in the industry."

"I could do some research," Etta said, "and ask around."

"You'll have to be snappy about it. There's an event

tonight that I need to infiltrate."

"Oh, man. Safiya and I were supposed to finish a series tonight."

"You can sit on your ass and watch television, or you can do some damn work and get paid." He raised his voice. "You need to sort out your priorities."

"I'll be there. No question. The problem is, I need to figure out how to break it to Safiya."

"The best thing to do is get rid of her for keeps. If she gets sticky about it, send her to the store, then dump her stuff on the street, and change the locks before she gets back."

"You are such an asshole."

"She's like mistletoe on a scrub oak," he said. "Bleeding you dry."

"Don't tell me how to run my love life. Are you at the office? I can come by now to do the planning."

A while later there was a firm knock at the door. It was too soon for Etta, and she had her own key. He got up and pulled it open a few inches, keeping his boot firmly planted on the inner side to make it harder to bust in.

A guy in a bicycle helmet stood there. "Ibáñez?" He handed him an envelope.

"Is that a summons?" Slater said, not reaching for it.

The guy waved it. "It's from Monta."

"I didn't know she delivered."

He took hold of it, and the guy walked away. At his desk he ripped open the envelope and looked over the business cards. They were sleek and glossy and professional.

When Etta arrived, she called a greeting, and he heard her dump her stuff on the front desk. When she stepped into his office, she was wearing a blue rugby shirt and jeans, and sat across from him. "So what's the job?"

Slater sat back. "A fashion show. We need to blend in."

"Is it connected to Artémise and that enby long drink of water I met the other day?"

"Gene. It is, indirectly."

"What are their pronouns?"

"She or they," Slater said. "You want her number? Redheads are fun."

Etta waved a hand. "It's like going to a sports car showroom. Nice to look at, but way too fast for me. Where's the fashion show?"

"At Stenman's on Wilshire."

"I know that building. It was a department store, but it's supposed to be architecturally significant."

"Stenman's has been closed for forty years. Doris talked about it. She barely remembers it from when she was a kid."

"The building is still there. I've seen stuff about other events once in a while." Etta furrowed her brow. "Why don't they use it for retail? Even a dumb chain store. The place is a landmark."

"Max worked with a guy who owned a building like that. If there's no tenants, it means the owner doesn't want to do the earthquake retrofit, or can't afford it. There's this gray area where you can still use the place but you can't run a business inside. Events and filming rights pay enough to cover the property taxes and the maintenance."

"What's the show about?"

"Let me send you the link." He grabbed his phone and tapped at it.

Etta pulled out her own and studied the screen. "There's three different lines in this show. Which one are you stalking?"

"A Touch of Class."

"That sounds so trashy."

"It's exactly the opposite. It's right there in the name." He threw up a hand. "It's classy."

Etta chuckled. "Did you click through to the company's bio?"

"Hit me."

She read from the screen. "The collection invokes imagery that is neither rational nor consequential. The fashion house is based in Los Angeles but transcends the bounds of geographical location and the meaning of time itself. Presenting and dispersing conceptual garments as nonhuman entities through discursive movement, A Touch of Class women's sportswear enhances the porosity between the creator and the observer."

"Are you kidding me?" Slater demanded. "That makes absolutely no sense."

"This is the way people in the art world describe things. In extremely abstract terms. It makes me think it'll be interesting."

"Can you parse what they're talking about? I get that clothes are nonhuman entities, but was that ever in question? And how do textiles transcend time itself?"

"I can't translate it," Etta said, "but when it comes to art shows, there's an inverse correlation between how little I understand in the description and how much I enjoy the work."

"So if they explain it clearly, it's usually boring."

"Exactly."

Slater scoffed. "It's clothes. How complicated can it be?"

"It sounds like workout clothes."

"In the industry, sportswear means casual clothing. Clothing for actually doing sports is called activewear."

"Listen to you. You sound like an insider."

"It's weird how much of this I know just by osmosis from working in this neighborhood."

"So what do you need me to do at this show?" Etta said.

"Partly it's just to have a second set of eyes. I was thinking you could infiltrate the space where the models are getting dressed. It would look sleazy if I did that. It's less louche for a woman to be hanging around a women's changing room."

"The problem might be getting through the door in the first place. This listing says invitation only."

"Rats."

"You think we can legitimately crash?"

"We'll have to look the part," he said. "I had that zodiac zombie make some industry business cards for me. We'll need some for you. Unfortunately that means another trip to the print shop."

"Show me the cards," Etta said.

He sat up and slid the envelope across the desk.

She pulled the cards out and looked them over. "We don't need Monta or the print shop. I can run them off here. I have cardstock. They'll look almost as good."

Rising, she went out to the front desk, and spent a minute at the computer. Slater heard the printer hum to life, and when she returned, she showed him the business card:

Etta Wood
Slade Wholesale Women's Wear
Del Rio Building

"These are great."

"I should go," she said. "I need to get dressed, and eat, and return Safiya's wheelchair."

"Do you know what to wear?"

"I know who to ask."

He frowned. "Wait—why is Safiya in a wheelchair?"

"Was in a wheelchair. She had toe surgery."

"It's in your car?"

"The rental place is on the way home."

Slater got up. "Show me."

He locked the office, and they rode down to the street, and crossed to the parking lot. Etta had parked next to the Continental, and she opened the back of her car, and pulled out the wheelchair. Setting it on the ground, she pulled on the armrests to fold it open.

Slater sat in it, and flipped down the footrests, and pushed the wheels to roll it a few feet. He rolled it backward, then swiveled it sideways.

"We can use this."

"I'm supposed to turn it in today."

"I'll pay the overtime on it."

Standing up, he folded it closed, and loaded it in the trunk of the Continental. Etta climbed in her Prius and backed out, and he headed back across the street. His phone buzzed in his pants, and he dug it out—Helen.

"*Dígame,*" he said when he picked up.

"I know damn well you don't speak Spanish," she said. "Nobody says that anyway."

"What do you need, Helen?"

"Come to my place. We need to talk."

It wasn't far enough to protest, and he walked over to her storefront. The door was unlocked now, and a woman with dark hair stood near the cash register.

"I'm here to see Helen," he said, and she gestured toward the back.

When he stepped through, he saw Helen doing something near the rear door, and called out a greeting. She walked over to her desk and waved him to the chair in front of it, dropping into her own and scooting it close, then resting her arms on the desktop.

"I looked up the company you're stalking," she said. "They're listed under fabric sales."

"Is that problematic?"

"It's also what I do. It would work better if you were posing as a buyer, not another fabric vendor. If they think you're a competitor, they'll clam up."

"Will your credentials give that away?"

"We'll see what they print on your pass, but I doubt it'll be obvious. You can get onto the floor with me, but you should tell A Touch of Class that you're shopping. Ask them about whatever they have on display. They'll be much more engaging with a potential customer."

"So I should say I'm a designer," Slater said.

"That would do it. Although they might want to look up your previous work."

He waved a hand. "I'm working on my first collection. I just finished up at Fashion Institute."

"There you go." She sat up. "We'll meet here. That way you can get your pass when I get mine, and I won't have to come out and deal with it while I'm working the show."

"I know that place is huge."

"I'm taking a van over to get set up. My worker will be here at seven. You could come around seven thirty. The van should be loaded by then."

"That seems early," Slater said. "You definitely have Steve's work ethic."

Helen scowled. "You think all the Asians are the same? You racist trash bag."

"Steve is Nisei, and if I had to lay odds, I'd bet you're Korean. Don't they hate each other? I was talking about you personally, and Steve personally." He threw up a hand.

"With the absurd early mornings. No comment on anybody's ethnicity."

"Fine." Her expression softened. "I'm sure I sound hypersensitive. It's just a constant abrasive grind. I'm sure you're on the receiving end of it too."

"All the damn time." He stood up. "See you in the morning."

TWELVE

, Slater got settled at his desk. He heard Etta's keys in the door, and her familiar voice. When she stepped into his office doorway, he had to sit back to take it in.

She was wearing a stretchy form-fitting minidress, black with asymmetrical blocks of pink and lime green and sky blue. Her hair was in a sharp wedge cut, dark but with gray streaks in it. Not gray, he realized, but silver—the strands glinted like metal when they caught the light. On her feet were incongruous high-top black boots.

"I didn't realize you had breasts," he said.

"Man, shut up. I'm already uncomfortable enough. It clings everywhere. Except my crotch. That part is completely exposed to the elements."

"Where did you get it?"

"A couple of blocks from here. I'm assured it's avant-garde."

"Did you get a haircut?"

Etta scoffed. "It's a wig, genius."

"You look like a fashion victim."

"Thank you. That's what I was going for. What are you wearing?"

"I've got those 1970s suits."

He rose and walked over to Max's office. A little wardrobe sat in the corner, and he pulled out the two suits he kept there. One had an oversize houndstooth pattern in green and brown, and the other was a red and purple plaid. Stepping into the front office, he held one in each hand.

"Which one?"

"The plaid," Etta said. "But not with that shirt. You'll look insane."

He put the houndstooth back, and carried the plaid one into his office, and got undressed. Pulling on the white shirt he kept with the suit, he stepped into the suit pants. They were flared toward the bottom, and felt thin and insubstantial. The jacket had absurdly wide lapels, and once he'd put it on, he stepped into his boots and went out to the front office.

"Can I wear these?" He lifted a foot and waggled it. "The other option is black derbies."

Etta looked him up and down, then cocked her head. "It looks a little nuts, but it's a fine line between nuts and high fashion."

"Sold," he said, and squatted to tie his boots.

They rode down to the street, and as they stepped outside, Slater spotted a guy up the block, dressed in black, with a long lens in hand.

"Fucking paparazzi," he muttered, then shouted at him. "Yo, fuckface."

"I don't think that's a camera," Etta said. "He's doing something with the bus."

The guy was standing next to a city bus that was parked

at the curb. He turned to look at them, his brow furrowing, and Slater spotted the transit agency logo on his shirt.

"False alarm." He looked away and headed across the street toward the parking lot.

"It's been, what, three days since those photos of you dropped?" Etta said, walking abreast. "In social media time that's like a decade. Nobody's looking for you."

They climbed into the Continental, and Etta pulled her door closed.

"This skirt is so short, if I sit the wrong way, they'll put me on the sex-offender registry."

"Have you never worn a skirt before?"

"Not since I was in eighth grade. In Samoa people wear *lavalava* all the time. It's open like a skirt but at least it covers your knees and your cha-cha. Plus everybody wears them, not just women."

Slater reached over and opened the glove box, and scrabbled around, then slammed it again. "Fuck me."

"What's missing?"

"I left my camera-jamming glasses at my place."

"We probably have time to swing by there."

"I can live without them," he said. "I don't think any-one's looking for me specifically. It's more about public places and data collection."

"Max uses facial-recognition sites sometimes on cases. It's scary how quickly you can identify someone from a photo."

"I hear you."

Slater nosed the big vehicle into the street, and got on Olympic, and headed west. The sun was low in the sky but it was still a while until dusk. As they rolled up Wilshire on the Miracle Mile, he muttered, "Idiots."

"You see someone you know?"

"The crape myrtles." He gestured to the trees in the median. "It's a stupid thing to plant. They do it because they're zero maintenance. They look flashy for two weeks, then they drop their leaves and look like freaking sticks all winter. Even when they're half dead they still hog up the water."

Slater pulled into a lot a block from Stenman's, and they climbed out. It felt weird to be dressed this way, especially since it was still broad daylight. The distinctive suit was endemic to the dark.

As Etta climbed out, she glanced around, then leaned down to tug on the hem of her skirt, shifting her hips as she hiked it down. "That's the last time I'm going to do that."

"You definitely look the part."

Opening the trunk, he lifted out the wheelchair, then folded it open, and sat in it. Etta watched as he practiced rolling it around on the asphalt.

"It's a solid cover," she said. "You look like you know what you're doing."

"This is hard freaking work. My hands are already getting sore."

Halfway up the block to Stenman's, Etta looked him over. "You're working up a sweat. Want me to push you?"

"I don't, but do it anyway."

She got behind the chair and got him rolling faster.

"I hate this," he said. "Being at your mercy."

"That's because you're a control freak. Just lean into it."

The broad main entrance to Stenman's was closed up and looked abandoned, with leaves and trash littering the doorway. Etta pushed the chair to the alley at the side of the building. Partway down he could see a door was propped open. A half dozen people were standing around the alley nearby, smoking and vaping.

Just outside the door stood a guy with his hair in knobby twists, dressed in black, wearing a headset and holding a tablet. He couldn't be older than thirty. Etta rolled Slater up next to him.

"John Slade plus one," Slater said.

The guy looked at Etta. "The name again?"

"John Slade," she said, enunciating slowly.

He tapped at his tablet. "I don't see it here."

"Big Fella invited us," Etta said. "He told us we'd be on the list. I've been looking forward to this all week."

"You're not on the list." He met her gaze. "I can't let you in."

"Is this place ADA compliant?" Slater said. "If I was going to file a lawsuit tomorrow morning, would I sue the building owner, or your boss, or both?"

The guy frowned at him, but there was uncertainty in his eyes. Slater heard Etta gasp, and twisted his head to look back. Her face was contorted, her eyes screwed shut. She put her hand over her mouth, then sobbed.

"I work so hard," she croaked.

"Oh, girlie." The guy with the tablet shifted on his feet. "Nobody needs the waterworks." He huffed and then lowered his voice. "There's an elevator next to the stairs."

Etta quickly stepped behind the wheelchair and pushed him through the doorway, the chair jostling him as it went over the sill.

This was definitely a back door, into a small space with an uncomplicated gray paint job and service stairs that led upward. Maybe it had been the staff entrance. Etta pressed the elevator button.

Slater rolled himself on, and once the doors had rumbled closed, he looked up at her. "The fuck is Big Fella?"

"One of the designers listed in the program," she said.

"You're better prepared than I am."

"We were a little rushed, but I took the time to read it."

"The tears were a great idea. You're so good at this."

She preened a little. "I know. But you can remind me of that anytime."

"Door dude hardly even looked at me," Slater said. "He was exclusively talking to you. It's the chair. Like I'm a piece of furniture."

"Welcome to how women experience the world, like, every day."

"I get it now. It's why wheelchair people are usually assholes."

"I'm thinking you're going to have to stay in the chair," Etta said. "It's your cover now."

"Unless circumstances demand otherwise."

"We didn't even need the business cards."

"Better to have it and not need it than to need it and not have it."

"Just like lip gloss," she said, as the elevator doors rolled open.

They were in a big room, the upper level of the old department store, long devoid of furniture and display counters. The open floor ran most of the length of the building, broken only by support columns painted pastel green. A long runway had been set up, about four feet off the floor, fringed with dark fabric. It ended at an arched entryway with a curtain of narrow gold ribbons that obscured the room beyond. A smaller door stood farther along the wall. No chairs were in sight, and there was already a crowd of people standing around.

"This is amazing," Etta said.

"There's nowhere to sit, and no bar."

"I mean the room. It hasn't been renovated since the department store closed. It's like a time capsule."

"I'm just seeing old paint and plaster."

She gestured to the pastel-blue ceiling. "It's paint and plaster from another time. It looks so 1950s to me. If we ever need to glow up the office, that's the blue."

"If you roll me over there," Slater said, "I can watch the door into the staging area."

Etta pushed him closer to the curtained runway entrance and the door next to it, and he grabbed his wheels and twisted them so that his back was to the elevated runway structure. Etta stood next to him, and they looked over the crowd.

"What are you seeing?" Slater said.

"Is this an exam?"

"On-the-job training."

"Most of them are in their twenties and thirties, I'd say. A decent ethnic mix."

"That tracks."

"They look affluent."

"The affluence thing is harder to pin down," he said. "They might just be dressy because they're in the industry."

"Nine o'clock." Etta leaned in. "Black guy with an orange necktie."

Slater looked at him. His head was shaved bald, and he wore a sharp dark suit, and round eyeglasses tinted the same shade as his tie. "He's fuckable."

"That's Big Fella."

"The name must be ironic. He's not very tall, and he can't weigh more than a buck forty."

"You obviously didn't read his biography in the show listing. With the assistance of medications, Big Fella has succeeded in his brave struggle with weight loss."

"I'd still fuck him."

"You'd fuck anybody." She gestured toward the doorway. "People are coming and going pretty regularly from the back room. I'm going to make my move."

He watched her wander over toward the wall, deftly making it look like she had no destination in mind. She paused to look at her phone for a moment. Eventually she followed the steps of a lanky woman in high heels, matching her pace and her sense of purpose, and went through the doorway.

It wasn't optimal to be sitting here when everyone else was on their feet, but at least he could see the door, and the people walking out of the back room. Etta wasn't among them. That was a good sign—she hadn't been immediately eighty-sixed.

Surveying the crowd, he saw a woman staring at him, with an odd look on her face. She quickly looked away when their eyes met. Then it happened again with someone else, and again. He couldn't quite decode the meaning, as he'd never really seen it before. It had to be about the chair. Maybe it was pity. People seemed interested in his situation but not enough to actually connect with him.

A guy with a Roman nose and unctuous brown hair that hung to his shoulders walked over, and leaned over him, and spoke in a loud voice. "I'm just going to roll you to the end of the runway so you can get a better look. How's that?"

Slater twisted his wheels to face him. "You lay a hand on this chair and I'll dislocate all your fingers."

The guy recoiled. "Dude. I'm trying to help you."

"Keep your grubby paws off me. You know, I actually envy you."

"Because I can walk?"

"Because you're stupid. Stupid people seem so carefree."

"Why are you being such an asshole?"

"Buy a violin, Long Hair," Slater said.

The guy scowled and stepped away.

THIRTEEN

CCESS TO THE BACK room wasn't really controlled, Slater decided, from what he could see as people came and went. Etta had been in there a while now.

A woman stepped over and stood next to him. "I love that suit. Are you in the industry?"

He looked up at her. "Isn't everybody?"

"I'm a journalist. I write about the industry. Have you had a look at Big Fella's line?"

"You're looking for a quote?" Slater said. "I can tell you that when it comes to designers, there's Yves Saint Laurent, and then there's everything else."

"You're absolutely right. But I can't print that." She looked past him. "There's Big Fella. I have to talk to him. Have fun tonight."

He watched her walk away and intercept the designer.

More people seemed to be walking out of the back than walking in now, he saw, and eventually Etta strode out the door, and paused to flick her weirdly long hair away from her face. She wandered through the crowd for a minute, then stood next to his chair, and leaned in.

"Did you finally get turfed?" he said.

"Affirmative. But I learned some things. Check out that guy. Ten o'clock. Black turtleneck, tall, big forehead."

It was probably a normal-size forehead, he thought, but the guy was losing his mousy brown hair.

"Why is he wearing a turtleneck in the middle of summer?"

"The same reason I'm wearing this wig," she said. "To project 'fashion insider.'"

She was right, he knew. Irving Irving had been working a similar look.

"They called him Boyd," Etta said. "He was in charge of dressing the models for A Touch of Class."

Andy had come up with that name too. He'd inferred that Boyd was a principal at the fabric store. Slater studied him as he paused to talk to someone. He seemed pleasant enough, smiling as he chatted.

"And that one," Etta said, "walking out now."

"The blue shirt?"

"No—the Brazilian mix, with the linen shirt."

It did look like linen, with linen's inevitable characteristic wrinkles. The guy was slight but muscled, and wore his shirt open a few buttons, with tan chinos, and a tight Black haircut.

"He's quite the slab of cream cheese," Slater said. "How do you know he's Brazilian?"

"I don't. The Brazilian mix is about ethnicity, not nationality. Iberian mixed with African mixed with Indigenous. It's a look. People from Brazil and Dominica and Puerto Rico."

"That sounds vaguely racist," Slater said, "but I know

who you're talking about."

"I'm not sure of his name. It sounded like Charlie."

They watched as the guy walked toward the opposite end of the room.

"One more person," Etta said. "One o'clock. The woman in the floral print with her hair up."

"I see her. At least you're not labeling her ethnicity."

"South Asian," Etta said. "Maybe Tamil or Sinhalese."

"Stop that," he said flatly.

The music in the room came up, and the lights dimmed.

"I'll fill you in on them later."

She maneuvered the wheelchair so that he was facing the runway, then stood erect and clapped with everyone else, even though nothing had happened yet.

A guy in a blue suit stepped through the gold curtain, and a spotlight illuminated him as he spoke. Slater couldn't see a mike, but he had to be wearing one, as his voice was amplified, booming through the sound system. He name-checked each of the lines, and talked them up for a minute, outlining how brilliant they were, and how they were changing the world.

"Up first is Vivi Kwong," the emcee said, and the crowd clapped and hooted as upbeat music started pumping.

A woman strutted out through the curtain, making the shiny gold strands flutter, and walked the length of the runway, spotlit the entire way. She was wearing a billowy white top and unbleached cotton capris. As she turned to walk back, the next model appeared from the curtain. There were maybe a dozen in total, clad in summery women's wear, with several sheer prints in fluorescent colors. To Vivi's credit not all the models looked like stick insects, and several of them had actual curves. As the last model disappeared through the curtain, the music faded.

A few minutes later the emcee appeared again to announce A Touch of Class, and read the same inscrutable description Etta had found in the show listing. The music sounded different, but it was similarly upbeat, and a model strutted out through the curtain. Unlike the first set, these clothes didn't seem to have a theme. It was all women's wear, but the first top was light and short-sleeved, and next came one that looked heavy and dark. The third model to walk the runway was wearing a top made from Artémise's paisley. It had baggy sleeves and was gathered at the waist. Of the dozen or so outfits that appeared, that was the only garment in Artémise's print.

The third line was Big Fella. His stuff was menswear. All the models were built like linebackers, but at least they could walk, their movements fluid, not overly muscle-bound. They all wore boring suits in the usual bland grays and browns and muted dark blues. The only color and variety was in the neckties and pocket squares.

After the last model walked, the music stopped, and a few minutes later the emcee appeared again.

"Let's give it up for these creative geniuses," he called, and named the lines again as the designers stepped onto the runway.

The woman in jeans had to be Vivi Kwong. She was soon joined by Big Fella. He'd swapped his tinted glasses for rhinestone-framed dark sunglasses. Next the guy in the turtleneck stepped out—Boyd. He and Vivi beamed and waved and bowed from the neck at the applauding crowd. Big Fella looked a little disinterested, and held up a hand in an extended half-hearted wave.

When they eventually retreated into the back, the spotlights faded, and the applause died out. People were milling around and talking in loud voices, amped up from the show, lots of them not ready to vacate quite yet. Etta grabbed the handles of the wheelchair and rolled him toward the elevator.

Several people boarded with them to ride to the ground floor. Etta stepped off after them, and Slater wheeled himself. It was dark outside now, the alley lit by the glaring light of a fixture over the door. He rolled the chair into the crowd of people standing in the alley, oblivious to him.

"Step aside," Slater called, but they were either not hearing him or not interested. He rolled the chair between two guys, bumping into their legs, and winced at the cloud of skunky pot smoke enveloping them.

One of the guys stepped back and gave him the once-over. "You don't need to be a dick about it. Just because you're in that chair."

Twisting his wheels, Slater turned to him. "I thought weed was supposed to mellow people out. You need to inhale deeper."

He held Slater's gaze, and flicked the little butt onto the concrete, and raised his eyebrows. "Dick."

Slater leaped out of the chair and slapped him hard, left and right, a rapid kovac. "Why do you make me do this to you?" he demanded, and shoved the guy, making him stumble back, then slapped him again.

The guy he'd been smoking with shouted at him. "You're not even crippled, you freak."

Slater turned and lunged at him. He managed to deliver a kovac before the guy pushed him away.

"You want me to break you, is that it?" Slater demanded. "Why do you do it?"

Other people in the crowd had moved back, clearing the space around them. From behind, Etta pulled on his shoulder.

"You are not going to start a brawl," she said intently.

The first smoker grabbed the empty wheelchair, lifting it by the armrests, and hurled it with both hands, spinning around like the hammer throw in the Olympics. The chair sailed high, and struck the looping razor wire that lined the top of the fence across the alley. It hung there, a dozen feet off the gritty concrete, bouncing gently for a moment amid the coils.

The guy looked to Slater, eyes wide, the aggression gone. He hadn't expected that.

Etta shouted at them. "Not everybody in a chair is incapable of walking, you morons. His disability is mental, and it's dangerous."

"You're the reason wheelchair users are assholes." Slater jabbed a finger at him and raised his voice. "You."

When Etta tapped his arm, he turned and strode toward the street, and she matched his pace. Before they turned onto the sidewalk, she looked back.

"They're not following us. You're lucky they're hipsters and not gangbangers. We'd be bleeding already."

"The jazz cabbage makes people slow and stupid," Slater said. "Neither one of those stoners could slap-fight their way out of a nursing home."

"They did manage to trash a perfectly good wheelchair. That was a rental." She gestured up Wilshire. "There's a diner a couple blocks up."

He took deep breaths as they walked, working to dispel the adrenaline. As they stopped at a red light, he glanced sidelong at Etta.

"That hair is so wild. It really makes you look like a different person."

"Most people tonight were looking at my curves, and this crazy dress."

"You've got the gams to pull it off."

"Actually I don't. But thanks for saying that."

"I never come over here." He waved at the street. "There's a lot going on."

"It's cool, right? The Miracle Mile has its own energy."

She pointed out the doorway to the diner, and they stepped inside. The place was quiet, with just a couple of people at a table near the front window.

"Get me a soda water," Etta said, and walked over to a booth by the wall.

Slater went to the counter, and ordered two soda waters, and paid for them. As the clerk stepped away, he noticed the tablet next to the register. The screen said, "Add your music to the queue." He tapped in "Oh, You Beautiful Doll," surprised that it came up in the database. He added the song, and it started to play as the clerk came back with the drinks.

This rendition had fast-paced music, with lots of brass, and a man's tenor voice performing it in traditional style. It was nowhere near as mesmerizing as Artémise's version for Rocky.

Sliding into the booth across from Etta, he set one of the glasses in front of her.

"You picked this song," Etta said. "I watched you do it."

"It's got a good beat, and you can dance to it."

She laughed. "Maybe if you're wearing a corset and twelve pounds of formalwear, like it was 1900."

"It was written back then, but you can still feel the vibe. That never gets stale."

"You're a romantic, Ibáñez. You can't deny it. The song you picked is romantic." She jabbed a finger at him. "That's who you are."

"It's a technique to disarm everyone else." He raised his

eyebrows. "When they're focused on that funky ragtime beat, I can focus on serving up some knuckle sauce and knocking skulls together."

"Deny it all you want, but deep down, you're soft."

"That's never going to happen."

Etta sipped at her drink. "So there were four models for A Touch of Class, and the two guys were organizing things. Boyd is the one in charge."

"He was the only one who took a bow."

"Boyd was being hard on the models, even though I don't think he knew them. My sense was that they were working the show for him but they weren't regular staff."

"Was he harassing them?"

"Not like a letch. But the one with the black pomp— he called her Chloe—she was changing into an outfit, and Boyd says, 'You've gained weight.' Chloe is pissed at that, and she says, 'I haven't gained an ounce. Your clothes are cut weird.'"

"What about the other guy?" Slater said. "Charlie."

"It was more like a *sh* sound. Like Charlotte, or Sharla. He was taking direction from Boyd. 'Go find this belt,' that kind of thing. Boyd was definitely calling the shots, but he wasn't haranguing the guy like he was the models."

"You pointed out a woman too."

"I overheard her talking to Charlie. When Boyd was busy with the models, Charlie called her Tamara. She said to him, 'My laptop is still running slow. It's almost like you didn't do anything.'"

Slater frowned. "That makes him sound like an IT guy."

"Who knows. They're already doing apples and oranges. Selling fabric and doing a women's wear line."

"With stolen fabric designs," he said. "One of those tops was in the paisley print that got jacked from Artémise."

"Do you want me to make notes about all this?"

"That would be great, you beautiful doll." He sat back and drained his glass.

Etta chuckled. "Let's go."

As they walked back to the Continental, Slater said, "What do I owe you?"

"Well, it was short notice, and I had to buy the dress and the wig."

"You can bill separately for the drag."

"Four yards?"

"It's great that you know what you're worth," he said, "but I freaking hate that you're expensive."

"Pony up, buttercup."

He dug out his wad, and peeled off some C-notes, and handed them over.

"This is five hundred," she said, riffling through them.

"The extra C-note is for putting up with the miniskirt. I would have hated that."

———◆———

BACK IN DOWNTOWN, SLATER pulled into the lot across from the office and parked in the spot next to Etta's Prius.

"Are you going upstairs?" Etta said, as they both climbed out of the Continental.

"I need to change out of the suit."

Her car chirped as she unlocked it. "You owe me a wheelchair."

"Get Max to open the safe. There's lots of lettuce in there."

She chuckled. "It was funny, watching those pot-heads get slapped around."

"Open-handed." He held up his palms. "And they started it."

Once he'd changed clothes, he drove to his house, and found Pike upstairs, stretched out on the sofa. As he walked in, Pike set his book face-down on the faux grass.

"I love that shirt."

"It's fun, right?" Slater sat with him and kissed him. "Nobody's making anything like this today. Cassidy says that's symptomatic of a society that's lost its way."

"So you're infiltrating the fashion industry."

"I took Etta to crash a fashion show tonight," he said, and told him a little about it. "The women's clothes were fun, but the menswear was so damn boring."

"The flip side of that is that it's easier for men to get dressed. Imagine the amount of work women have to do." He massaged the back of Slater's neck, eliciting a contented sigh as Slater dropped his chin to savor his touch. "I was thinking about that dream you had this morning. You weren't sure what I was up to. You found it unsettling."

"Of course it was unsettling. You have to admit you were being kind of glib." He waggled his fingers in air quotes. "'You can hang out if you must.' Fuck that."

"It feels like deep down, you're suspicious of my motives," Pike said. "Like you think I'm up to something."

Slater glanced sidelong at him. "Are you?"

"You know better. Even if your subconscious doesn't believe that. If I have something to say to you, I'll say it."

"You make it sound like it's about trust. Like you think I don't totally trust you."

"Based on that dream, I don't think you do. Or at least your subconscious mind doesn't."

"I know you," Slater said. "I do trust you. All the way, with my life. But there's still this concern that I'll come back one day and find all my stuff dumped on the street, and then my key doesn't work in the door."

"I couldn't really do that, since it's your house."

"You know what I mean."

Pike shifted position, and pushed him onto his back, then lowered his weight onto Slater's body, pinning his arms to his sides with his elbows. He could feel the heady heat of Pike's skin, even through his shirt, felt his breathing next to his own. It felt good to be compressed a little. Pike had figured this out at some point, and knew that it chilled him out.

FOURTEEN

SLATER WOKE BEFORE PIKE did, and drew the curtains a crack for the early light. He pulled open the closet to look through his clothes. Business casual, Helen had said, which meant white-collar drag, but he also needed to look fashionable. He put on another of the 1970s shirts, polyester with long sleeves, in a print with blue and green peacock feathers. The thin fabric of the black chinos felt weird, but he pulled them on anyway, and a pair of derbies. He hated how light and insubstantial they felt. He wasn't going to be kicking down doors in these.

Upstairs he grabbed a bagel, then hustled down to the garage, where he opened his gear cabinet. It was really a gun safe, built of heavy steel and bolted to the floor, but it was designed to look like a sheet-metal box from an office-supply store. Rather than firearms he kept his illicit tech gear inside, hidden cameras and trackers and lock-picking tools. Once he'd pulled his camera-jamming glasses off their charging cable, he locked it up again.

The frames of the glasses were thick, and a series of

minuscule ultraviolet and infrared lamps surrounded the lenses. The light they emitted wasn't visible to the human eye, but the glare was intended to mess with surveillance cameras, and Svetlana assured him the colorful pattern on the frames would inject mathematical confusion to facial-recognition software.

Climbing in the Continental, he drove to his office and parked in the lot across the street. He walked to Helen's shop and rapped on the glass door. When Helen stepped up, she twisted the bolt and pulled it open. She was wearing a skirt, and a loose blouse open a few buttons, and white tennis shoes.

"You're here early." She grinned. "I like your glasses. Can I see them?"

As he stepped inside he pulled them off and handed them over. "Most people think they're odd."

"They are odd, but in a good way. Why are they so heavy?"

That was from the batteries in the arms, he knew, to power the tiny LEDs, but he said, "I'm not sure."

She handed them back and then bolted the front door. "Where did you get them?"

"One of those shops in Santee Alley."

"Come and meet Ron. He works for me." Helen leaned in and lowered her voice. "I didn't tell him you're undercover. I said you were an aspiring designer who was too broke to buy his way into the show."

"That's an excellent cover story."

He followed her into the back room and saw that the door to the alley was propped open. A white van was parked outside with its side door rolled open. A guy was loading a big plastic tub into it, and he paused as Helen introduced them.

Ron was totally fuckable, short and built, wearing jeans and a work shirt. He had solid pecs, and not the kind you got from blue-collar work. Those were from the gym.

Helen's phone sounded, and she dug it out and stepped toward her desk.

"Tell me what to move," Slater said, waving at the stacks of tubs and boxes and bolts.

Ron looked him over. "You're not really dressed for work."

"I'm not going to sit on my ass and watch you do it."

He laughed and pointed to the plastic tubs. "You can load those toward the front."

They weren't heavy, he found, tentatively lifting one, and he carried two of them over to the van. Once they were loaded, Ron put a tarp down on the floor of the van, and Helen came back, and the three of them loaded rolls of fabric. Some were sealed in plastic sheeting, and some were taped.

Eventually Ron rolled the door closed. "That's all of it."

"Let me get my shoes," Helen said.

Ron got in behind the wheel of the van, and Helen came back with a bulky handbag over her shoulder. As she walked to the passenger door, she stopped.

"I forgot. There's only two seats."

"There's room for me in the back," Slater said. "Just don't get pulled over."

He rolled open the side door, and sat on the floor against the tubs, and rolled it closed again. Ron got the van moving, and through the back windows Slater could tell they were headed to the convention center. Eventually they turned onto a ramp leading underground. Pulling his stealthy glasses off, he found the little power switch, and clicked it on with a fingernail. There was no way to know how effective they were, or if the tech industry had changed the camera tech to defeat the ultraviolet and infrared glare since Svetlana had put them together. But there were cameras absolutely everywhere, and these were better than nothing. Eventually the van stopped, and they climbed out.

It was an underground garage, and Ron had parked in the lengthy loading zone, next to a sidewalk. There were a couple of freight elevator doors a ways in front of them. A flatbed truck was parked there now, with a planter box perched at the end of the bed, and in front of that a pickup with a couple of people unloading it.

Stretching his back and rolling his shoulders after sitting on the hard floor, Slater stepped over and looked up at the foliage on the truck. It was a slender podocarp, in good shape, healthy and trimmed. It must be for a display upstairs.

Behind the one at the end of the flatbed was an identical boxed podocarp, and somebody was behind it, shoving it toward the end of the bed. Ron stepped up next to him.

"The people in the pickup are almost finished, but these guys need to move this truck before we can unload."

"They need to unload the plants first," Slater said.

Ron wasn't looking at the truck, but Slater was, and saw the podocarp tip toward them. The planter box was falling off the edge of the flatbed. Moving fast, he planted a palm on Ron's chest and shoved him into the lane next to the truck, then tried to twist sideways to avoid the impact. But the mass of greenery slapped into his face and knocked him backward.

As he tumbled onto his butt, he could feel the cool leaves enveloping his head, and the planter box hit the concrete with a *crack*. Then the podocarp was snatched away.

The box had righted itself, he realized, and watched it snap upright. Standing above it on the truck bed was a guy in jeans, his eyes wide.

Almost instantly Ron was yelling at him in Spanish, waving his arms around. He was talking fast, but some of the words stood out, like *estúpido*. Helen stepped over to Slater. She was holding his stealthy glasses. At least they didn't look busted.

"Are you OK?" she said.

He reached for her hand and let her help him to his feet. "I'm fine. Podocarps don't have prickles."

Helen was peering at him. "You don't look scratched or bloody."

Handing him the glasses, she turned to the flatbed, and talked to the other guy with the truck, the one Ron wasn't yelling at. Slater pulled on the glasses and looked over his shirt. There was no damage except some stray leaves, and he brushed them off, then swatted the dust off his butt.

"Why did you do that?" Ron said, stepping over to him. "Did you hit the pavement too?"

"Not that. Why did you shove me out of the way and let the tree land on you?"

"I've done a lot of yard work," Slater said. "I'm used to getting smacked around by shrubbery."

"You think I'm a weakling."

Slater raised his voice. "You're welcome."

He huffed. "Right. Thanks for that."

The pair with the flatbed had offloaded the other boxed podocarp, and lifted them onto a hand truck, and rolled them toward the elevator. The flatbed started up and pulled away.

"I'll move the van up," Ron said.

Helen stood next to him on the sidewalk. "I know why

you did that. Pushed him out of the way."

"You're smarter than I am," Slater said. "I have no idea why I did that."

"You think he's hot. I saw the way you looked him over. Like you wanted to sample the merchandise."

"I'll admit Ron is a snack, and he's not stupid, which is actually breathtakingly rare. I do like the way his pants fit. Those glutes. You know what they say—a pretty face is like a melody, but a pretty ass is like a symphony."

Helen frowned. "Nice."

He waggled his left hand and tapped the ring on his finger. "I can't really act on it, Helen, no matter how much Ron wants me. I'm wearing the old ball and chain here."

"Ron's wife and kids will be relieved."

He followed her up to where the van had stopped. Next to the elevators was a booth with plexiglass windows and a guard sitting inside. Helen approached the booth, and talked to the guy through the opening at the bottom of the glass, then walked past the elevator.

Standing nearby, Slater waited for Ron or Helen to tell him what to do. The guard jutted his chin at him and said something in Spanish.

"I know I look like I should understand you, but I don't."

"*Este pocho,*" the guy muttered.

Slater lunged at the booth and banged his fist on the plexiglass. "Come on out of there. We can have a conversation about who's a *pocho.* Come on."

Grabbing his shoulder, Ron pulled him back. "Chill out, man. He doesn't mean anything by it."

"Do I need to call the cops?" the guard said.

Ron stepped over and talked to him, through the glass, in Spanish. Slater glared at them for a moment, then forced himself to look away.

When Helen returned, she was pushing a hand truck, and parked it next to the van, and rolled the side door open. The three of them moved most of the bolts onto it. When a woman stepped off the elevator, pushing an empty hand truck, Helen went to talk to her, and had soon commandeered it. It was roomy enough to load the rest of the bolts and the tubs onto.

"I'll move the rig," Ron said, and climbed behind the wheel.

Helen pressed the button to call the elevator, and by the time the doors lumbered open, Ron was back. They pushed both carts into the big space and rode up to the convention floor.

It was a huge room, with displays along wide aisles stretching out on both sides. Helen pointed the way, and they pushed the trucks. Some of the booths looked like they were already complete, and others had people working on them. Helen's booth was maybe ten feet square, with a couple of tables already set up.

Once they'd unloaded, Helen said, "The carts have to go back first."

"We can do that," Slater said, and pushed one of them. Ron took the other, and they rolled them back toward the elevator. Once they were in the garage, they parked the trucks along the wall.

Walking back, Slater looked toward the little booth, and caught the guard's eye. The guy scowled at the sight of him, safe in his little plastic box. Slater pointed two fingers at his own eyes, then jabbed a finger at him: *I'm watching you.*

"Leave the man alone," Ron said, and pushed open a door marked with an exit sign. "We can take the stairs. It's faster than that *pinche* elevator."

They climbed up several flights onto the convention

floor. Helen had her stuff partly set up: a sign for her business on an easel, fabric swatches arranged neatly on the tables and hanging nearly to the floor, and a metal rack. From the shape of it, it was meant to hold several bolts of fabric in a cascading arrangement.

Repositioning the rack, Ron gestured to the pile of fabric bolts. "Grab me the jacquard."

"The fuck is that?" Slater said.

"*No te hagas,*" he said. "The thick one, fool. Off-white. It has a pattern in it."

Slater saw the one he meant, and pulled it from the pile, and handed it to him. "You actually know this stuff."

"I hope so. I'm going to be standing here all weekend trying to sell it to people." Ron grinned. "You thought I was a day laborer?"

"You're dressed like one."

"Only for setting up. I have my office-boy clothes in my bag." Once he'd positioned the jacquard at the bottom of the rack, he stood erect. "I know you hear it too. People deciding who you are by the look of you. Like that guard. You don't speak the language but you know what a *pocho* is."

"I should be used to the smack talk," Slater said. "I'm not thrilled that I'm the one making the assumptions, though."

"Jacquard is a fabric with a design woven into it."

He watched as Ron squatted again to pull some of the fabric from the roll, draping it on the rack.

"You're in good shape. Do you work out?"

Ron glanced up at him. "Yes, but no."

"The fuck does that mean?"

"Yes, I work out, and no, I'm not going out with you. Keep it in your pants, cowboy."

"How do you know that's what I meant?" Slater demanded.

"Do you know how many gay guys work in this industry?"

"Your loss."

Slater helped him set up some other bolts on the rack, and unroll a few feet to display them. Helen was working on organizing a couple of yards draped on the tables, then stepped back to look over her work.

"It looks messy," she said.

"I saw a roll of packing tape somewhere." Slater gestured to the plastic tubs. "Use that underneath. It'll keep the fabric in place."

"Then you can't pick it up."

"Tape it at one end. It'll mostly stay in place, and the chumps can't walk away with it."

She clicked her tongue, not looking convinced, but then found the packing tape and attached the swatches. After she'd finished she moved the empty tubs under the tables.

"The credentials desk should be open now."

She called to Ron, and the three of them walked toward the front of the hall. There was a crowd milling around a row of tables, and in a few minutes they got to the front. Helen recited her name, and Ron's, then eyed Slater.

"John Slade," he said, and spelled it.

The clerk got Helen to pose briefly for the camera, and then Ron, and then Slater took his place and looked into it. A minute later they each got a laminated exhibitor pass on a lanyard. It had his photo, and JOHN SLADE in big lettering, and in smaller text the name of Helen's business. It didn't say anything about his job title.

"I need to get changed," Ron said. "My stuff is in the van."

Slater walked with Helen back to her booth, and she

stood in the aisle, looking it over. "I think it looks OK."

"It looks great. You'll blow their socks off."

She chuckled at that. "Thanks for helping."

"It's just moving some boxes and bolts. I'm here anyway."

"Plus I'm doing you a favor." She tapped the pass hanging around her neck.

"Technically you're doing Steve Kawada a favor," he said. "That set of tits Ron is the real sherpa. I hope you pay him well. The guy works hard."

"Talk him up all you want. He's not going to put out for you."

"That seems like an awful waste," he said, and walked away.

The show really was all about fabric, he saw, walking the floor. Some of the displays were obviously big players, with lots of signage and floor space and smiling staff in matching outfits. At the far end a runway was set up. Somebody was going to do a fashion show later. Cassidy had said most of the industry was in New York, but there was obviously lots of it happening in this town.

He found the sign for A Touch of Class Textiles, printed in the same wedding-invitation curling script as on the storefront. The booth was the same size as Helen's. Several bolts of fabric were on a display rack, with more piled on the floor. Prominently placed was the bolt of Artémise's paisley. Either they'd pulled this one out of that display window or somebody had manufactured more than one roll of it.

Just one person was here, standing behind a table and looking at his phone. This was the one Etta had called Charlie. Not the one in charge. He was wearing a bowling shirt, tan with white panels and a chevron pattern, snug enough to reveal his lithe musculature.

The guy tucked his phone away and smiled as Slater approached. "I like your glasses."

"I like this fabric." He stepped over to the paisley and felt it, running it between his fingers.

"You're a designer? I didn't think the doors were open yet."

"Women's wear. I got in early because I helped a friend set up this morning."

"What kind of women's wear?"

"I'm doing a line of tops," Slater said. "So I'm looking for fun fabrics."

"Casual designs, or more formal?"

"Sportswear." He put his hands on his hips. "I take my cues from the OGs. There's Yves Saint Laurent, and then there's everything else."

"I get that." He nodded. "Do you have a card?"

Digging in his pocket, he handed him one of the John Slade cards.

The guy studied it. "You're in the Del Rio Building. I've had clients in there."

"Can I have a swatch of the paisley? I want to show it to my production people."

He stooped to grab a pair of scissors from under the table, then went over to the paisley. Stepping closer to it, Slater saw there was a white label inside the end of the heavy cardboard tube. The guy cut a six-inch square from the roll, then folded the end under again.

"We call it Cabernet Chew," he said, handing Slater the swatch.

"Is that the manufacturer's name for it?"

"It's just a nickname." He turned to the table and grabbed a business card, then handed it to him.

"Shaula Shargaz," Slater read aloud. "Is that Brazilian?"

He frowned. "I don't think so. It's just my name."

"I'll put it in my phone." Pulling it out of his pants, he opened the camera, then dropped the card. It fluttered to the floor.

"Whoops," Shaula said, and stooped to snatch it up.

As he did that, Slater quickly snapped a photo of the label inside the roll of fabric. When Shaula stood erect and handed him the card, he took a photo of it too, then tucked his phone away, and read the text under Shaula's name. The address was for the shop with the display window, but the business name was different.

"Neutral Hermeneutic Services," Slater read. "That doesn't sound like a fashion business." He flipped the card over, but the back was blank. He gestured to the sign on the booth. "You're not full-time with A Touch of Class?"

"We provide various other services. You know how the economy works now. You have to diversify. The business name is kind of complicated."

"I've run into hermeneutics before. The idea that any-thing can be read like a text." Slater held his gaze. "Not for what it is, but for what it means."

Shaula's eyebrows shot up. "Very good."

"What's the neutral part about?"

He took a breath. "It would be easier to explain it over a drink."

"I can do that. When are you done here?"

He laughed. "The show just started. I'll be here until they lock the doors."

"So that's when I'll be back."

Walking away, he had to grin. The guy was hitting on him. That made it easy.

FIFTEEN

I T TOOK SLATER A while to walk out of the sprawling convention center, and even then he wasn't at the street, but in some kind of courtyard. This place really took up a lot of real estate. He could walk to his office from here, he decided, and headed east.

It was weird to walk in these shoes. They felt tentative, like he could feel the surface of the sidewalk through the thin soles. When he got up to his office, the lights were off. He clicked his tongue to greet Rey Pascual, placidly watching the door, scythe at the ready.

The heft of the stealth glasses made his ears sore, and he pulled them off, and clicked off the power switch. They didn't look any worse for wear even though the podocarp had knocked them off his face.

He set them on his desk and dug out the swatch of paisley and his phone. Pulling up the image of Shaula's business card, he texted it to Andy, and added:

Can you look into this guy?

He'd taken the surreptitious photo of the fabric roll in a rush, and he thought it might turn out blurry, but when he zoomed in on it, the text on the label was legible. There was a set of Chinese characters, then an eight-digit number, and below that a long string of jumbled letters and numbers. He forwarded the photo to Andy, and sent another text:

What does this mean?

Sitting back, he took a breath. Hugo, the friend of Doris's who'd schooled him on synchronicities and coincidences, had also laid out hermeneutics for him. Now it felt like they were piling up, the coincidences, and nagging him for attention, insisting that things were connected. He'd been thinking about Hugo because Athena had appeared more than once in unrelated contexts, an undeniable coincidence. And now the coincidence was that Shaula's company was named after the same obscure concept Hugo had talked about. Pay attention to synchronicities, Hugo had told him. Do a hermeneutic reading, tease out the patterns, look for hidden information.

There was a manila folder on his desk, he saw, and grabbed it. The first sheet was a printout of the photo grid of facial-recognition matches to Cassidy's dirtbag boyfriend. He'd almost forgotten about that. Below it the other pages were printouts detailing the guy's criminal convictions.

Pushing himself out of the chair, he scooped up the folder and went down the hall to Cassidy's studio. A woman sat under the windows running a sewing machine. She didn't look up when he rapped on the open door. Cassidy was at the cutting table, and greeted him as he stepped in.

"Groovy shirt," she said.

"Have you got a minute?"

Her brow furrowed, and she leaned back against the

cutting table. "What's in the folder?"

"I get the attraction. The guy you've been seeing is totally fuckable."

"Frank."

"Frank is an alias," Slater said. "His legal name is Edward Brinsley Cramp."

"Are you kidding me?"

"I am not."

"So he is shady."

"Shady as fuck," Slater said. "He spent five years as a guest of the people of California at Susanville."

"That's a prison?"

"Up by Reno."

Her face contorted, and reddened, and she wiped at her eyes.

Slater took a breath and eyed the woman on the sewing machine. She sat with her back to them, oblivious to their conversation.

"Sorry," Cassidy croaked.

"You don't have to apologize for that. Betrayal hits hard."

It took her a minute to recover her composure, and eventually she looked toward the ceiling and let out a guttural roar.

"You can read about it if you want." Slater waved the folder. "This stuff is all from public records. Except the facial-recognition thing. That's a paid service. But the matching images are all from publicly available websites."

"You're saying I need to ditch him."

"That's none of my business. I'm saying he's lying to you. If you want the editorial, he's lied to you about his name and his rap sheet, so he's probably lying about other stuff too. You don't deserve that."

"I'm not so sure."

"Listen, toots—you're smart, you work hard, you're passionate about this business. When you found the dead stock upstairs you managed to sell Max and me on two dozen outfits. Including this one." He tapped the collar of his shirt. "Even though we were just minding our business, not even looking for clothes."

"That was a pretty exciting day." Cassidy chuckled. "Straight guys are usually less interested in the smarts and more into the packaging."

"Lucky for you, you're rocking that too. You need to find a guy who understands what you're doing in here. Somebody who's going to lie to you about how well your pants fit, not about their criminal record."

"That sounds right." She wiped at her eyes. "I'm going to break it off tonight."

He left the folder on the cutting table, then walked back to his office, and sat at his desk. Picking up the swatch of the paisley, he looked it over. Malcolm said the design was based on almonds, but only generally. Almonds were symmetrical, like seeds always were, but paisley had asymmetrical twists in it. He ran the fabric between his fingers. It felt artificial. There was a little sheen to it but it was also rubbery. This was definitely not silk.

His phone buzzed in his pocket, and he pulled it out to check. It was a text from Pike:

Want to go to Greenleaf tonight? I want to watch you dance the shimmy.

He texted back:

I want to impale you with my rock-hard tool and watch you shimmy.

Pike's response came soon after:

These things are not mutually exclusive. Best handled sequentially.

Slater chuckled. Such an idiot. He wrote back:

Maybe on hitting Greenleaf. I'll let you know.

He tucked the swatch into his pocket, and went down to the street, and walked over to Artémise's design studio. When he stepped in, the boss, Athena, stood near the front door, talking to the guard. The guy was still dressed in black, his ersatz badge printed on his shirt. He eyed Slater and scowled in recognition. Athena was wearing a top that looked like unfinished raw cotton, a loop of cowrie shells loose around the collar.

Slater gestured to her shirt. "Is that couture?"

"It was in Artémise's collection last year," she said. "I guess you're not a fashion person."

"I wasn't hired to learn the clothes."

"So what have you learned?"

"Things are progressing," he said. "Did you know there's a statue of Athena in the central library? Up the back stairs. She's got two sphinxes with her."

Her brow furrowed. "Fascinating. What can we do for you today?"

"I need to see Malcolm."

Slater jutted his chin toward Malcolm's office and walked away. The door was open, and he went in, and tossed the paisley swatch on the desk. Looking up from his computer screen, Malcolm's eyebrows shot up. He took the swatch and peered at it.

"This is not what I envisioned for the fabric," he said. "It's too heavy. Is this polyester? Maybe it's acrylic. The colors are all washed out. It's just ... wrong."

"Who calls it Cabernet Chew?"

Malcolm was still focused on the swatch, rubbing it between his fingers. "I'm sure we called it that around the office."

"But it's somebody else's trademark, so you didn't put it on the sell sheet, or on a media release."

"That was a completely informal name." He met Slater's gaze. "Where did you hear it?"

The guy was breathing hard, Slater saw. He'd set the swatch down but was absently tapping a finger on the desktop.

"What do they pay you here?" Slater said.

He frowned. "None of your business."

"You went to Fashion Institute. That couldn't have been cheap."

"Who told you where I went to school?"

"Is it supposed to be a secret?"

Malcolm looked away and took a breath. "I wish I'd done an internship instead. I could have learned the same stuff in someone's factory. It would have cost a lot less."

"I've heard fashion isn't all that lucrative anymore."

"It's called late-stage capitalism. All the assets and all the money are gradually being extracted and concentrated in fewer and fewer hands."

"I remember," Slater said. "You're a pinko."

"There's lots of money in the industry for business activities, but salaries are low. Technically I'm earning below the poverty line in LA County."

"Seriously? Here? Why would you work for poverty wages?"

"Why does anybody? There's not a lot of other opportunities in the industry. Plus I get to be in the glow of Artémise. That's worth something."

"Her aura isn't going to pay your phone bill."

Malcolm sat back. "Do you ever eat Filipino? I know a great adobo place in HiFi."

"Are you asking me out?"

"I heard you hit on Artémise's bodyguard. I thought I'd try my luck."

Slater stared at him for a moment. "I've got a lot on my plate."

"You're not into twinks? Or am I too swishy for you?"

"I like twinks as much as I like bodyguards," Slater said. "And there's no such thing as too swishy. I'll fuck you, Malcolm, if that's what you want. But it'll have to wait until all this is sorted out." Grabbing the swatch from the desktop, he walked out.

Up the block he saw a taco cart, and crossed to it, and took a minute to convince the vendor that he really wouldn't miss the beef, then stood over the gutter to eat a couple. It was still a while before the trade show would close, so he walked back to his office.

Once he was at his desk, he looked up income statistics, and what level was considered poverty. It varied wildly in different parts of the country, but a designer with computer skills should be making a lot more than what the official poverty line was in LA. It meant Artémise was stiffing Malcolm.

Next he looked up Cabernet Chew. He had no memory of the candy bar, but it was a thing, and had a serious online fan presence, with people reminiscing about the taste and the texture. Some entrepreneur was selling unopened boxes of the candy, claiming he'd found them in a food warehouse. In the photos the expiration date was over twenty years ago. Who the fuck would eat that? He scoffed and clicked away.

Malcolm was right, he saw, when he read about paisley. The design was ancient, and it was probably inspired by almonds. Something had made the guy fidgety. Maybe Malcolm had leaked the print design, or maybe he'd just been nervous in psyching himself up to hit on Slater. Lots of people found that stressful for some reason.

Eventually he got up, and went into Max's office, and opened the little wardrobe. He pulled out his other seventies suit, with the oversize green and brown houndstooth. The fabric was lumpy and thick, almost like wool, and had absurdly wide lapels.

Cassidy hadn't had to sell it too hard that day. It was a beautiful suit, and it felt like it was right on the razor's edge between extremely chic and a little weird. He pulled on the white shirt, then the suit, and the stupid derbies. Across the street he climbed into the Continental, then drove to the convention center, and nosed into the underground garage.

This was different from where they'd unloaded Helen's van. It felt more consumer-facing, with potted plants positioned near the escalators that led up to the convention hall. He held up his event pass for the staffers at the doors, then walked the aisles of the show. There were people around but the place felt quieter now, with the scheduled closing time imminent.

When he walked up on the A Touch of Class booth, Shaula was still on his own. He glanced up at him, then did a double-take.

"I like the drip, John."

"It's vintage. Nineteen seventies."

"It definitely transcends time."

"Are you ready to roll?" Slater said.

"I just need to cover up our stuff."

He spent a minute draping white sheets over the table

where he'd been sitting and over the fabric display. Eventually he lifted a day pack from under the table and stepped over.

"Where's your car?" Slater said.

"I took the metro."

"That means I'm driving. I'm in the lot."

Shaula slung his pack over his shoulder and they walked out to the escalators. As they descended, he stood on the step in front of Slater and looked back at him. Slater couldn't parse his expression. He wasn't wound up. He was too calm to be tweaking. It was more like he was confident, or pleased with himself.

Slater jutted his chin. "Where did you leave your car?"

"I don't actually drive."

"That's unusual in this town."

"There's lots of other ways to get around."

"I can imagine you doing all kinds of things."

Shaula chuckled. "You're so direct. I thought you were with someone."

He touched his ring with the tip of his thumb. "I am. Can I ask him to join us?"

"Why not?"

They stepped off the escalator, and Slater gestured toward where he'd parked.

"Do you know a place called Greenleaf? It's on Broadway."

"I've never heard of it."

"You'll love it. It's where the hep cats go to groove."

"Is that why you changed into the suit?" Shaula said. "Is there a dress code?"

"What you're wearing is fine."

Slater dug out his phone and thumb-typed a text to Pike:

Headed to Greenleaf now. I've got a target in tow.

Thinking about it, he sent him a second text:

Tonight my name is John Slade, clothing designer.

They walked up to the Continental, and Slater unlocked the passenger door for him, then walked around to the driver's side. Shaula climbed in and looked in the backseat.

"This car is huge."

"Thank you."

He chuckled. "Fuel must cost a fortune."

Slater backed out and rolled up to the street. On the block in front of Greenleaf he spotted a car pulling out from a meter up ahead, and he tromped on the gas to roar up to the space, and nosed into it.

They climbed out and walked toward the corner. It felt weird coming here when it was still daylight, although it wouldn't be for long, with the golden light of the end of the day bathing the tops of the buildings.

Stepping into Sackett's, the cafeteria on the ground floor, he led Shaula past the steam tables and the cash registers and into the dining room.

"This is a restaurant," Shaula said.

"Greenleaf is upstairs. You can take the elevator, but this is the scenic route."

The dining room was decorated like the forest, with faux conifers and taxidermy bears and racoons, and Shaula paused to look around.

"This place is wild."

"I'm told it hasn't changed in a century," Slater said. "It definitely looked like this when I was a kid."

They walked through to the staircase, and up to the more utilitarian auxiliary dining room, and then up another flight to Greenleaf. The guy on the door didn't bother to card them, instead giving them each the once-over before he waved them in.

A long wooden bar lined the back wall, and at one side was a bandstand in an alcove, fronted by the dance floor. Beyond that was an array of tables.

"This place looks like it hasn't changed either," Shaula said.

"This was restored. They had to pull down eighty years' worth of redecorating."

Piped music was playing on the speakers, and the bar was busy, but only a few tables were occupied. The host took them to a table, and they sat adjacent.

"I love the vibe in here," Shaula said. "There's a band?"

"They're totally hotcha. They'll be on later. Some nights there's a floor show too."

The server came over, and Slater ordered a gin and tonic and a plate of fries.

"Gin and tonic for me too," Shaula said, and after she'd stepped away, he eyed Slater. "What's tonic?"

Slater frowned and studied his face. He wasn't joking. The guy wasn't a kid, but maybe he didn't hang around bars.

"It's a mixer. It has a bitter taste. I think it's made from tree bark. Before there were drugs, it was a treatment for malaria."

"That sounds toxic."

"One glass of it won't do you any harm."

Shaula dug out his phone, and peered at the screen, and tapped his unlock code. He didn't even try to conceal it. Either the guy wasn't a total lowlife, or he wasn't very bright. Sitting at his elbow rather than opposite, watching him sidelong, Slater could see the numbers, and memorized the code, repeating it in his head. He pulled out his own phone and typed it into a note.

Stuffing it back in his pants, he didn't bother to watch what Shaula was doing on the device, and instead surveyed the people at the bar, and looked over the bandstand. Soon Shaula tucked his phone away and looked at him.

"Tell me about your clothing line."

"I'm just getting started," Slater said. "Looking for inspiration. I'm more interested in you. What's your story?"

He laughed. "You mean Neutral Hermeneutic Services."

"How is that connected to A Touch of Class?"

Shaula paused as the server set down their drinks, then lifted his glass.

"Should we toast to something?"

"To the fashion industry," Slater said. "And confusion to our enemies." He tapped his glass against Shaula's and took a sip.

"It's bitter. I don't mind it."

"You were talking about your company."

"Actually, you were," Shaula said, raising his eyebrows. "You were encouraging me to talk about it."

"So sing, brother."

"I have a business partner. Boyd. We collaborate on both companies."

"I didn't see him at your booth."

"We have a studio. Boyd was there today while I was working the show."

"Is he a partner in the sack too or just in business?"

"I would never get romantic with that guy. Lucky for me he's pretty much only into women."

The music stopped, and they looked toward the stage as a string of people filed onto it. There were eight of them, wearing the dark-green uniform of the house band. One of them sat at the drum kit, and another went to the piano.

There was also a guitar and a lot of brass—a trumpet, a trombone, and a couple of saxes.

Once they were set up, a woman strode out onto the stage and stood at the mike. Her dark hair was styled to tumble back, and her makeup gave her a bronzed glow. She was wearing a midnight-blue velvet gown, off the shoulders, and jewelry glittered at her neck.

"She's so glamourous," Shaula said.

"That's Les. She owns the joint."

"Welcome, friends," Les said. "Thanks for being here. Later on we've got the talented songstress Roquelle to light a torch for you. Right now, join me in welcoming the Greenleaf house band."

She raised her hands to delicately clap them together, and people around the room clapped too. As Les walked off the stage, the band started with an upbeat song.

"They sound great," Shaula said, raising his voice.

"There's nothing like live music."

They watched the band through the song and the next one. Slater spotted Pike over at the top of the stairs and waved to him.

"That's your man?" Shaula said. "What should I call him?"

"Reddy Kilowatt."

SIXTEEN

〰〰〰〰〰〰〰〰〰〰〰〰

P IKE WAS WEARING DARK pants and a shirt with short sleeves and a random black-and-white print. It looked like a sprawling inkblot from a shrink's test kit. As he walked up, he flashed that easy smile, then leaned in to give Slater a brief kiss.

"This is Shaula," Slater said.

Pike sat next to him, opposite Slater. "You're in the schmatte trade?"

"We met at the fabric show."

"You sell fabric?"

"Among other things. It's just a job."

He wasn't exactly contradicting what he'd just told him, Slater decided, but that definitely sounded like an obfuscation. At least Pike had taken the hint, and was asking questions that wouldn't trample his cover story.

"Reddy Kilowatt must be a nickname," Shaula said.

Pike laughed. "I'll answer to that. Or call me Pike."

"Where did the nickname come from?"

"The day I met John here, I had to tase him."

153

"You didn't have to," Slater said. "It was a choice. But it's hard to question that decision, because here we are." He threw up his hands.

The plate of fries arrived, and the server eyed Pike.

"Can I get you a drink?"

"What are you two drinking?" Pike said.

Shaula lifted his glass. "Gin with tonic sauce."

Pike frowned. "Squares." He eyed the server. "Get me a blended margarita, and that roasted vegetable thing."

As she stepped away, Shaula said, "Why is gin and tonic square?"

"I'm just messing with you." He reached for a fry. "And it's tonic water, not tonic sauce."

Shaula took a handful of little packets from the side of the plate. "So much plastic for so little ketchup. In the future there's no single-serving packaging."

"The man can predict the future," Pike said. "That's remarkable."

"I've been there. I'm just visiting here."

Pike raised his eyebrows. "You're a time traveler. Good to know. I'm going to need lottery numbers, or at the very least some stock tips."

Shaula chuckled. "It doesn't work that way."

"How far in the future are you from?"

"I'm not supposed to say." He reached for a fry.

"You're serious."

"Why do I always get the crazies?" Slater said, and threw up a hand.

Shaula frowned at him. "I'm not crazy."

"When you have to say it, son."

"Don't worry about him," Pike said, and got up. "This song is so hot. We have to dance." He eyed Shaula. "Come with us."

He flashed his palms. "I can't dance."

"Anybody can dance." Stepping around the table, he tapped Slater's shoulder.

Rising, Slater pulled off his suit jacket, and hung it on his chair, and followed him to the dance floor. A couple of other people were fast dancing, and Pike started into the frug. It was about the footwork and mostly about the hips, bouncing on one side and then the other. It definitely required this fast beat. Slater got into it too. It had been a while, but it came back quickly.

Pike had a dumb grin on his face, and did the monkey with his arms, and then the hitchhiker. They were both low-impact upper-body moves that were easy to combine with the frug. Pike had once said you couldn't stay cranky when you were dancing, and it was obvious why. Slater followed his lead, with the monkey, then did the jerk with his arms.

The instructor who'd taught it to them said you had to thrust out your chest as you threw an arm up over your head, then drop it and throw up the other one. Pike eventually morphed into the jerk, holding his gaze for a moment, then laughing. It was so much less controlled, and felt liberating, like a good workout.

When the band started the next song, the beat was slower, and they went back to the table, sweating and breathing hard. Shaula was beaming like a goon when they sat down.

"That is so much fun," he said. "You're so good at it."

Pike slurped at his margarita. "We're actually not. The moves are pretty easy. Anybody can look good at it."

"Dancing just looks so hot."

"You can dance. Come on." He reached for his hand, and Shaula didn't hesitate, letting Pike pull him up. Slater watched as he showed the guy how to do a simple two-step to the sedate song. Shaula picked it up quickly. It was hard to believe the guy had never done that before.

When they came back to the table, Shaula dropped into his chair and slurped at his highball.

"Who knew I could dance?"

"It feels good sometimes," Slater said.

"I have to admit I'm a little disappointed. When I met John today, I thought I might get lucky, despite that ring on his finger."

"You're making a lot of assumptions," Pike said. "Maybe your luck will double." He eyed Slater and raised his eyebrows.

"Fine with me," Slater said.

"You mean I can sleep with you both?"

"As long as you don't actually fall asleep." Pike waved a hand. "I want to dance some more, and my food's not even here yet."

Shaula picked up his glass. "No rush. It gives me something to look forward to."

From the direction of the bar, Les James walked over, and stopped behind Slater's chair. Taking his hand, she squeezed it, and leaned in to kiss his cheek. He got a whiff of her perfume.

"It's good to see you here," she said.

"The band sounds great tonight."

"They'll get sweet later, if you want to dance some more. Can I get you another round?"

"That would be nice," Pike said.

She stepped around and squeezed Pike's shoulder. "Have fun."

"She likes you two," Shaula said, watching her walk toward the bar.

"I did some work for her," Slater said.

"Whatever it was, I think she appreciates it."

"She appreciates that I didn't rip her off."

"It's more than that," Pike said. "That elusive thing about trust. She trusts you. I bet she'll comp the next round."

"She left lipstick on your face," Shaula said.

No way was he going to rub it off. It'd get everywhere, on his hands and on his suit. "Why does everybody wear that stuff?"

The drinks came, and then Pike's dinner. After he'd eaten part of it, he got up, and motioned to Slater. "Come on."

Slater followed him to the dance floor. The song was slow, and he put a hand on Pike's waist, and took hold of his other one. He had to concentrate to get his muscles to remember the steps they'd learned, but eventually he got into the rhythm.

He mouthed Pike's ear. "Thanks for remembering my alias."

Pike laughed. "You have a complicated life."

The place was filling up, he saw, and the bar was crowded. After the song ended, they went back to the table. Les strode out onto the stage again.

"Please join me in welcoming the lovely Roquelle."

People clapped and hooted, and a woman walked out, wearing a summery dress with a tight waist that accentuated her curves, her Black hair swept back. The band started up, with a slow beat, and Roquelle launched into a song. The lyrics were about man trouble, the feel of it heartsick and angry in turns, and she belted it out. Afterward there was a lot of applause.

Roquelle did several more numbers and then spoke. "Thank you. I'm going to take a break. See you on the other side."

"We can go," Pike said.

They walked down the stairs. It was dark out and almost chilly when they got to the sidewalk. Pike crossed the street to the structure where he'd parked, and Slater walked up the block with Shaula and climbed in the Continental.

"Where do you live?" Shaula asked, fumbling for the seat belt.

"Echo Park."

"Is Glendale Boulevard on the way?"

"I can go that way," Slater said. "You need to stop somewhere?"

"Just for a minute."

When he turned onto the boulevard, Shaula sat up.

"This building. Stop here for a minute."

Slater pulled to the curb. It was redbrick, two stories, old but renovated, with big glass windows. A cell phone store occupied the ground floor. It was closed now, with only dim lights on inside.

"My business partner and I bought this building," Shaula said. "We're going to open a hermeneutic services office."

"What's the revenue model for that? Hermeneutics isn't really a tangible product."

"We'll consult with people. It's like any service provider. Lawyers and therapists and coaches don't have tangible products either."

"Are you waiting for the lease to run out on the cell phone store?"

"We need to make some more money to launch the business and cover operating expenses. Right now we can cover the taxes."

"It's a good location," Slater said.

"You can keep driving. I just wanted to see it. It's quite exciting."

He pulled into the street. "Is it rude to ask what you paid for the building?"

"Four million. Once we scrape together another million, we can launch the business."

At his house, Slater pulled into the garage. Pike's rig was already here. He led Shaula up the stairs and into the bedroom. Slater kicked off the derbies, and pulled off his suit jacket, and started to unbutton his shirt.

Stepping out of the bathroom, Pike was still dressed. "So this is happening."

Slater tossed his shirt toward the closet. "Unless you need to vacuum or do the laundry first."

He eyed Shaula and shook his head. "He's got a maid who does all that. It's disorienting sometimes. My sex life has changed a lot since I met John."

"Well, I'm not shy." Shaula pulled his shirt off and dropped his trousers.

Stepping behind him, Slater was naked now, and ran his hands over his back, then reached around and caressed his torso. Shaula leaned back into him, pressing his ear to his cheek.

Pike got undressed and approached them, and squeezed Shaula's cock, then met his mouth. Grabbing Slater's shoulders, he pulled the three of them tight together.

"This is so hot," Shaula mumbled.

Pulling back, Pike moved to the bed.

"So what do you want to do?" Slater said.

"I want to be between you two. That felt amazing."

Pike waved him over, and Slater climbed on the other side of the bed. He was getting hard, and pressed his cock into his thigh. Shaula pulled himself close to Pike, running his hands over him, caressing his skin.

Eventually Shaula pulled back. "Can I fuck you?"

Grabbing a condom from the bedside table, Pike handed it to him, and shifted onto his side. Once he'd rolled it on, Shaula pressed into him, pulling himself closer.

Slater watched as they got into it, and caressed Shaula's back. It pissed him off to be left out, and he pressed his cock between his legs. Shaula looked back at him.

"Yeah, like that. Do me."

Slowly at first, Slater pushed into him, and gradually started to increase the pace. He worked up to pounding him, and Shaula yelped as he climaxed. That pushed Slater over too, and he strained into him, then shifted onto his back. Shaula had Pike in his mouth now, he saw, working him, and eventually Pike grunted as he came, and put a hand on the guy's head to slow him down.

Shifting between them, Shaula was red-faced, and rested his head on Slater's arm. The heat of his skin felt intense. This was as close to euphoria as it got. He rapidly drifted off, but then started awake when Shaula spoke.

"When I woke up today I did not see that coming."

"So your knowledge of past events is incomplete," Pike said.

"You people didn't actually keep good records. The transition from paper to digital media involved a lot of transitory formats. Information was just lost. Plus the people who win conflicts rewrite the truth to suit their own agendas."

"Fuck me," Slater said. "You're really attached to this."

Shaula turned to him. "It's safe to talk about because nobody ever believes it."

"We'll call you Cassandra," Pike said.

"Why have I heard that name?"

"In Greek mythology, Apollo gave her the gift of prophecy. But part of the deal was that nobody would ever believe her."

"I'm not really prophesizing."

"Just don't kill your grandfather," Pike said, "and mess up the time line."

"I know that's a popular theory, the multiple time lines. But that's not how reality works."

"I guess a time traveler ought to know." Pike shifted to sit up on the pillows. "How does it really work?"

Shaula held his palms a few inches apart, like he was holding a box. "The universe is like a glass block. Time is one of the dimensions. Everything moves through the block on a fixed path."

"If everything is already fixed," Pike said, "that means there's no free will. Why would I bother getting out of bed?"

"Because you'd starve or get evicted for not paying rent. You're still responsible for your actions. Even if the future is fixed, your actions help make it happen."

"It sounds like you want it both ways, babe," Slater said.

"You just gave it to me both ways. That was freaking hot."

He sat up, and climbed over him, and walked toward the bathroom. A moment later came the sound of the shower.

Slater quickly got up, and grabbed his suit pants from where he'd thrown them on the chair, and pulled out his phone. Once he'd found the note with the unlock code, he stepped over and picked up Shaula's trousers from the floor, and dug out the guy's phone.

"What are you doing?" Pike said.

"Hang on to your plausible deniability," he said, his voice low. "If he comes back before I'm done, distract him."

"So you're not going to tell me what you're doing, but you want me to run interference."

"You catch on quick."

Pike groaned.

The code worked, and the screen resolved into a grid of icons. It took Slater a minute to download and install Svetlana's tracking software on the device, but the shower was still running when the last screen popped up, asking, "Installing certainty and secret?" Svetlana's software developers were probably still in the motherland, and her stuff was usually a mishmash of broken English and Cyrillic. But it always worked. He hit the button labeled FINALIZE, and the app disappeared.

He tucked the phone back in Shaula's pants, then set his own on the bedside table, and climbed on the bed.

Watching him, Pike laughed.

"What?" he demanded.

"I guess you did tell me he was a target."

The water went off, and Shaula reappeared, and started to pull on his shirt. "I have to go."

"I'm going to come by your shop," Slater said.

"The address on my card is for our studio. You liked some of the fabrics?"

"The fabrics, the sales rep, his effortless foxiness."

Shaula chuckled. "Do I need a key for the front door?"

"Just flip the deadbolt," Pike said.

He heard him trotting down the steps, and the front door open and close. Pike got up.

"Do you need to shower?"

Slater followed him, and enjoyed washing his back, running the soap and the loofah over Pike's skin. The guy was so hot he could almost go again.

After he'd toweled off, Slater climbed the stairs and poured his ration of bourbon into a tumbler. He hated that it was so paltry, but those were the booze rules. Walking over to the French doors, he stepped onto the deck, looking out at the city. He sipped at his glass and savored the burn in his nose and his throat.

Hopefully Doris was right, that the guys with the cameras had moved on already. If they'd staked out the house right now, they'd get nudes, full frontal snaps of his junk. Sipping the heady elixir, he chuckled at the thought. Shaula said he hadn't anticipated what had gone down tonight. The last few days felt like that. A week ago he couldn't have imagined being photographed with a damn pop star.

SEVENTEEN

B RIGHT DAYLIGHT WAS FLOODING the bedroom when Slater woke. Grabbing his phone, he checked Svetlana's tracking app. Installing the hidden tracker on Shaula's phone had worked, and it showed his location as a green dot on a map. It was at the convention center. Shaula must be doing another day at the trade show.

Forcing himself out of bed, he pulled on another of the 1970s shirts, a shiny polyester number with a big checkerboard of black and white. Inside each of the white squares was a stylized red or yellow flower. It felt loud, but he had to trust Cassidy's advice, that it would look avant-garde. Jeans and boots went well enough with it, he decided, and went upstairs.

The kitchen smelled like burned toast. He could see Pike out on the deck, enjoying the sun, wearing fugly dark-green cargo shorts and a T-shirt. Slater filled a mug with steaming-hot joe, and grabbed an apple and a bagel, and walked out to join him at the patio table.

Slater sat adjacent. "Were you preparing an offering

for Hades this morning?"

"It was a toaster malfunction. It smells worse than it was."

"A skilled craftsperson doesn't blame their tools."

Pike laughed. "There may have been some human error involved. I love that shirt."

"It's from the seventies dead stock. You're not dressed for work."

"It's Saturday."

"I should probably know that." He slurped at the java.

"So what's up with Shaula?"

"I know, right? Gams for days, and then those glutes."

"I remember that part. How does Shaula figure into your Artémise case?"

"He was shilling Artémise's fabric at that trade show," Slater said. "Him or his shvantz business partner either pirated it or bought it from someone who did."

"It seemed odd that he didn't ask me anything about what I do, or my background, or what I'm all about. I asked him about his stuff. I talked about tasing you, and even that didn't elicit any questions."

"Most people are self-involved. Doesn't that feel like the norm? But I can definitely see it with Shaula. Dude seems so cerebral sometimes, and other times he's kind of clueless."

"Lots of smart people are like that."

"Or maybe time travelers are like that."

Pike chuckled and lifted his coffee mug. "I got the sense you didn't believe him."

"It just doesn't wash. If he can do it, why aren't there legions of others walking around?"

"Maybe there are."

"It's easy to pick out tourists from overseas," Slater said. "Even people from other states. I think I'd be able to spot drop-ins from the distant future."

"Maybe our era just isn't very interesting."

He gestured with his apple. "So you believe him?"

"It struck me as fiction," Pike said. "When he was explaining it, it sounded kind of familiar. Like, oh, right, I think I read that book."

Once he'd finished his breakfast, he kissed Pike good-bye and headed down to the garage. Backing the Continental into the street, he drove to the Fashion District, and parked at his office, and walked the few blocks to the A Touch of Class storefront.

Artémise's paisley was still in the window. If it hadn't been moved, that meant they had more than one bolt of it, since Shaula had one at the trade show. The door was unlocked, and Slater stepped inside and looked around. It was an open space with a high ceiling and a counter toward the back. Behind it were a couple of desks and a doorway into a back room.

For a fabric dealer it felt like there wasn't enough inventory. Helen did the same thing and her place had bolts and bundles stacked to the ceiling. This place had just a few things on display. At one side of the space stood a rolling rack hung with an anemic selection of clothes. It looked like the women's wear from the show at Stenman's.

Boyd was sitting at one of the desks, wearing little round glasses today, and a drab gray polo shirt. At the fashion show he'd been dressed like a fashionista, but now he just looked like an office drone. His skin was a little wan in the fluorescent lighting. The guy needed to go outside sometimes and get some color.

Rising from the desk, Boyd stepped to the counter, and flashed a smile as he greeted him. It kind of worked. The guy wasn't really hot, but he knew how to act charming.

Up close Slater could see the lines on his face. In his fifties, maybe, his mousy hair was cropped short. That was the smart thing to do when you were balding in front.

From the doorway into the back Shaula appeared, wearing a bowling shirt again, brown and beige with red embroidery on the breast pocket. He cracked a broad smile.

"Hey, John."

Boyd eyed him. "You two have met?"

"This is John Slade. We met at the fabric show."

"You're not doing the show today?" Slater said.

"We hired somebody to work the booth. I was there this morning. One of us will go back later."

Boyd braced his arms on the counter and glanced down at Slater's jeans. His brow furrowed. "Why are you interested in fabrics?"

"I do a clothing line. Women's sportswear. I'm always looking for new ideas." He shifted on his feet. "I actually saw your line in that show at Stenman's."

"What did you think of it?"

"It was unique. I'd never seen anything like it."

"I'm glad you thought so." Boyd waved at the room. "I'm sure Shaula took you through our products."

"He showed me a lot." Slater eyed Shaula. "You never explained the Hermeneutic Services thing. It doesn't sound like a standard fashion industry offering."

"He told you about that?" Boyd said.

Shaula waved a hand. "It's printed on my business card."

Boyd met Slater's gaze. "It's an esoteric concept."

"When I gave him my card," Shaula said, "he already knew what hermeneutics was."

He raised his eyebrows, still studying Slater. "Seriously."

"I don't look like the type?" Slater said.

"No judgment."

"Are you sure about that?" Slater put his hands on his hips. "You're right in thinking that I spend more time with my hands in the dirt than I do focused on abstractions that contribute absolutely nothing to the world. I can't calculate anyone's *I Ching* bubble quotient, but my hydrangeas look amazing this year."

Boyd chuckled. "The *I Ching* is about divination. Hermeneutics is a tool to understand the world."

He waved an arm. "Well, that sounds completely unrelated."

"It's not just an abstraction, John," Shaula said. "It's tangible. We use hermeneutics to assess the meaning of situations and life experiences."

"That's the services you provide? People actually pay you for that?"

"We do other stuff. Hermeneutics is layered into it."

Boyd shot him a look. "It's more about our outlook. The central question is, do our minds arise from the material world, or do our minds create the material world?" He rapped on the countertop with his knuckles.

"That's easy," Slater said. "The world was here first. Your brain grew out of it." He held his gaze. "You think you're special. The center of the universe, maybe, or some cosmic exception. But you're actually not. Next question."

He laughed. "Most scientists think that way too. One strand of New Age thinking is that human consciousness is the fundamental thing, and it generates everything else."

"That's exactly the wrong way around," Slater said. "How does your hermeneutic process fall into that?"

"We think both of those views aren't quite accurate," Boyd said, his eyes bright. "There's a third option. Reality and the mind are both derived from elsewhere. That's why we use the term *neutral.* Both consciousness and the material world emerge from something deeper. The true universe that we can't usually detect."

"Now it sounds like a religion. Jesus created the earth in seven days, that whole gimmick."

"It's not about gods. It's about the true nature of reality."

Slater threw up his hands. "How would you know what's real if you can't detect it?"

"I said you can't usually detect it," Boyd said. "There are techniques."

"It's interesting that you're a determinist," Shaula said.

Slater frowned at him. "I'm a what, now?"

"You think consciousness arises from matter. That means everything is determined by the laws of nature and what happened before. And that means you have no free will."

He pushed a hand through his hair. "This is starting to feel like talking to a shrink. I did a lot of that in my youth. What kind of services do you provide besides pushing fabric and your clothing line?"

Boyd shifted on his feet. "Can I ask, where's your studio?"

"He's in the Del Rio Building," Shaula said.

"I know that one. It's right around the corner. Think about that building for a minute. When you're in front of it, on the street, what else does it resemble? What natural forms?"

"Why does that matter?" Slater said.

"It's a hermeneutic interrogation."

"I don't need that."

"There's no harm in it," Boyd said. "You said you get your hands dirty. That you grow azaleas. That means you work with natural forms."

"I said hydrangeas. Azaleas are up in the Sierra foothills." He took a breath and furrowed his brow. "I'm not sure my office building looks like any natural forms. It has dark vertical lines, up the stacks of windows. I always wondered whether the architect was trying to represent redwood bark."

"It doesn't matter what the creator's intent was," Boyd said. "Only what it means to you."

"That sounds very New Age."

"To me this neighborhood feels like the canyon country along the Colorado River. The steep walls, and the color palette, and the dust. On a deeper level they serve the same purpose. The canyons and the Fashion District. The land is vast enough to inspire creativity without stifling it, but the vertical limits on the space induce focus, unlike wide-open places where your mind can just wander."

"Maybe that's why I like the Mojave," Slater said. "It's wide open, away from the grind. I don't have to focus."

"So your office building evokes a redwood. What about the street in front? If you look beyond its obvious use, what's deeper than that?"

"There's sewer pipes and stormwater tunnels."

"He doesn't mean literally," Shaula said.

"He knows that," Boyd said. "He's just not ready for a frank interrogation."

"Tell me about the fabric in the window," Slater said. "The paisley."

Boyd glanced toward it. "That's quite new. It's a nice high-poly blend."

"Hermeneutically speaking, what does it mean? What symbols arise when you study it?" Slater raised his eyebrows. "Where did it come from?"

"Aren't the colors great?" Shaula said. "Like a Cabernet Chew. The candy bar."

Boyd frowned at him. "It doesn't have a name."

"I might need a lot of it. Do you have more than a bolt or two?"

"We can price it out for you," Boyd said. "What are your production quantities?"

"I'll let you know," Slater said, and walked out.

On the way to his office, he thought about the conversation. Boyd hadn't deliberately been trying to muddle things, he decided. He just really liked talking about hermeneutics because he was into it. Hermeneutics was loopy, and the time travel thing was definitely bullshit. A lie or a delusion. Thinking about it, Slater knew a guy who knew plenty about loopy.

When he got upstairs, he pulled out his phone. Andy had texted:

Got some info for you.

Swiping it away, he found Mason's number, and dialed, not sure whether he'd pick up. He'd never slept with the guy, so he might not even remember him.

"How are you doing, Slater?"

"I need your expertise."

"I'm at my office today if you want to meet."

He knew where his building was. It was too far to walk. Down at the street again, he drove over and parked under Pershing Square. Mason's office was in an art deco tower in the liminal zone between the Historic Core, with its century-old office buildings, and the Financial District, where they'd built all the shiny new glass-walled office towers.

When he stepped into the lobby, the guard on the desk glanced up at him but didn't try to slow him down. He rode the elevator up and found the right office. It was hard to miss: the door was black and bore Mason's name in bright yellow lettering, with PSYCHIC INVESTIGATIONS under it.

Slater rapped on it, and tried the handle, and stepped inside. It was one big room with windows over the square. Farther back was a desk and some bookshelves, and under the window was a tired-looking plaid sofa and a wing chair. A bicycle was parked next to the circular conference table.

Mason rose from the desk and greeted him with a big dumb smile. Tall and built thick, he was a redhead, and a nebbish, even though he had great legs. That kind of musculature was inevitable when you cycled everywhere.

A potted *Monstera* sat between the desk and the lounge furniture, and Slater dropped to one knee to check the dirt. He frowned and looked up at Mason.

"What is wrong with you? The soil is soaking wet."

"Am I overwatering it?"

"Once a week or so is plenty."

"Understood."

"Put a pole or a trellis in the pot. It'll climb up it."

"Who knew you were so passionate about plants?" Mason said.

"They can mostly take care of themselves. Except in the face of human stupidity."

"Sit down." He gestured to the sofa.

He sat at one end, and Mason took the adjacent wing chair.

Mason met his eye. "Someone told me to say 'What happened to you' instead of 'What's wrong with you.' It shifts the focus to your experiences rather than perceived defects."

"I can tell you see a shrink."

He chuckled. "Her office is right upstairs."

"I saw plenty of those when I was a teenager," Slater said, "to the point that shrink talk is infuriating."

He flashed his palms. "Enough said."

Slater held his gaze. "So what happened to you?"

He laughed again. "You called me, remember?"

"Are you still exclusive with that smoke-show banker?"

"He's a mortgage guy, but yeah."

It seemed obtuse, but people did that, walled off their sex lives. Even Pike leaned that way.

"I remember you once talked about time travel," Slater said. "A target in my case says he's from the future. Is there any chance that's possible?"

"Sure it's possible. I'm not sure why you'd broadcast it."

"He says it's safe to talk about because nobody believes it."

"That's wild."

"How is it possible?"

"In my experience it's a state of mind," Mason said. "You can bleed through to the past by focusing on it in a specific way. Using psychic energy."

"So you've done this."

"Lots of times. Usually the bleed-through is a remote experience. Like what they call remote viewing. You're not really there. But if you push harder, you can actually be there, along with your body."

"How far back have you gone?" Slater said.

"Seventy years once. That took a lot out of me. I know a guy who went over two hundred years. Usually I use it as a viewing tool. Like looking at old camera footage."

Watching him talk, in the light from the windows Slater could see that the stubble on his jaw, even his eyelashes were electric orange, the same color as up top. It had to look like that all over. What was it about redheads?

"Reality isn't as simple and straightforward as our physical senses tell us," Mason said. "There's all sorts of other stuff going on. If you can shift into other psychic mental states, you can access some of it."

"Like traveling through time."

"One of my mentors said everything happens all at once, so there really isn't a past or a future. Looking at something from years ago isn't about moving or going somewhere. It's more like shifting your focus. Like if I look beyond your shoulder at the city outside. You're still here, but I'm focused on the Financial District now."

"You don't seem deluded."

Mason frowned. "Thank you?"

"I don't want to make the mistake of assuming my target is a deludenoid if he's not."

"He could be lying to you. But I know what he's claiming is possible."

Slater rose. "I should pay you."

"It doesn't really feel like this was a full-on consultation."

"You need to pay for this place, don't you?" He waved at the room. "And I don't want you to feel like you can say no if I need to talk to you again."

His eyebrows shot up. "In that case, give me fifty clams."

Digging out his wad of cash, Slater found a fifty, and handed it over, then walked out.

Andy's building was just a block from here, and on the way down in the elevator, he texted him:

On my way over.

The sidewalks were busy today, and not just with the desk jockeys and the suckers plying the retail stores. Lots of people lived down here now.

He strode into the lobby of Andy's building and went up to his loft.

"Advance warning by text means more than ninety seconds," Andy said as he pulled open the door.

"You're here, aren't you? And cool it with always changing the damn rules."

Andy dropped into his desk chair and swiveled toward him. "The picture of the label you sent was on a roll of fabric."

"Inside the end of it." Slater stood near his desk. "I already know that."

"It was the name of the manufacturer. A fairly big … company in Shaoxing."

"That's in China?"

"Near Shanghai. The first number is a … manufacturer's code, and the bottom one is an order number. The company … specializes in rapid turnaround."

"Good to know."

"Then the business card," Andy said, and swiveled toward his array of monitors, his head gently undulating with his random muscle movements. He read from the open documents on the screens. "Shaula Shargaz is the registered owner of the … company on the card. Neutral Hermeneutic Services. The street address in the … incorporation documents is the same as on his … business card, and the same as that fabric store. A Touch of Class."

"There's nothing about an address on Glendale Boulevard?"

"Only one address comes up for … both. More interesting, it seems like Shaula Shargaz didn't … exist before two years ago."

"Who was he before that?"

"Good question." Andy swiveled to face him. "Maybe if you had a photo of him."

"He's not online?"

"Not linked to that name. If you can … get a photo of his ID, that might lead to his real identity."

"Could it just be a pseudonym?" Slater said. "People come to LA to reinvent themselves all the time."

"He used the name on legal documents. Like the business registration. So he has to have an ID with … that name on it. To me it doesn't look like a legit identity because … there's no history. That implies subterfuge."

"I don't know why I'm surprised. Everybody lies to me."

"There's more. You've seen the stars in the sky."

Slater narrowed his eyes. "I have."

"Dim stars have … catalog numbers, but bright stars have names."

"Like Castor and Pollux. In Gemini."

"Sure. In the constellation Scorpius there's a … star named Shaula. That's an Arabic name, and it's the official one that … astronomers use. Right next to Shaula is a star that's officially named Lesath. The ancient … Babylonian name for that one is Shargaz."

"Fuck me."

"Maybe his mama was an astronomer," Andy said.

"Maybe. But I know he wasn't born two years ago." Slater took a breath. "Bye, beautiful."

Slater walked back to the square, and down to the parking, and drove to his house. Pike's rig was in the garage but there was no sign of him upstairs. It felt warm inside, and he propped open the French doors for the breeze, and stretched out on the sofa.

On his phone he looked up the stars Andy had talked about, and read about Shaula and Lesath. The name Andy had used, Scorpius, was the name astronomers used, and it was the same as the stars in the astrological sign Scorpio. But Scorpio was just the shape of the scorpion, and Scorpius designated everything in that clearly delineated patch of the sky.

Those two stars were part of the scorpion's shape. Because they were close together, astronomy nerds called them the cat's eyes, and some of the original Australians called them the falcons. They never got very high in the sky from LA's latitude, but they got higher if you looked at them from the southern hemisphere. That explained why the Australians would have noticed them, and why Shaula was one of the stars on the Brazilian flag.

Thinking about it, Etta had said Shaula looked like he had the Brazilian mix. Black and Indigenous and Iberian. Brazil had come up twice around this guy. Was this one of Hugo's synchronicities?

Setting his phone on his belly, Slater rubbed his eyes. It was too much, this alternate version of reality. Looking for secondary meanings, speculating on signs and symbols, excavating tenuous connections. He needed to stick to the parts that had solid evidence.

EIGHTEEN

◨◧◨◧◨◧◨◧◨◧◨◧◨◧◨◧

SOMETIME LATER SLATER WOKE when he heard footsteps on the stairs, and voices. That was Pike. The other voice was a woman's. Rising, he went into the kitchen. Pike stepped in from the stairs, looking sweaty, still wearing the cargo shorts and a T-shirt. Behind him was his colleague Brewster, wearing jeans and a tank top, her hair tied back. She greeted him with an air kiss.

"You two are dressed down today," Slater said.

"I borrowed your hedge trimmer," Brewster said. "Your man was helping me knock back the foliage at the side of my yard. It grows so fast in the summer."

"What kind of hedge is it?"

Brewster frowned. "A green one. I didn't conduct a DNA test."

"Got it."

Pike opened the Frigidaire, and grabbed a can, and handed it to her.

"I'm not stopping," she said. "I brought your man back, and he offered me a soda water."

"I was drinking from the garden hose," Pike said, "but Brewster is too fancy for that."

She popped open the can and took a sip. "Your hedge trimmer worked great."

"It should," he said. "It's pro gear."

"It did get bogged down a little trying to cut through all that rusted-out barbed wire. Somebody must have built a livestock fence at some point."

Slater narrowed his eyes. "My power tools are like my children."

She laughed. "I'm just yanking your chain. How cool is it that you're in a job where you got to meet Artémise? I saw the photos."

"Your job is cooler. You get to walk around with a gat on your hip, and you're legally allowed to slap lowlifes around."

"You could probably get a concealed-carry permit if you wanted."

"Oh, hell, no," Pike said. "I like the current Pax Ibáñez. Slater isn't armed, and that means there's fewer bullet holes in people and other things."

"He's right," Slater said. "I wouldn't even make it out of the gun store parking lot before I'd need another crate of ammo."

"What was she like?"

"Artémise? It's hard to say. I only talked to her for a few minutes. She's not dumb, and she doesn't act entitled. I don't think she's lying to me. That alone is vanishingly rare." He gestured helplessly. "She's good to her dog."

"Rocky is such a cutie."

In his pants his phone chirped loudly. That specific alert meant proximity to one of his trackers. The only one he was running right now was on Shaula's phone. Digging it out, he checked the tracking map. The green dot was right in front of this house. What was he doing in this neighborhood?

"Damn it," he muttered.

The doorbell rang, and Pike headed down the stairs.

"Are you expecting packages?" he called back.

"I feel like you knew that was going to happen," Brewster said. "You got a notification on your phone."

"That was just an email." Slater tucked the phone away and frowned. "You're such a cop."

Downstairs he heard a loud greeting, and Shaula came up, still wearing the brown and beige bowling shirt, his backpack on one shoulder, followed by Pike.

"Hey, John," he said as he stepped in.

Brewster eyed Slater and cocked her head.

"What are you doing here?" Slater said.

"Is it strange to just drop in?"

"I'd say it's borderline," Pike said.

"I figured it was still daylight out."

Pike introduced him to Brewster, and she affected a casual tone.

"Where did you grow up, Shaula?" She gestured with the soda can. "I can't quite place your dialect."

It was like cop mode was hardwired, Slater thought. She couldn't switch it off on the weekend.

"Michigan," Shaula said. "But I've been out here for a while."

"Oh, cool." Brewster nodded. "I went to school in Lansing. Where in Michigan are you from?"

He gestured with his index finger. "The other side."

"Lansing is kind of right in the middle."

"Do you know Detroit?"

"Not really well," Brewster said.

"I'm from Detroit."

"Did you have any trouble transferring your driver's license? When I first got here, the woman at the DMV counter told me to my face that I was stupid."

"Seriously?" Slater demanded. "When somebody who works at the DMV thinks you're stupid, sister, you've got problems."

"It doesn't mean she's actually stupid," Pike said. "It means Angelenos are not kind."

Brewster threw up a hand. "Maybe I was being stupid that day. She wanted my passport or something."

"I don't actually drive," Shaula said.

"I see." Brewster drained the last of the soda water, and set the empty can on the counter, and eyed Slater. "Thanks for the loaner, John."

As she headed down the stairs, Slater jutted his chin at Shaula. "What's going on?"

Before he could answer, Pike clapped his hands. "We were going to eat." He eyed Shaula. "Do you like soul food?"

"If it's vegan."

"John here is vegan, so that's how we order it." He stepped over and pulled open the icebox.

"In the future, everything is vegan."

"So says the man who outsmarted Chronos." Pike took out a pitcher and gestured with it. "Lemonade?"

Once he'd poured him a glass, Shaula took it and stepped into the room past the dining table.

"I didn't see this level last night. Do you host yoga classes?"

"Why would I do that?" Slater said.

"The wood floor. People are really into yoga these days."

"How would you know, future boy?"

Shaula waved at the space. "There's no furniture. What's

the purpose of this room?"

He put his hands on his hips. "What does it say to you? Think about it for a minute. What natural features does it remind you of? What kind of symbolism bubbles up in your mind?"

Shaula chuckled. "You're trying to do a hermeneutic interrogation."

"It's a way to distract myself from punching you in the face."

Stepping in front of him, Pike handed him a glass of lemonade, and pulled his attention away. "Can you put in the food order?"

Digging out his phone, he looked for the vegan soul food restaurant. Pike took his own glass, and led Shaula to the lounge furniture farther in, and sat in one of the chairs. Shaula dropped onto the sofa.

"What's a hermeneutic interrogation?" Pike said.

Still tapping at his phone, Slater followed them, and sat in the other chair. "His business partner pulled that on me today. They're opening a shop."

"Basically it means reading something for other interpretations," Shaula said. "Beyond the literal sense. To get to a wider subjective meaning."

"That implies the meaning of something can change," Pike said.

"Very good."

"I deal in the firm and fixed kind of reality. Motives and time lines and facts."

"The problem with time lines is that you see them flowing only in one direction," Shaula said.

"Right—as a time traveler, you can mess with that."

"Not really. But things aren't always linear."

"You're going to do hermeneutics in a storefront?"

"We bought a building on Glendale Boulevard," Shaula said. "It's going to be a hermeneutics center. Like a consulting business, not like a shop where people just wander in."

"How long have you worked with Boyd?" Slater said.

"A couple of years. Me and Boyd are on the same wavelength. We build on each other's understanding."

"Is hermeneutics from Hermes?" Pike said.

"I'm not sure where the word comes from. Boyd would know."

"I bet it is. Hermes is the god of crossroads, and boundaries, and liminal spaces. Places where meanings can change." Pike gestured to the French doors. "Down the block there's a crossroads that the neighbors disagree about. Is it in Echo Park, or is it in Angelino Heights? The meaning changes depending on who you talk to."

"Did you see Hermes there?" Slater said.

Pike laughed. "In spirit, maybe."

"I like how you say Hermes *is* the god of the crossroads," Shaula said. "Not was. Like he's still valid."

"We are sitting here talking about him," Slater said.

Pike sipped his lemonade. "Tell me about hermeneutic interrogation."

As Shaula got into it, Slater tried to absorb the details. His explanation got animated as he punctuated it with gestures. Pike was good at this, drawing out information, whether he was actually interested in the subject or not. He asked questions and got the guy talking. That alone was building intel. Thinking about it, Pike was probably doing this to help him out on his case. He really should be more grateful. Having the guy around was beneficial in so many ways.

When the food arrived, Slater hustled down to the front door to grab it, and carried the bag out to the deck.

They sat at the patio table as the sun crept lower in the northwest.

As they were eating, Shaula held up a little dowel. "This is a piece of wood."

"It's so you can have a chicken-leg experience without an actual chicken bone," Pike said.

He rolled it between his fingers, peering at it. "That is so damn weird."

"Don't eat it," Slater said.

Shaula frowned. "I figured out that part."

Once he'd finished, Pike sat back. "So imagine this: I find a handgun in an evidence locker, and I tuck it in the back of my belt, and I take it on a time trip to last year. Then I accidentally leave it on the table in a coffeehouse."

"That would be really irresponsible," Shaula said.

"I'm really flaky sometimes in hypotheticals." He waved a hand. "So then some knucklehead finds the weapon in the coffeehouse, and uses it to rob a pot dispensary. Of course he gets caught, and the weapon winds up in the evidence locker. Where I found it." He threw up his hands. "Where did the weapon come from?"

Not hesitating, Shaula said, "From the neutral space."

Pike laughed. "Where's that at?"

"The neutral space is the unseen deeper reality that gives rise to the physical world and to consciousness."

Slater eyed Pike. "You really asked for it, son. This stuff gets Jesusy." He jutted his chin at Shaula. "Pike worships the old gods. Ares and Aphrodite and Hestia. Just this morning we were talking about making an offering to Hades. You have to burn stuff first."

"Is that true?"

"No," Pike said flatly. "About Hades, yes, but I don't worship them. We've been reading about them. I'm Jewish."

"I don't know much about their beliefs."

"Neither do I, but I'm still Jewish."

"Why are you reading about the Greek gods?"

"They're interesting, don't you think?" Pike said. "For mortals, breaking their moral codes or disrespecting them means you're in big trouble. But you never know how the gods are going to react, and how they're going to mess with you."

"The neutral space isn't a religion," Shaula said.

"But you can't see it. You just have to believe it." Slater threw up his hands. "Like a religion."

"You can see it. You can be totally immersed in it. But you have to be in an altered state of consciousness."

"Like meditating?" Slater said.

"You take DMT."

"Here we go," Pike said. "It's all about drugs."

Shaula laughed. "You think DMT makes you hallucinate, but it actually opens a door into the deeper reality. It's always here, all around you." He waved a finger in a circle. "But DMT lets you experience it with your conscious mind for a short time."

"Did you study philosophy?" Pike said.

"I think Boyd did. I'm just a chrononaut. These ideas are the best fit for my personal experiences."

"Your lengthy life experiences?" Pike narrowed his eyes. "Are you even thirty?"

"Your hypothetical story is technically possible. The handgun emerged out of a loop. It came from where all new things come from."

"The magical land of neutral," Slater said.

Shaula frowned. "Think about where a painter gets inspiration. They create images you've never seen before. Or a new band that has a sound no one has ever heard before.

That comes from the neutral space. The true higher reality."

Pike eyed Slater. "Are you buying this?"

"I'm not even shopping, baby. It's way above my pay grade." He jabbed a finger at each of them in turn. "You two are in a boutique on Rodeo Drive, highbrow and high-end, and I'm down a back alley in Chinatown, looking at the rack of plastic trinkets they put out on the sidewalk."

Pike sat up. "Should we do the naked thing?"

"I was hoping that might come up," Shaula said. "John?"

Pike waved a hand. "You don't even have to ask him. The answer is always going to be yes."

"You make me sound sleazy," Slater said.

"Your word, forty-niner, not mine."

They got up and carried the aftermath of the meal into the kitchen, then trooped down to the bedroom.

Pulling off his shirt, Shaula eyed Slater. "Can I fuck you this time?"

"Bring it."

He ditched his boots and his jeans, then unbuttoned the vintage shirt and draped it on the armchair. Climbing on the bed, he pulled Shaula on top of him and mouthed his neck.

Already hard, Shaula pressed his woody into his thigh. "You want to be on your back?"

"It's called family style."

Pike was naked now too, and climbed on the bed, and caressed his back.

"You should do me," Shaula said, meeting his gaze.

"Are you sure you can handle all that at once?"

"I can try."

Pike laughed and wrapped his arms around his torso, running his hands over his chest. Shoving Slater's knees apart, Shaula pressed into him, and he winced at the intensity of it. Shaula was soon pounding him, and stroking him at the same time. He paused a moment and groaned as Pike penetrated him.

As he climaxed, Slater grabbed his hand, and Shaula strained into him, his face red and contorted. He leaned back into Pike. A minute later Pike came, his body spasming, and he slumped back.

Breathing hard, Shaula stretched out between them.

"Why did you call him forty-niner?" Shaula said.

"It's a nickname. Because he only wears pants that date to the gold rush."

"There's been a few of those."

"The one in the Sierra in the nineteenth century. The people who came out here looking for gold were called forty-niners."

"Classic style is timeless," Slater said.

Shaula turned to him. "To a point."

"He looks good in denim," Pike said.

"That big empty room upstairs. I'm still trying to parse it."

Slater rubbed his eyes. "I don't have to explain myself to you."

"Why you did it doesn't matter. What matters is what it represents. What it means."

Pike shifted onto his side, propping his head on his hand, and looked at them. "When I walk through that room, it feels like a blank canvas. Like you could do anything with it. Make anything happen there."

"Preach, brother," Slater said.

"I can see that," Shaula said. "It echoes the gold rush. The colonists who came here thought California was that way. Unused land to exploit."

"My living room didn't colonize anybody."

"By extension it kind of does. If you go back far enough, the land was someone else's."

"Buzzkill," Slater said flatly.

"That room also has all the glass at the far end. The French doors. It's open to the sky and the outside world. Then at the opposite end is the kitchen. Symbolically that's the hearth, the traditional human gathering place. Maybe the room represents humanity's path from the natural state toward technology and civilization. Like you're reenacting that path upstairs. You yearn for the freedom of the primitive world, but you also need to come back to civilization. You've left all that space to accommodate the transition."

"Fuck me," Slater muttered.

"This room is curious too," Shaula said. "The color. It's kind of purply-blue."

"It's called periwinkle," Slater said. "You should know that, seeing as you're in the schmatte trade."

"The purple tint implies that you're in charge here. There's no equivocating. The blue cools things down. It blends in yin energy, balancing your sexual activities."

Pike laughed. "I like that. It kind of fits."

"And the drapes," Shaula said.

Slater sat up and grabbed his phone. "Nobody gives a damn about the drapes."

"I do," Pike said. "When the sun comes up, if they're not closed."

"Now is a good time." Slater tapped at his phone and got up. "Put your shoes on."

Pulling on his jeans, he stepped into his boots.

Shaula sat up. "Where are we going?"

"Not far. You can interrogate the subjective meaning of the highest reaches of the house."

Once he'd tied his boots, he didn't bother to put on

a shirt. Pike pulled on a pair of gym shorts, and Shaula stepped into his pants. Slater led the way up to the kitchen, then opened the door in the side wall near the dining table. Outside was a metal-grate landing and a set of utility stairs that led up the side of the house to the flat roof. He climbed up, with Shaula and Pike following.

Stepping onto the roof, he walked over to the middle of it. The dregs of the lingering summer sunset still glowed on the horizon in the northwest, but it was dark enough, and the sky was clear.

"You could make use of this space," Shaula said, looking around. "It needs a railing, though."

"You can't really walk on it too much," Pike said. "There's no decking. The roof will start to leak." He eyed Slater. "What are we doing up here?"

Looking at his phone, Slater held it toward the southern sky. "You can't see them from the deck, and it's hard to see them in the glare of the city, but they're right there." He pointed them out. "See that star?"

"I do," Shaula said.

"Lo, that's Shaula. And the one right next to it is what the Babylonians called Shargaz. Your surname."

"What can I say? My parents were hipsters."

"Hipsters who were into astronomy?"

"Are they in Sagittarius?" Pike said.

"Scorpius." Slater kept his gaze on Shaula. "The scorpion. In Arabic, Shaula means 'the stinger.'"

"It's odd, right?" Shaula said. "People usually name their kids after their relatives."

"Yes, Shaula, it's odd," Slater said intently. "Almost too odd to be credible."

"My understanding is that the Babylonians named them for two weapons. One was for offense and one was for defense." He briefly held up his fists in a boxer's stance. "One, two, *bam*."

"I like the symbolism of that," Pike said. "It's elegant, and well-rounded."

Shaula dropped his chin. "Something like me?"

"Stop flirting with him," Slater said flatly.

He chuckled. "I have to go."

They headed down the stairs, and once they were all inside, Slater closed the door.

"I'm going to get dressed and bounce," Shaula said, and walked toward the stairs.

Slater watched him step out of sight, then went to the kitchen cabinet and pulled out the fifth, waggling it toward Pike.

"Want a nightcap?"

"Sure."

If they were both drinking, he could pour the good stuff instead of his cheap quotidian bourbon. He put the bottle back and grabbed Pike's scotch, and poured out his ration, and one for Pike. Handing him a tumbler, he clinked them together, and took a sip, savoring the heady burn.

"I get why people have to wear clothes," Slater said. "Seeing you standing around shirtless is awfully distracting."

The sound of footsteps on the stairs came from below, and then the front door opened and closed.

Pike gestured with his glass. "He did a hermeneutic analysis of this room."

"And the bedroom. He's totally committed to it. I just can't figure out how it makes money."

"The hermeneutic stuff sounds like psychoanalysis. I bet he could be like a life coach. Tell people what's wrong with them through hermeneutic interrogation."

"It seems more like astrology or tarot card readings,"

Slater said. "There's just enough tangible stuff mixed in that it sounds plausible. Mars and Saturn really are up in the sky, and the cards are right in front of you on the table, made of real paper. But mostly you just have to believe it." He waved a hand. "In the end the neutral space is completely unverifiable."

Pike tipped his glass toward him. "Unless you take DMT."

He scoffed. "I've got enough damn problems."

NINETEEN

WHEN SLATER WOKE IN the morning, Pike was already gone, and he lay there for a while. It took a minute to swim up to full consciousness. He needed to talk to that brick roof again, he realized, and he grabbed his phone and texted Mason:

Are you around today?

His reply came a minute later:

Do you know Waterman's deli? I'm headed there now. We can get breakfast.

"Idiot," he muttered. Of course he knew it. The place had been there for a century. In his childhood Doris used to haul him in there on Saturday sometimes before grocery shopping. He texted back:

I might have heard of it.

Rolling out of bed, he pulled on his jeans, and found another seventies shirt, with long sleeves and a diamond pattern in several shades of orange and dark yellow. Upstairs he saw that Pike wasn't around. He'd left him coffee, room-temperature and still in the pot. Pouring some, he slammed it, then went down to the garage. Pike's rig was gone. He backed the Continental into the street, and drove to Downtown, and found a street spot.

The deli was crowded, but Mason had scored a table for two, and waved at him as he stepped in. As if he needed to draw more attention to himself, the big mook. He was the size of a rugby player, and then there was that orange mop. Slater sat across from him and flipped his coffee cup over.

"Great shirt," Mason said.

"I know. It's vintage seventies."

The server stepped over and poured java for him. "What can I get you?"

"Oatmeal," Slater said. "Can you do it with oat milk or soy milk?"

"Sure." She eyed Mason.

"Bring me the same." As she walked away, he said, "When you texted, I felt like I couldn't say no."

"Good." Slater waved at the room. "I assume you were coming here anyway."

"So what's up?"

He slurped at his java. "What do you know about DMT?"

"You're going down some curious rabbit holes."

"My target is into it."

"From what I understand, everyone who does it has the same kind of experience," Mason said. "It's usually pleasant enough. You meet these entities. They're typically doing stuff, but what they're doing is hard to describe. Some people call them mechanical elves. Others call them aliens."

"But they're hallucinations."

"That's the straightforward explanation."

"Have you done it?"

"I don't think I need to. I can get to altered mental states without drugs."

"If you don't buy the straightforward explanation," Slater said, "what do you think is going on?"

"It's compelling that people report the same environment, the same entities. I'd say that's evidence it's a window into some other layer of reality."

Slater raised his eyebrows. "That's what he said."

He chuckled. "When you take LSD or mushrooms, it's not like that. It's more like your mental state shifts. You get more perceptive, and the trip can be about anything. Upbeat or dark."

Mason waited as the server set down their bowls of oatmeal, then dug into it.

"So people who do DMT find themselves in the neutral space?" Slater said.

"I haven't heard it called that. The complaint I've heard is that you can only be in that experience for a few minutes before the drug wears off. Some researcher is talking about extending the dose so you can stay there longer. But who knows what that might do."

He scoffed. "Have you ever run into people who got burned out on acid? It's not pretty."

Once he'd finished, Mason wiped his mouth with a napkin. "Did you look in the deli case? They make amazing conchas."

"Those are never vegan."

His eyebrows shot up. "Small vegan world. Your pastry karma must be maxed out, because Waterman's makes vegan conchas."

"Fuck me. Why did you tell me that?" Slater demanded.

"Now I have to buy some."

Mason laughed, and sat back as the server stepped over.

"Can you box up a dozen of the vegan conchas? And I'll take the check."

"Thanks for breakfast," Mason said.

"What do I owe you?"

"Nothing. An AI search could have told you the same thing in fewer words. And you bought my breakfast."

A minute later the server handed him the check, and a paper bag with handles, branded with the Waterman's logo. It was written in hot-pink looping script. It probably hadn't been reworked since the place opened.

Once he'd paid, he walked out with Mason, and they parted on the sidewalk. Setting the bag on the passenger seat, he drove to his office. The parking lot was almost empty on Sunday, the only day the clothing factories took a break. As he climbed out, he grabbed the pastries. The summer heat would trash them if he left them in the car.

He expected the lobby to be deserted, based on how quiet the street was, but a guy was standing in front of the elevator door. Wiry and not very tall, he had a shaved head.

"You actually have to push the button," Slater said, and pressed it. The sound of machinery starting to move came from somewhere overhead.

The guy shifted on his feet. "Right."

Slater looked him over. Basically fuckable. Why did this guy look familiar? Then it struck him—this was the lowlife Max had investigated for Cassidy. Frank. She'd planned to ditch him. That meant he shouldn't be here. What was this idiot's real name? Briefly digging out his phone, he found the documents Max had sent. His criminal record called him Edward Brinsley Cramp.

Frank was breathing hard, like a man with a lot on his

mind. Plus he hadn't called the elevator. Maybe he wasn't sure he really wanted to go upstairs, and he was psyching himself into it. Slater's heart started to pound when he saw that his shirttails were out, hanging over his belt, and there was a telltale bulge in the small of his back.

When the elevator arrived, Slater gently set the bag of pastries on the floor and stepped toward it, then turned and punched the guy in the face. Frank shouted in surprise but reacted with flying fists, landing one on his ribs, and a left to his face, then the side of his head. Moving in, Slater tried for a dick punch, but the guy blocked him, so he grappled with him instead.

Frank knew how to brawl, but Slater had the weight advantage. Using a wrestling maneuver, he tossed him on his belly, quickly snatching the handgun from his belt, and stepped back.

The guy had definitely felt the weapon leaving him. When he twisted around and flipped onto his butt, he braced his hands on the floor, not making any move to come at Slater. Instead he looked up at him, breathing hard, his face red.

Slater waggled the weapon to make sure he knew who was in charge, then scooped up the pastry bag, and jutted his chin toward the street. "Out."

Slowly getting to his feet, fists balled, Frank trudged out to the sidewalk. In the daylight he turned to face him. His jaw was set, and a drop of blood hung at one side of his mouth. Slater could taste blood in his own mouth. The guy had struck his lip, and it was numb, and undoubtedly starting to swell. He tucked the weapon into the pastry bag on top of the pink box.

"Give that back," he said, his voice low.

"You don't really want it," Slater said. "Frank might be a

bandito, but Edward Brinsley Cramp is still on parole. The heater is a one-way ticket back to Susanville. They'll tack on another five years."

"The fuck are you?" he demanded.

"I work for your ex-girlfriend. Emphasis on the ex. To you I'm the elbow man. The game is over, and you need to beat it."

"Are you the one who told her about my record? She dumped me because of that. Right on the sidewalk, like I was garbage. No warning, no apology."

A prowl car rolled up to the curb, and the side window slid down. The cop in the passenger seat called to them.

"Hey, fellas. What's going on?"

"We're just talking here," Frank said.

"You're bleeding," he said. "Do you need assistance?"

"I'm fine. I fell."

"It's just a superficial wound." Slater waved at the lobby. "There's a loose tile on the steps."

"It looks like that loose tile took a poke at you too," the cop said. "What's in the bag?"

Slater briefly held it aloft. "The best conchas in town. Unfortunately I can't share them. They're for church later."

The cop scoffed, and looked away, and the prowl car pulled out from the curb.

Slater eyed Frank. "You're welcome."

"You're the one holding the rod. You should be thanking me for not mentioning that."

"My prints are on the grip, but Edward Brinsley Cramp's are on the rest of it, and on the mag. If I see you around here again, or Cassidy even gets a whiff of your stank in the neighborhood, I'll deliver this to the cops myself."

It was just bluster. Slater would never get into it. He wasn't even sure where his prints were or weren't. But clearly the guy believed him. Staring at him, he was still breathing hard, murder in his eyes.

"Let it go, man," Slater said. "It's not worth it. There's so many other women in the world. A month from now you won't even remember her name."

Wiping his bloody mouth with the back of his hand, Frank turned and strutted away. Slater stood on the sidewalk and watched him round the corner. He felt a little dazed. His ribs were starting to hurt, and his mouth. The guy had slugged him good.

At the curb where the cops had been a moment before, a sedan rolled up, a rideshare logo displayed in the windshield. The back door opened and Cassidy climbed out. Heaving her bag onto her shoulder, she flashed a smile.

"I love that shirt," she said. "You look like a total boss."

"I had a highly skilled stylist source it for me."

She chuckled. "Are you on your way in or on your way out?"

"I just got here too. You know it's Sunday, right?"

"When am I not working? I'm out here trying to make some scratch."

"I hear you, sister."

He followed her into the lobby, and boarded the elevator with her, and pulled the scissor grate closed.

Cassidy peered at him and tapped her lip. "What happened here?"

"One of the hazards of the job." He gingerly pressed a finger to his mouth.

"I thought you were embedded in the fashion industry right now, not cage fighting."

"Those fashionistas take things seriously," Slater said. "I told somebody I thought Yves Saint Laurent was a hack, and the claws came out."

"Oh, that would do it. You're lucky to be alive." She gestured to the bag in his hand. "You've been to Waterman's. Is there anything in there you'd like to share?"

"Not at this time."

Cassidy laughed. "I don't need to be snacking anyway."

They stepped out on their floor, and Slater unlocked his office and flicked on the lights. Sticking his head into Max's office to make sure he was alone, he went back to his own desk, and dropped into his chair. His head was starting to throb. Rolling open a drawer, he found a bottle of ibuprofen, and shook some into his mouth.

The weapon, he remembered. Rising, he took it out of the pastry bag. It was an odd one, tan and metallic and black, with the slide and the frame and the barrel each a different color. He popped out the mag and cleared the chamber. There were only a few rounds in it, but that would have been more than enough to put him on a slab.

The sound of keys in the lock came, and he dropped the rod and the mag into his top desk drawer, and rolled it closed.

TWENTY

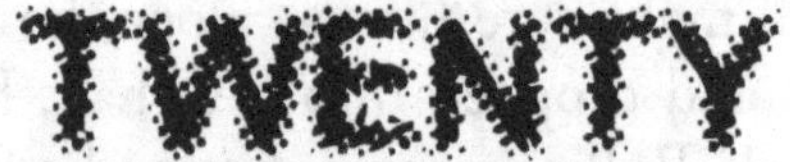

S THE DOOR OPENED, Max called a greeting.

"You're working Sunday," Slater said, stepping into the front office. "You must be busy."

"I have to finish a report for a client. A window-shade job."

"I know you hate the paperwork. Can't you get Etta to do the writing?"

"She wasn't involved in this one. Explaining the details to her would take longer than just writing it myself." Max's eyes narrowed. "Who clocked you?"

"Edward Brinsley Cramp. I bumped into him just now in the lobby. He was looking for Cassidy. I took his heater away and eighty-sixed him."

"Does Cassidy know he's a lowlife?"

"I filled her in on Friday. Frank said she dumped him."

"Are you going to tell her he was here?" Max said.

"She's a civilian. Do I really want to give her something to stress out about? I told the dirtbag I'd take the heater to the cops if he came around again."

"He's definitely not going to want to violate his parole. Do you think he bought it?"

"He knows his prints are on it."

Max nodded. "He won't be back."

"This world we're in, brother. Sloshing around the cesspool. Taking out the trash. We're like the garbage collectors, except we don't get to drive around in that cool truck."

"I hear you. If people like Cassidy knew half the stuff we do for them."

Slater huffed. "Are we sure that telling her the truth isn't the better option?"

"You got rid of the guy, so it's the right call. You don't need to set her up to be looking over her shoulder for the next decade."

Back in his office, he sat at his desk, staring absently at the turquoise walls. Etta had picked that color, and the furniture, and the light fixtures. He needed to get rid of that rod. More important, he needed to tell Cassidy something. Just not the whole truth.

Rising, he went out and walked down the hall. Cassidy was at the cutting table, working on a pattern with a pencil. She stood erect and smiled as he stepped in.

"We're becoming good friends."

Slater put his hands on his hips. "There's a way to audition guys to assess how risky they are."

Her expression sobered. "Like Frank. I broke up with him, by the way."

"This applies to all guys. It's not foolproof, but it works."

"Do tell."

Looking at her desk, he stepped over to it, and tapped a dark green binder sitting on the desktop.

"I'm going to help you with his," Slater said. "Try to talk me out of it."

She frowned. "OK."

"This binder should be on the shelf, Cassidy. I'll just move it over there for you."

"You don't have to do that."

"No, no, it's OK; it's no trouble." He picked up the binder.

"I don't need it moved."

"You don't have to do everything yourself. I can help."

"Put it back," she said.

"But it really does belong on the shelf. I'll just take care of that for you."

Cassidy waved an arm. "You're being really annoying."

He set the binder on the desk. "Now I'm a different guy. Do it again. Try to talk me out of it." He tapped the binder. "I'll just move this over to the shelf for you."

"No thanks," she said. "You can leave it where it is."

Slater flashed his palms. "Got it. If you change your mind, just let me know. I can help."

"I get it. It's much less trad male that way."

"You can give a guy that test by saying no. If he doesn't respect your no for the little things, it's more likely he won't take no in a dark alley, or in the bedroom."

"That's actually a good insight." She folded her arms. "You really do know the gritty side of things."

"Yeah, Max and I call it the cesspool."

"Why do you do it?"

"Great question." He rubbed his forehead and huffed. "I work and I work till I'm half dead, grinding the gears to keep all this going." He waved at the room. "And guys like Frank keep showing up, grifting and chiseling and coming at me."

"I shouldn't have asked you that," Cassidy said. "I know why. You do this because you're good at it."

"I'm glad somebody thinks so."

Walking out, Slater went back to his office, and heaved his feet up on the desk. He needed to think. His face hurt, and his lip was throbbing. He gently prodded it. It was definitely swelling.

He had so much going on. He didn't need to be scrapping with lowlifes, and all the bullshit about time travel, and hidden layers of reality, and shifting meanings. He needed to focus on the case. Thinking it through, he realized he'd neglected some obvious interviews. He dug out his phone and dialed Etta.

"You never made notes for me from that stupid fashion show," he said when she picked up.

"Didn't I give you those? I wrote them up. I'll send them now."

"Why are you whispering?"

"I'm at church. Mass just ended."

"Are you fucking kidding me?" Slater demanded. "You need to get away from those sickos."

"I'm hanging up now," she said.

Looking at the screen, he saw that she really had ended the call. He couldn't figure out why she still went. Etta used to work for those sexless degenerates, and they'd threatened to shit-can her for sleeping with women. In his hand the phone buzzed with a notification, and when he checked, he saw that it was Etta's notes.

Sitting back in his chair, he read through them on the little screen. She'd written Shaula's name phonetically, as she'd heard it, "SHAW-luh." That was pretty damn close. Scanning farther, he saw Tamara. That was the name he needed. He read through what Etta had overheard the woman say to Shaula. It was about a laptop, and that it was still running slow. Etta had recorded Shaula's response too: "When the machine runs slowly, what fills the gaps? What thoughts or feelings does that allow time for?" She hadn't noted the woman's response. If it were Slater, he would have punched the guy in the face. He'd heard way more than enough of the hermeneutics bullshit.

Etta had added a note about Tamara: "Several people with that name in the industry. Was able to identify the target." Below that was a link to a news item. When he clicked on it, the headline read, "Is fast fashion taking over?" The text was an interview with Tamara, and it had the name of her company up top, along with a photo of her. At the show he'd only caught a glimpse of her from a distance, but this woman had the South Asian look Etta had described. She'd even added the company's address. It was just a few streets away—he could walk there.

Sitting up, he sent Etta a text:

Excellent research in the notes. Hit me up for another hundo.

Thinking about it, he sent a second message:

Are you still at the cathedral? Get up and beat it. They're messing with you.

He tucked his phone away. No way was she going to respond to that.

It was Sunday, but if Tamara was working for herself, and grinding like Cassidy, she might be at work today. He locked up the office, and went down to the street, swinging his arms around in the sunshine and breathing deeply to dispel the fog of getting pummeled by dirtbag Frank.

Tamara's place was a storefront business, he saw, walking up on it, but it wasn't set up as retail. It had planter boxes on the sidewalk out front, the big heavy ones that property owners put out to discourage graffiti and prevent homeless people from pitching tents. There were windows up high and the name of her business painted on the door. He rang the bell next to it.

A woman with dark hair pulled it open and greeted him in Spanish.

"Is Tamara here today?"

She turned and shouted the name, then retreated as Tamara walked up. Her black hair was tied back, and she was wearing a denim jacket. Slater handed her his business card, the one with his real name on it.

"I wanted to ask you a couple of questions," he said. "It'll only take a minute."

"You're an insurance investigator." She studied the card, then looked up. "Did someone file a claim that involves me?"

"Is there somewhere we can talk that's not in the doorway?"

"It would be good to get out of here for a minute. Let's go for a coffee."

She called something in Spanish to the woman inside, then stepped out and pulled the door closed.

"What's open today?" Slater said.

"There's a place up the block for people who come into the neighborhood to shop retail."

They walked abreast, and he felt Tamara's eyes on him.

"I love that shirt."

"It's 1970s dead stock." As they stepped into the coffee place, he said, "I can order."

"Get me a skinny latte."

Slater ordered at the counter and carried the drinks over to where Tamara had sat, near the front window. She sipped at the cup as he sat down.

"What kind of insurance claim are you investigating?"

"I'm researching a couple of companies," Slater said. "Not yours, but I know you're a player in the industry."

"That's flattering, and maybe not entirely accurate."

"There was a show Thursday night at Stenman's."

"I was there. I don't remember seeing you."

"I wasn't on the catwalk."

She chuckled. "There was some great new stuff. Especially Big Fella. He's very creative. I do women's wear, for an older demographic, but I can see the ideas he's bringing out."

"What about A Touch of Class?"

"Are they friends of yours?"

"Not at all," Slater said.

"I don't really want to gossip."

"And yet I really want you to gossip." He spoke louder. "Sing, sister."

Her eyebrows shot up. "Well, to be candid, their work isn't very original. And it's kind of all over the place. A couple of garments with similar lines and similar structure, and then other pieces in completely different styles."

"That's unusual?"

"Very. The prints are all over the place too. Light and summery, then dark and formal. One of the Touch of Class prints at that show looked a lot like one of mine. Something I designed. But the colors were different. I couldn't believe they came up with that too. I started questioning myself, like maybe I'd subconsciously copied somebody else's print."

"Have you ever had dealings with a guy named Shaula Shargaz?"

"He works in the neighborhood. He was at the show on Thursday too. He said he was helping out one of the lines. Either Big Fella or A Touch of Class."

"You've worked with Shaula?" Slater said.

"He does IT. He's fixed my computer a couple of times.

Although he didn't do a very good job. It's still running slow."

"What's the name of his IT business? Or does he just do it freelance?"

"I can't remember." Tamara furrowed her brow. "It's something completely obtuse. It doesn't sound like computers at all."

"Neutral Hermeneutic Services?"

She snapped her fingers. "That's it."

TWENTY-ONE

SLATER WALKED BACK TO his office and was about to climb in the Continental when he remembered the conchas. He hustled across to his building, and once he'd retrieved the bag, drove to his house. Pike's rig was here, and he found him upstairs, shirtless, standing in front of the closet.

"I'm looking for a shirt with the right vibe," Pike said, and eyed him. "Whoa—who punched you?"

"A rat-fuck parolee who's stalking my office neighbor."

"Did you get him popped?"

"It's not worth it. I think I scared him off though."

"Is that the shirt you're wearing?"

"I want one with short sleeves."

Slater dug through the closet, and found another of the vintage shirts Cassidy had talked him into. It had a warm green and blue pattern of thick angular tubes that wound around his torso on a cream-colored background.

Pike pulled on a shirt with a random pinky-red pattern. "Does this make me look like a hoochie daddy?"

"In no way is that hoochie."

"The sleeves are really short."

"It shows off your arms," Slater said. "The only downside is I'm going to be looking at it, so I'm going to have a stiffy all afternoon."

Pike pulled on a pair of golf shorts, and Slater let him talk him out of the jeans, instead putting on a pair of off-white chinos. As he was transferring his keys and his cash, he found the swatch of paisley Shaula had cut for him, and tucked it into his hip pocket.

"I like the white pants," Pike said, looking him over. "I never see you dressed that way."

"It feels like Purim up in here."

"Think of it as being undercover. Like infiltrating the fashion industry."

Eventually they climbed in the Continental and headed west to Sunset Plaza. Up in the hills a line of vehicles was backed up on the narrow street, slowly crawling ahead.

"Is everybody looking for street parking?" Pike said.

"I'm thinking it'll be valet only."

As they got closer, a guy in a black vest stepped up to the driver's door and handed him a valet tag. They climbed out and walked up the driveway, not far behind a couple of other people headed in.

"At least we dressed like they did," Pike said under his breath.

The front door was propped open, and they walked into the house, then through to the back, with the sprawling grassy yard and the patio around the pool. Nobody was in the water, but dozens of people were standing around talking or sitting on the patio furniture, their conversations almost drowning out the music. Coming through a big set of speakers near the house, it wasn't live, and sounded upbeat, and instrumental, like acid jazz.

"There's the bar," Slater said, and they walked over to it.

"I've got mimosas," the bartender said as they approached, "or something else?"

"Let's do a mimosa," Pike said, and they each took one. They stepped away, sipping from the flutes and looking over the crowd.

"I love that Artémise's guests look like the real world," Pike said.

"They all look monied to me."

"I mean the ethnic mix. This is what the metropolis looks like. Every color of the rainbow."

"Her staff are pretty eclectic too. The handful that I met at least."

Pike was looking past his shoulder. "Is that who I think it is?"

"Probably."

"I guess it's no surprise she's friends with other celebs."

"Who are you talking about?"

"The woman with her hair pinned up. She's definitely on a TV show. The one where they drive around solving crimes."

"There's a few like that," Slater said, and turned to look.

"Her name is Mel something."

"She looks like an actor. The proportions and the good looks."

Pike gestured toward the house. "I kind of want to look around inside. That foyer was so dramatic."

"Text me if you get thrown out."

"That won't happen," Pike said. "I'll claim I was looking for the head."

Slater watched him walk into the house. He knew he wouldn't get busted, knew that he'd get away with it. The guy had that unfathomable ability to charm people, the same way Doris did. He could talk to them for a minute and suddenly they were like old friends.

The mimosa wasn't very strong. He slammed the rest of it, and wandered toward the bar, and asked for another. As he stepped away, a server with his hair pulled tightly back approached him. He was carrying a tray loaded with little canapés.

"Are any of these vegan?" Slater said.

"Everything's fully plant-based today. From Artémise's catering line."

"I'll be damned." He took a little fried ball of something on a toothpick and tried it. As the server started to turn away, he spoke through the food. "Hold up, toots." As the guy paused, he took two more. "Do you know where the bathroom is?"

"Inside there and to the left." He nodded toward the house. "All the way down the hall."

Slater ate the canapés as he walked to the house. They were made of garbanzos, maybe, and spiced with curry, and totally delicious. He should have taken a handful.

Inside he walked the length of the hall and turned a corner. At one side was an alcove, under a bright window, with a set of white sofas facing each other across a low table. Perched on one of the sofas and leaning over the table was a guy wearing a Hawaiian shirt. He had a great head of dirty-blond hair and several days' worth of stubble on his face. Totally fuckable, Slater decided. He was holding a credit card, and two neat white lines were laid out on the tabletop.

The guy looked up at him. "Do you have any cash?"

Slater groaned and dug in his pants. He found a newish single in his wad and peeled it off.

"Aren't you the big spender." The guy frowned at the

bill as he took it. "Benjamins are usually in better shape. Do you want a bump?"

"No," he said flatly.

"Maybe you have something softer." Not looking at him now, he focused on rolling up the bill. "I feel like I should shift down. Maybe take a school bus."

"The fuck is that?" Slater said.

"A Xannie. It's a downer. How can you not know that?" He jutted his chin. "What are you carrying?"

"You need to stick to one drug at a time, Slick. Otherwise your heart stops beating."

The guy frowned. "Thanks, Dad."

Slater walked away and found the bathroom. It was surprisingly small for such a big house, really just a powder room. Maybe it was meant for the maids and the gardeners. He couldn't see the source of it, but the room had a strong smell of patchouli.

Outside again, he found Pike over by the bar. He had two glasses in hand, and gave one to Slater.

"I switched to white wine."

He sipped at the glass. "Fuck me. This is really good."

"I know. When it's open bar you expect it to be cheap and acidic."

"Now I can't drink cheap white wine anymore, since I know what the good stuff tastes like," Slater said. "These people really are trying to break me."

"So I did coke with that TV star."

"That's a lie," he said flatly.

Pike laughed. "It's a total lie. But it was nice of him to offer."

"That blond wastoid? I saw his setup. I wasn't sure if it was coke or meth."

"I asked. He said it was cocaine."

"He asked me for Xanax," Slater said. "Is he famous for real?"

"Not famous enough that I remember his name."

"I suppose we'll hear all about him when he overdoses. What did you find inside?"

Pike leaned closer. "Nothing remarkable. The house has been cleaned and organized."

"You sound like you're on the job. So why did the bathroom smell of patchouli? Is that some rich-folks thing that I'm not sophisticated enough to understand?"

"I wasn't sure if it was patchouli or sandalwood. I assumed it was Black culture."

"I thought patchouli was a hippie thing."

"Some of Artémise's personal fashion is hippie-inspired." Pike gestured to the other side of the patio. "Did you see the food? There's a whole buffet laid out."

They walked over to the tables, set up along a neatly trimmed Mediterranean cypress hedge. It was a good choice if you needed a green wall since it wasn't a water hog. Someone was taking care of it too, as it was free of crabgrass and cobwebs.

"I wonder if there's anything for you to eat?" Pike said.

"It's all for me today, babe. Artémise runs a plant-based catering line."

"Of course. I knew that. Didn't the ranchers' league sue her for slander because she won't let her kids eat hot dogs?"

"Look at this stuff," Slater said. "I wish I'd brought a backpack. I could load up."

Standing at the table holding a plate and a set of tongs was the woman Pike had recognized. Mel.

"You're the dog walker," she said, eyeing Slater. "I saw those photos."

"That's not what I do."

"Rocky is such a great pup. I could tell he likes you."

Pike waved at the table. "What should I try first?"

"This jackfruit pancit is better than my mother's," Mel said. "Don't tell her that. She'd put a hit on me."

"I won't breathe a word."

"Unless you're in Manila, you probably won't run into her."

"My mother wouldn't know jackfruit or pancit if she had to pick them out of a police lineup," Pike said.

Mel furrowed her brow. "That's funny. Do you do stand-up? I feel like I might have seen you."

"I'm not actually part of your world. That was a non-revenue joke."

"Do you have stage presence?" she said. "You could probably do it if you wanted to. You're not weird-looking."

Pike furrowed his brow. "I appreciate that."

"I don't mean you personally. I mean what the camera sees." Mel gestured with the tongs. "Of course everyone is beautiful, in their own special way, blah, blah. But some people just look weird on camera. It's not about good looks or ugliness."

"It's all new to me," Pike said. "But I don't usually love photos of myself."

"Nobody does. I refuse to watch my own series." She leaned toward him. "Don't tell my producers that. Anyway, I bet you wouldn't look weird on camera."

Slater was across the table, munching on a chunk of spanakopita. "No freaking standup. Comedians are nuts."

"That's kind of a sweeping generalization," Mel said.

"Every one of them I've met is completely unhinged." Slater threw up a hand. "I'm crazy, so if I can detect it in other people, it has to be extreme."

"You're labeling a whole creative field. It's just rude."

"It's true, though," Pike said. "He is a little crazy."

"It's rude to trash-talk other performers."

"You mean it's rude to ruin the grift for other people," Slater said. "If you point out the racket, everybody becomes suspect."

Mel scoffed. "Try the pancit," she said flatly, and carried her plate away.

Pike gestured with a piece of pineapple on a toothpick. "You have such a way with people."

"You're welcome," he said, chewing the last of the spanakopita. "I just saved you from a world of misery. Hanging around comedy clubs, drinking watered-down booze, hurling insults at strangers."

He chuckled. "It's hard to believe you and Doris are related."

"Doris lives in some heymish parallel universe where people are basically decent, and interesting, and guileless," Slater said. "Over here in reality, I know you're either the grifter or the mark."

Stepping close to him, Pike leaned in and mouthed his ear. "I'm going to grift you big time when I get you alone," he murmured.

"It's on, son."

"First I need to check for open-mic nights at comedy clubs."

Slater had to laugh. He squeezed the back of Pike's neck. "That's not funny."

Someone was approaching them, Slater saw in the periphery, and pulled back. It was Artémise, wearing pink-tinted glasses and a sheer lime-green dress with a slit up to the belt. A white bikini was visible underneath. Maybe the green thing was meant to be a wrap, part of a swimwear ensemble.

"Look at you two," she said. "Cuddling up on each other like a couple of teenagers."

"Yeah, we got it bad, and that ain't good," Slater said. "This is Pike."

"I love that shirt," Artémise said.

Pike stood up straighter. "That's high praise, coming from someone with a successful fashion line. It's off-the-rack."

"I like the fit." She swirled her palm at his chest. "You're a real person, not a torso model."

He laughed. "I definitely try to keep it real."

She turned to Slater. "I heard you got a swatch of the fabric with my stolen design."

"I did."

Shifting on her feet, she raised her eyebrows. "Do you have it on you?"

"Are you sure you're ready for that? You're having a party here."

Artémise waggled her fingers. "Hand it over."

Reaching into his hip pocket, Slater gave it to her, and watched as she studied it, and ran it between her fingers.

"Fuck this," she said.

"I know it's infuriating."

"It's so cheap. The colors are all washed out. Where was this made?"

"The manufacturer is in Shaoxing, China. But that's not who pirated it."

"What are you going to do about it?" she demanded.

"I'm not there yet."

Waving the swatch, she raised her voice. "Surely you have a plan. That's what I hired you for."

Slater matched her tone. "You hired me because I'm not a yes man. Let me do my job."

She huffed and handed it back, then closed her eyes for a moment. With a single deep breath, when she opened them again, she looked visibly calmer. "This isn't really the time. Can you talk to Gene? Let her know if you need more money."

"Where's Rocky, anyway?" Slater said. "Have you got him locked in a closet somewhere?"

Artémise laughed. "I thought all these people might be a little overwhelming for him. He's at our place in Topanga with my kids and Nadège. There's lots of space for everybody to run around." She looked to Pike. "It was nice to meet you. Try the watermelon salad. It's the bomb."

Pike watched her walk away. "You asked about her dog and not about her children."

"Rocky is a great dog. Her kids are entitled brats."

"Who's Nadège?"

"The nanny. Or one of them."

They took plates, and loaded them up, and stood nearby to eat. Eventually they wandered back toward the bar. Slater asked for an OJ. He couldn't drink anymore if he was driving later.

Pike stopped to talk to someone. He didn't recognize her, and stood nearby, and sipped his orange juice. They were talking inanities, he decided, and tuned them out.

A while later the blond who'd been doing coke walked out of the house. The guy was flying high now. Slater could see it in his eyes, the way they darted around the crowd. His eyes met Slater's, and narrowed, and he strode toward him. Slater set his glass on a table and planted his feet apart.

"You." The blond pointed a finger at him. "You have a school bus for me."

"Spread out," Slater said.

He leaned toward him. "I'm asking nicely."

This close to him, he could see the thin sheen of sweat on his skin, and a vein throbbing in his neck, revealing his rapid pulse.

"I'm not a fucking drug dealer."

The guy pointedly looked him up and down. "Are you sure about that? Why else would a guy like you be in a place like this?"

He knew it was a mistake, knew there could be expensive consequences, but he just couldn't hold back. Slater slapped him hard, right and then left, a firm kovac. The guy put a hand to his cheek, his eyes wide, and stepped back.

"You can't just hit me," he shouted.

"You'll take it and you'll like it," Slater growled.

He lunged at him and managed to land another slap before the guy ducked and hustled away.

"Fricking junkie," Slater shouted after him.

He could feel a lot of eyes on him now. He took a breath and looked around. Artémise was standing near the bar, watching him along with everybody else. Of course stuff like this would happen when his client was nearby.

Artémise threw a hand in the air and raised her voice. "That's how you do it, people. Keeping the drug use in check. I hired that guy."

Laughter rippled through the crowd, and the tension was broken. He remembered that about entertainment people—they liked a little drama.

"You know better, Benny," Artémise called toward the house.

The blond hustled to the door, and went inside, ignoring her. Slater ran a hand through his hair and grabbed his OJ. Pike stepped next to him.

"We can go," he said quietly.

"Good plan."

He drained his glass, and set it down again, and they walked into the foyer.

"You got the host's stamp of approval," Pike said. "That means nobody's going to call the cops."

"It was open-handed anyway. Not really assault."

"That's debatable. But at least you won't have to explain it."

He pushed out the front door, and they walked across the courtyard toward the driveway, their shoes crunching on the gravel.

Slater huffed. "Didn't I embarrass you? Why aren't you mad at me?"

"Why would I be mad? It wasn't about me." Pike chuckled. "Benny was being a little racist. I'm sure Artémise has seen plenty of that. Besides, we've been here long enough."

The valet at the end of the driveway took the chit and hustled up the street. While they waited, Pike draped an arm around his shoulder and pulled him into an embrace. When the valet returned with the Continental, Slater palmed a bill, and the guy deftly retrieved it in a feigned handshake. He held the car door for him, closing it as he got in.

As Slater navigated the winding streets down to Sunset, Pike leaned back on the headrest.

"Oh, this shirt? Artémise was telling me how much she liked it."

"That is a great shirt."

"Artémise thought so," Pike said. "She liked the fit."

He chuckled. "She didn't really need to point out that you don't have a model's body."

"If you think about her world, though, she probably only sees model types. I'm sure the gravitas of my pedestrian manliness was quite refreshing."

"It definitely puts lead in my pencil."

At the house he parked in the garage, and as they were climbing the stairs, Slater spoke.

"Those were high-tone snacks, but do we need to eat? I bought some conchas today."

"I was just talking to Artémise about eating," Pike said. "We talked about salad. Did I mention that actor, Mel What's-her-name, actually tried to get me into standup?"

"Artémise actually asked me to tell you to quit name-dropping so much."

"You know I'm going to be eating out on that story for months."

He stopped on the landing and put his hands on Pike's belt, pulling him close. He kissed him and nuzzled his jaw. "Fan boy," he murmured.

"I really hope Artémise slaps a maître d' or throws her phone at somebody soon," Pike said. "Because the moment her name comes up in conversation, I can say, 'I was just at her house. We talked about salad.'"

Slater mouthed his neck. "You taste better than any salad. Better than any high-end plant-based catering smorgasbord."

TWENTY-TWO

〰〰〰〰〰〰

IN THE MORNING PIKE was gone when Slater woke. He had more Fashion District skulking to do, so he put on another seventies shirt. This one looked like Shaula's bowling shirts, with vertical blue bars and a big asterisk pattern.

He drove to his office, and parked the Continental, and walked over to Irving Irving's place. Inside the same woman was on the desk, and she buzzed him in.

"Is he around?" Slater said, approaching her. "I don't have an appointment."

"You were here last week."

"The name's Ibáñez."

Rising, she walked into the back. Slater stepped over to ogle the underwear on the headless mannequins. The clerk returned a moment later.

"Go on back," she said. "He's in his office."

As he walked into the hall, he saw that the small office they'd been in last time was dark and unoccupied. Farther up on the opposite side was an open door to a much larger room, with wood paneling and rosewood furniture. It looked like the offices of lawyers and politicians he'd been in. Irving was parked behind the desk and looked up as he stepped inside.

"Such a delightful shirt."

"It's 1970s dead stock."

"It suits you." He gestured to the chair in front of his desk. "Sit down. I just got back from New York last night. You're lucky to catch me here."

"Have you ever worked with a company called Neutral Hermeneutic Services?" Slater said as he sat.

"I think that's the outfit I hired to install Wi-Fi in this building," Irving said. "They called it mesh, like it was some kind of athletic wear. I needed to replace the ethernet. Technology changes almost as quickly as fashion. I don't have anyone in-house who can do things like that."

"Did they tell you what the name of the company meant?"

"I assumed it was some computer thing."

"Did you meet any of the workers personally?"

"I only dealt with one person. A man. He did all the work."

"What was his name?" Slater said.

"That escapes me." His brow furrowed. "He was wearing a box-cut camp shirt."

He gestured impatiently. "What's a camp shirt?"

"Straight cut, short sleeves." He gestured to his own neck. "A camp collar with a simple placket. They wear them on bowling teams. He was lightly built but muscular. Around thirty, I'd say. His skin tone was warm mocha. Slightly darker than yours."

"Have you seen him anywhere else?"

"I don't think so. Is he involved in your copyright

investigation?"

"I can't comment on that." Slater rose. "Thanks for your time."

"I'm never going to complain about seeing a pretty face."

He walked out to the street. The guy had no idea that Neutral Hermeneutic Services and A Touch of Class Textiles were the same people. Irving had raged about A Touch of Class last week, had wanted to sue them, but he described Shaula like he was just the IT guy. Tamara around the corner had talked the same way. She knew both companies but not about the overlap.

Slater walked to A Touch of Class. The shutter was up, and he tried the door. It was unlocked. As he stepped inside, Shaula rose from one of the desks behind the counter.

"Where's Boyd?" Slater said.

"He'll be back later." Shaula furrowed his brow. "You look steamed."

He put his hands on his hips. "You've been lying to me."

"About what?"

"You do IT work in the neighborhood."

"I didn't lie about that," Shaula said. "Why would I tell you about it? You never asked. It's one of the services we provide."

"Along with hermeneutic interrogations."

"The IT work pays the bills. Hermeneutics are the big picture."

"Who does the IT jobs—you or Boyd?"

"I'm more tech savvy."

Slater waved at the room. "The array of services explains why you don't have a lot of stock in here, considering you're a fabric supplier."

"We specialize in carefully curated fabrics." Shaula

raised his eyebrows. "Quality over quantity."

"You get fabrics manufactured?"

"Sometimes. Why does that matter?"

Slater scoffed and walked out.

"Who told you I do IT work?" Shaula called after him.

Back at his office, he flicked on the lights, and eyed Rey Pascual, standing there diligently watching the front door. He clicked his tongue in greeting, then walked through to his desk, and heaved his boots onto the desktop. Phone in hand, he texted Andy:

> Neutral Hermeneutic Services. You said Shaula is named in its incorporation paperwork. What about Boyd? And is Shaula linked to A Touch of Class?

Before he could set the phone down, it buzzed in his hand. Gene. He picked up.

"Artémise was happy to see you yesterday," Gene said. "Apparently you made quite an impression."

"One of her guests assaulted me. But the food was really good. Why weren't you there?"

"I need to take a day off once in a while. Artémise said you showed her a swatch of the fabric with the stolen design."

"She was not happy to see it."

"She said it looked common."

"What, she intended it for royalty, or the nobility?" Slater said. "We're all common, toots, since 1788."

"The opposite of common is exceptional," Gene said. "Artémise's clothing is exceptional."

"I've seen the look book. I know it's priced for the one-percenters."

"Our target demographic is actually the top nine percent."

"Good to know."

"Do you have anything new to report?" Gene said.

"I'm pretty sure I know how the bolt got into that display window. It's going to take a few more days to nail down the details."

"Do you need more money?"

"That would be great."

"Can I wire it rather than delivering cash? Another ten?"

"Cash is king," Slater said.

"If I can send it by wire, it'll happen today. Otherwise it'll be later this week."

"Fine," he said flatly. "But send ninety-nine hundred. That way the banks won't flag it for the tax people."

He spent a minute on his computer sending Gene his banking details, then saw Andy had texted:

Boyd's name is only connected to A Touch of Class. Shaula's name is only connected to Neutral Hermeneutic Services.

Sitting back, Slater thought it through. Apart from the shared street address, you'd have to dig to find out both companies were the same two guys. Irving didn't know that, and neither did Tamara. It had to be part of their racket.

His phone buzzed again, and he checked the screen. The caller ID said A Touch of Class. He picked up.

"Hey, John, are you around right now?" It was Boyd's voice. "I have some stuff to show you. I know that building—what floor are you on?"

"What stuff?" Slater said.

"I'm coming over there anyway. I'll just drop in for a minute."

Slater stifled a groan. This was a test. He'd confronted Shaula, and now they suspected his cover story.

"I'm on the ninth floor," he said. "Left off the elevator

at the end of the hall. The door is propped open."

There was always a risk Cassidy wouldn't be there, but she had been yesterday when everybody else took the day off. Locking his office, he hustled down the hall to Cassidy's studio. The door was open, and he rapped on it as he stepped in.

Music was playing on a portable speaker, and Cassidy was working at the table, carefully cutting a pattern. She greeted him as he walked in and tapped the speaker to kill the audio. It was good that she was alone. That meant fewer moving parts, fewer things that could go wrong.

"Can I work here like I'm part of your business?" Slater said. "Just for a couple minutes. I can pay you."

"Is this part of your undercover thing?"

"It's too much to explain. My target is on his way here."

"You can sit at my desk," she said, and gestured toward it. "And you don't have to pay me. You dug up that dirt on my creepy ex."

"That invoice is paid in full. It was payback for educating me about the industry. That Yves Saint Laurent line is genius. It makes me look well informed. People just stop asking me questions."

Cassidy chuckled. "I'm glad."

"So this is a separate and novel transaction."

"How much are you offering?"

"Name it."

"How long will he be here?"

"I'm thinking a few minutes," Slater said. "He's just verifying that I'm legit. We'll chat and I'll get rid of him."

"Three hundred bucks."

"Sold."

He dug out his wad of cash and handed her the C-notes. It was steep for a few minutes' use of her office, but he knew she was grinding and short on jack.

"What role am I playing?" Cassidy said.

"There's no role. Just be yourself. The only distortion is that I'm your business partner. And my name is John."

"It's less fun, though. I can do accents. I could be Lady Waverley, the wealthy heiress who can't return to Britain because of mysterious circumstances."

"No accents," Slater growled. "Stick to the truth. It's easier to talk about, and it feels less hinky."

He sat at her desk and shifted the laptop in front of him, and Cassidy went back to working at the cutting table. When Boyd appeared, he didn't even knock, and just walked in the door. He was dressed like a bank teller again, in a polo shirt and chinos. Slater sat up.

"Cassidy, this is Boyd. He works at A Touch of Class."

"The fabric supplier," she said. "I've seen your storefront."

"That's our studio." Boyd flashed a smile. "You should come in. I'm always happy to see industry professionals. You two work together?"

"We're partners. We do a couple of different lines."

"What did you need to show me?" Slater said.

"Right. I got distracted by the charming one."

He approached the desk and handed him a sheaf of paper. They were color printouts, stapled in the corner, a little curled from having been rolled up. Cassidy stepped over, and stood next to his chair, and leaned in to look as Slater flipped through it. Each page had a photo of a swatch of fabric with model numbers and prices.

"The Lyocell looks beautiful." She tapped the page. "What's the thickness on it?"

"I'd have to look at it," Boyd said. "The texture is definitely glamourous."

"I'm all about low-impact options."

"We have a similar color in polyester, and it's a lot cheaper."

She looked up at him. "Good to know."

"These are great windows," Boyd said, waving at them. "Is that why you chose this studio?"

Slater sat back. "You need natural light in this business."

"Plus the rent was within reach," Cassidy said.

Boyd held her gaze. "You seem like a calm person. Have you done entheogens?"

"What's that?"

"Hallucinogenic plants. Like mushrooms."

"Not since I was a teenager," she said. "Are those supposed to make you calm?"

"They definitely do that for me. Take me to new places and still my mind." He gestured to the windows again. "What does this say to you, all this glass, and all this light?"

"It makes me glad it doesn't get too cold here," Cassidy said. "Heating this place would cost a fortune."

"I mean the feeling of it. What's that like?"

"It's very energizing, if that's what you're talking about. I walk in here in the morning and it's like slamming a shot of espresso. I'm ready to get to work."

"The gridwork," Boyd said. "All the glass panes lined up. What does that say to you?"

"We've got work to do here," Slater said. "We don't need a hermeneutic interrogation."

Boyd chuckled. "I just wanted you to see the book." He picked it up, and called "Later" as he walked out.

Rising from the desk, Slater briefly stepped into the hall. "He's gone."

"For a fabric vendor, he's not really savvy about fabric," Cassidy said.

"Why do you say that?"

"I admired the Lyocell, and he countered with polyester. Lyocell is a thing because it's environmentally sound. It's made out of trees and doesn't require any crazy chemicals to produce. Polyester is basically plastic. If you're interested in Lyocell, you already know it's not the cheapest option. It's like he missed what I said."

"Or he doesn't know why they're different," Slater said.

"He strikes me as more a salesperson than a back-office type. That thousand-watt smile, and the indirect flattery. It felt like if I'd responded to that more, I'd have a new boyfriend."

"Still, even a sales type should know what he's selling."

"The look book was odd too. Most people selling fabric would glue swatches of the actual fabric to the book, not pictures of them. You need to feel the texture and the weight." She furrowed her brow. "That book was kind of nothing. Not something you needed to see urgently. Also, why did he take it with him? A look book is like a catalog. You want people to see it on their desk later and order from you."

"You definitely earned your three yards," Slater said.

She laughed. "Happy to help."

Walking out, Slater didn't bother to go back into his office, and went down to the surface lot, and climbed in the Continental. Once he'd parked in his garage, he climbed out and eyed the wall rack of yard tools. Working on the landscaping was a good way to clear his head, and there was always something that needed attention.

He left the garage open, and walked to the opposite side from his own front door, to the door for the ADU behind the garage, Grace's one-bedroom. He rang the bell, and eventually Grace pulled it open and greeted him. She had rheumy blue eyes, and her hair in a white cloud, today wearing a cardigan despite the summer heat.

"I need to cut back the toyon in the side yard," he said.

"It's your house, honey. You don't have to ask me."

"A heads up, then, since I'll be working outside your kitchen door."

"You know, I love that space," Grace said. "You've put in something that blooms every month of the year."

"I'm glad that's working out."

"I want to ask you about one of them. I'll meet you back there."

Slater walked into the garage, and grabbed a pair of work gloves, and kneepads, and the hand pruners, then rolled the door down. He let himself in the side gate and found Grace standing next to her little patio table. She gestured to the shrubbery.

"One of my girlfriends asked about this one. It's bloomed on and off for months."

"It's called an apricot mallow," Slater said. "Native to the Mojave. Maybe the low desert too."

"She said it looked like a local. I see butterflies on it sometimes."

"Good news. That's how it works in the desert."

There was a piece of art mounted on the wall next to Grace's kitchen door. That hadn't been there before. Made of greenish metal, like weathered copper, it was circular, with a benevolent face in the middle, and wavering rays extending in all directions.

He gestured to it. "What's this?"

"The sun," Grace said. "I don't know the artist. Pike put it up for me."

"Damn it."

"He said it just needed a couple of concrete screws. That it wouldn't cause any serious damage."

"I don't care about the stucco. He should have told me what he was doing."

"Because you want to be in charge of everything."

He narrowed his eyes. "You can see right through me, Grace."

She chuckled. "I know men, and how their minds work. If that one causes me any grief, you'll hear about it."

"He won't."

"I get that feeling too. You certainly picked a doozy."

Grace went inside, and he pulled on the work gloves and the kneepads. He knelt next to the toyon and started cutting it back. It liked it here, it seemed, as it was growing fast and lush.

As he got into the rhythm of it, snipping and plucking, he thought about today. It wasn't great that Boyd was suspicious of him. The guy might just blow things up. He knew he shouldn't have confronted Shaula in the first place. That had been rash.

The apricot mallow needed to be cleaned up too. It usually bloomed in spring, but a little extra water coaxed more out of it. It wasn't too dense, so the pruning went fast.

Getting to his feet, he surveyed the work. It looked better, and more important, it didn't look like topiary, just a cleaned-up version of what nature was doing. He could leave the California lilac, he decided. It was still blooming, in less dramatic shades of pink and white, but the dense clusters of little flowers gave the yard a nice scent.

He needed a rake to clean up the trimmings, and he walked back to the gate, and stepped out to the street, and let himself in his own front door. In the garage he hit the button to roll up the door, then walked over to the workbench. Setting the hand pruners on it, he pulled off the kneepads, and walked farther back to grab the rake.

From behind him came a shadow in the doorway, and he turned to see a guy strutting in from the street.

"Dude, what the fuck?" Slater demanded. "This is private property."

Stepping up to the workbench, the guy reached for the tool rack and grabbed his hatchet. With his head shaved and built thick, at first glance he didn't look homeless, Slater decided, and he didn't seem drug-addled. But the look in his eye was intent, his expression hard.

No way could he brawl with someone who had a bladed weapon in hand. Slater knew exactly how sharp it was. He stepped toward the front of the Continental, and the guy quickly moved toward him, up the side of the vehicle. Slater bolted around the front end, past the driver's door, then out to the street. Behind him he could hear footfalls as the goon chased after him.

Across the street was a utility pole, and Slater made the split-second decision not to try to outrun the guy. Instead he grabbed the rungs that studded the sides of the pole, and heaved himself up, scrambling to get a foothold and reaching for the higher rungs. He climbed far enough that he was out of hatchet range. From here he could easily kick him in the face if he tried to use the weapon on his boots.

As he twisted around to look down, he saw the guy standing right below, looking up at him.

"Come down," he said.

"Fuck you, you fucking psycho."

"Come on. I won't use the ax on you."

"It's a hatchet," Slater said.

He raised it overhead and slammed it hard into the wooden pole. It landed with a *thunk* and stayed in the wood. The guy flashed his palms.

"Come on down."

"The fuck do you want with me?"

"You need to back off. Keep your nose out of other people's business."

"What people? What business? I've got a lot going on."

"You heard me. Let it go, or next time I'll use the ax." He turned to walk away.

Pushing hard with his feet, Slater propelled himself off the pole. He landed a little short but managed to grab the guy's shirt. The impact made him pitch forward and sprawl on the pavement. Slater struck at him with both fists, landing a couple of punches.

"It's a hatchet," he said through his teeth. "Who are you working for?"

Twisting sideways, the guy slammed his jaw hard with an elbow. It really hurt. Slater groaned and rolled off him, and the guy scrabbled out of his grip. He quickly got to his feet and trotted up the street.

Slater stood and walked a few steps, but the impact of jumping from the pole had messed up his knee. He stood with his hands on his hips, breathing hard, and watched the guy disappear around the corner.

TWENTY-THREE

⌘⌘⌘⌘⌘⌘⌘⌘⌘⌘⌘

"D ID YOU BREAK ANYTHING?" Grace was standing at her gate.

"I don't think so," Slater said. "I bruised my knee."

"He wasn't a professional goon. A pro never would have turned his back on you. That's felony stupid."

Slater hobbled toward her. "I wondered about that too."

"He stopped by a few hours ago. When I was in the yard. He introduced himself as an old friend of yours, and asked me when you might be home."

"That's also a little sloppy."

"Completely ham-fisted. I assumed he was a bill collector or a repo man, not a thug." She waved a hand. "I played the myopic clueless neighbor, and laid it on thick. He walked up the block, and I was still in the yard a few minutes later when he drove past. Real slow, with his driver's window rolled down, rubbernecking at the house. It was a black SUV. I looked it up. It's one of the new Broncos."

He laughed. "Grace, you are the best, you know that?"

234

"It had California plates. Unfortunately I couldn't read it. I see now that I should have warned you about him. I assumed if he wanted money you'd hear about it firsthand."

"You got all the dope on him anyway. Like you were working a gimmick."

She shrugged. "Old habits."

Slater took a breath. "I might not finish the yard today."

"I'll deduct it from my rent," she said, and laughed.

"Do you think I'm a sucker for not charging you anything?"

"You know you are, so it doesn't matter what I think. But I'm grateful."

"Pike just thinks it's weird."

"He's a civilian, honey. An honest man. He's never going to get it."

"That rings true."

"Take care of that knee." Grace gestured across the street. "And don't forget your hatchet."

He hobbled across to yank it out of the pole, then hung it back on the wall rack, and hit the button to roll down the garage door. Climbing up toward the kitchen went slow. Why had he bought a house with so damn many stairs?

Eventually he got to the sofa, and sat down to massage his knee. It didn't matter that he didn't charge Grace rent. He didn't want to have that kind of relationship with her. The payback was that she worked as an operative for him sometimes, and she was a resource, like making note of the vehicle of the moron who'd come at him.

The assault had to be about Boyd and Shaula. Shaula knew where he lived. Was he stupid enough to think Slater could be intimidated? Digging out his phone, he checked Svetlana's tracking software. The dot for Shaula's location was in the old part of Downtown. When he zoomed in, he realized he knew that building. It was on a busy corner, and it hadn't been converted, still functioning as offices a century after it had been built. The one unusual thing about it was that the rooftop had a restaurant. Hunting for Shaula there was a gamble, but he really needed to look him in the eye.

When he stood up, his knee was already moving better. That was a relief. Trudging down to his car, he drove to Downtown. He couldn't find a meter, so he parked in a lot up the block and walked back to the building. There was no security in the lobby, and in the elevator the buttons were numbered up to twelve, with one above that labeled only with the restaurant's name. Its business hours were posted on the wall. The kitchen wasn't going to start up for a couple of hours, but the bar was open.

When he stepped off the elevator, the music was up loud. The tables on the open rooftop were empty, and a guy with a cart was setting cutlery and wineglasses and napkins on them. Slater had never eaten here, since it was all about meat, but he'd seen this place from the street. A glass barrier ran around the edges of the roof. From below it looked insubstantial and ephemeral, but up close he saw that despite its transparency the wall was solid, and several feet high.

There was foliage up here, in planter boxes, a few with smoke trees and several with fountain grass. At least somebody had the imagination to think beyond the usual ubiquitous horsetail. As he walked in he saw a couple of people sitting at the bar. Shaula was one of them, with a half-empty beer glass in front of him on the bar top. He looked up as Slater approached.

He jutted his chin. "Boyd seems to be getting suspicious of me."

"This isn't really the place to talk business." Shaula

looked around, then got up and grabbed his beer glass, and waved for him to follow. He walked to a table along the glass railing, shielded from view from the bar by a boxed hedge, and took one of the chairs.

"Boyd's not convinced you're in the fashion business." Shaula frowned. "Are you going to sit down?"

He pulled out the opposite chair and sat. "The fuck does Boyd know about me?"

"He ran your face through one of those facial-recognition sites."

"How did he get an image of my face?"

"The camera in the studio. A search for your face comes up with a different name, and a lot of court records. Boyd thinks you work as a fraud investigator, and you changed your name."

"You don't seem surprised."

"I told him maybe you switched to fashion after all that legal trouble. Is your name really John, or is it Slater?"

"Let's say I use both. John is no more fake than your name. Shaula Shargaz sounds as phony as a three-dollar bill."

He frowned. "It's not fake. It's just not traditional. I'm a little sad that you lied to me."

"You want to talk about lying?"

Slater jumped up and lunged at him, grabbing him by the collar. Dragging him out of his chair, he shoved Shaula into the railing, then lifted him by his armpits until he was sitting on it.

"Whoa." Shaula pitched toward him, grabbing his shoulders. "Let me go."

Slater moved closer to him, and held firm, and spoke through his teeth. "Why did you send a thug after me?"

"What are you talking about?" He glanced sideways.

"It's a long way down, Slater. My heart is pounding."

"Unless you know how to fly, you need to squawk."

Shaula met his eye. Slater couldn't quite read his expression. There was fear in it, and surprise, but something else too. Like he was offended.

"I'm not sure you won't actually croak me."

"That's how threats work." Slater shook him. "You know you're going to talk. I'm going to make you talk."

"I know you live beyond today. I don't actually know about my own future."

"So your magic has its limitations."

"It's not magic. The distant past is vague."

"So I've heard."

Slater shoved him farther, and Shaula overbalanced, slipping until the backs of his knees hung on the railing. He leaned over him, his grip the only thing preventing him from falling.

"OK," Shaula yelped, his arms flailing. "I'll tell you what I know. Pull me back. Come on, pull me back."

He heaved him up, and when his feet hit the ground, shoved him away. Shaula collapsed into a chair, and spread his hands on the tabletop, red-faced and breathing hard.

The guy who'd been setting out cutlery walked over, his brow furrowed. "Are you two doing OK?"

"We're just talking here," Slater said. "You can bring me a soda water."

"We're not actually doing table service yet. You can order at the bar."

He scoffed and sat across from Shaula, then jabbed a finger at him. "If you lie to me, it's not going to go well for you."

"You're so irrational." He adjusted his shirt. "Just give me a minute."

Slater folded his arms. "The truth doesn't need a minute. It's the bullshit that takes time. All that effort to keep the details straight." He raised his voice. "You need to come across."

Shaula closed his eyes for a second and took a breath. "We use the IT gigs to get into people's networks and computers."

"What people?"

"Businesses. Mostly in the neighborhood. Mostly in fashion. We copy files that might be valuable. So we can release knock-offs at the same time the brand-name garments come out."

Watching him talk, he decided it fit with everything else he'd gleaned.

"People keep everything on their computers," Slater said. "Do you steal their identities, drain their bank accounts?"

"It's more subtle than that. Boyd calls it the long game. If they have a lot of subscriptions on a credit card, we set up similar recurring payments that will blend in. It's amazing that people don't even notice."

"So you're a damn nickel rat."

"I don't need to be judged right now."

"My whole life I've been told I don't really understand people, or how to deal with them," Slater said. "It means I'm not a very good judge of character. Maybe I've lost objectivity, sleeping with you. Deliberately putting myself in the thrall of those gams, that sweet little caboose. But I just can't see it in you. I can't see you as the mastermind of this grift."

"Boyd is the one with the ideas. My job is to get access to cloud drives and accounts. Once we're in, Boyd does the digging."

"Tell me about the paisley fabric in the front window."

"I don't actually know where that one came from. Boyd found the pattern in a design file. I know he thought it was valuable. He had a manufacturer put a rush on production."

"He didn't find it," Slater said. "He stole it. The fact that you're collaborating with him makes you a crook too. You get that, don't you? What's with your loyalty to Boyd anyway?"

He held his gaze. "We have the same outlook."

"Hermeneutic interrogations, the neutral space, time travel."

"I don't think he's completely sold on the time-travel thing."

"If you know you're putting yourself at risk, why not just walk away?"

"It's more than the risk involved." Shaula huffed. "I know it's morally messed up. I can't fix this, Slater. I'm in too deep."

"No one is beyond redemption."

"You really believe that?"

"If I didn't, I'd already be toast." Rising, he walked to the elevator, and went down to the street.

On the drive back to his house, he thought it through. Shaula seemed sincerely clueless about the guy who came after him with the hatchet. Maybe Boyd had set it up without telling him.

Was he losing perspective? He knew he couldn't believe anybody about anything without double-checking the story, and he knew he'd gotten too close to this guy. But even without that, in his gut he could feel it. The hatchet man wasn't about Shaula.

Eyeing his phone, he dialed Pike, glad that he picked up.

"That woman across the street has an automated license plate reader," Slater said.

"Her name is Tilly. You know this."

"You actually know her. Can you ask her for the LPR data from earlier today?"

"You can talk to her yourself," Pike said. "You're her neighbor too."

"She already likes you. She lets you raid her citrus trees, and the pair of you have your whole neighborhood-watch cabal going on."

"You really should get to know the neighbors a little too. Besides, I can't do it right now."

"I'm disappointed, Reddy Kilowatt. I'm also deeply hurt, and angry."

"You don't even need to mention the angry part," Pike said. "Seething rage is kind of your personality resting point."

"That's fair. But the heaviest load is the disappointment."

Pike laughed. "You'll just have to power through it. Do you need Tilly's digits?"

"I've got her number. I love you, you big mook."

"Forever, forty-niner."

As he turned the corner and cruised up his block, he saw Tilly was working in her yard. He didn't even need to call first. Pulling into his garage, he climbed out, and took a deep breath to steel himself.

He walked across the street and stood at her gate. "Hey, neighbor."

Tilly straightened up and stepped over. Wearing jeans and a baggy long-sleeved shirt, she had her dark hair tied back. She was taller than he remembered.

"Slater, isn't it?" she said. "I see you coming and going sometimes. You're always so busy."

"Yeah, it's my crazy life." He waved a hand. "Pike said you have an LPR camera."

She turned and pointed it out. He hadn't noticed it

before, high on a *canariensis* palm that stood at the edge of her yard along the sidewalk. A little solar panel was attached to the trunk above it.

"Your palm is in great shape."

"My insurance woman said I had to keep it trimmed or my rates would go up. That plate reader was such a great investment. It records tag numbers and takes a photo of the vehicle, night and day."

"Can I get you to pull up the hits from earlier today?"

Tilly pulled out her phone. "I'm surprised Pike didn't just give you the login. He has a guest user account. It's all web-based. You can check it anytime you want. What's your number?" As he recited it, she tapped at the screen, then looked up. "I sent you the details. Why do you need to see a vehicle from today?"

"Somebody's been throwing cigarette butts into my side yard." He gestured vaguely toward his house. "I thought I might recognize the scofflaw."

"Where Grace lives? That's rude. She's a senior. Randy up the block used to do that, but he switched to vaping. I can actually smell the weed sometimes when he walks by. Let me know if you need help identifying vehicles. I know most of the neighbors' rides."

"That's helpful."

He crossed back to his house, and went upstairs, and grabbed his laptop. Walking through the big room and out onto the deck, he sat in a chaise longue and pulled it open. Once he was connected to the plate-reader site, he went through the records.

It only took a few seconds to find the black Bronco and get the thug's plate number. Max could pull the record and get the owner's name, but he didn't necessarily need that. He just needed to know where the guy hung out.

Tilly's system only showed hits from her device, but there were aggregated LPR databases that he and Max bought data from. Those might show the car's other habitual locations.

Anonymity on the streets was a thing of the past. Plate readers were everywhere now, mounted on lots of private vehicles, all the taxis and tow trucks and delivery vans. The owners sold the data to aggregators. It was just another revenue stream. It wasn't really regulated either, as the laws were written with the intention of preventing the cops from becoming Big Brother, but the tech bros were doing it in their stead. He'd be surprised if police detectives didn't buy these records the same way he and Max did.

It had been a while since he'd looked at one of these sites, and it felt like there was a lot more data now. When he entered the Bronco's plate number, it showed a map with dots for sightings of the vehicle all over the city, including on his street. When he tapped that dot, it said the plate had been read three times, all today. That meant Tilly's system had submitted this stuff automatically. He wondered how much they paid her for that.

Scrolling around the map, there were lots of hits for the Bronco in Downtown, but not on the street where A Touch of Class was. Near there, though, it had been recorded twice on the block where Artémise's design office was—once this morning, and once a half hour after the guy had come at him with the hatchet. He'd driven there right after he'd been here. Slater could feel his heart start to pound. This was no coincidence. It had to be about Artémise.

He'd only talked to three people in that office. Athena didn't even know what he was up to, and acted like he was wasting her time rather than posing any kind of threat. Lenore had talked freely with him. It hadn't felt like she had anything to hide. Then there was Malcolm. The guy seemed like a cake-eater, but he had acted a little squirrely.

It was him, Slater decided. Malcolm had hired the assault goon, not Shaula or Boyd. He really wanted to go punch him in the face right now, but it was too late in the day. He wouldn't be in his office, and it would take too much work to find out where he lived. From downstairs he heard the front door open. That settled it. He could figure this out tomorrow.

He folded the laptop closed, and soon Pike came out onto the deck, still dressed for the office. He leaned in and mauled him for a moment, mouthing his neck and kissing him, then sat in the adjacent chaise longue.

"How did it go with Tilly?" he said.

"Tilly informed me that you already have a login for her LPR."

Pike made his eyes wide. "Do I? I guess I forgot."

"You deliberately manipulated me into dealing with her."

He laughed. "You make it sound like it was traumatic. She's right across the street. It couldn't have knocked more than a ten-minute hole in your day."

"I only have a limited reservoir of civility," Slater said. "When I have to be nice to people, it depletes it. Eventually it's going to run dry."

"It was mostly self-serving. If you talk to her, she'll feel familiar with you, and she won't quiz me about my shady boyfriend with the old car."

"The correct term is classic car. I did give her my number. That's pretty damn familiar."

"Excellent," Pike said. "Now she can contact you directly when she spots suspicious middle-schoolers on the street."

"Great."

Pike chuckled. "Have you seen the new paparazzi photos?"

"Again? Fuck me."

He dug out his phone and tapped at it, then wordlessly handed it over. It was a photo of him standing with Pike, wearing the groovy blue-and-green shirt and the off-white chinos. Pike was in the pinky-red shirt and golf shorts. This was in the driveway at Artémise's place, after they'd left the party, taken while they'd been waiting for the valet to bring the Continental. In the photo Pike was in profile, looking up the block, and Slater had an odd look on his face, squinting at something across the street.

"Did you notice a photographer?" he said.

"I didn't." Pike raised his eyebrows. "Did you see the caption?"

He scrolled to it and read aloud. "'Rocky's dog walker escorted from Artémise bash by plainclothes security.'"

"I do kind of look like I'm detaining you, with my hand on your shoulder."

Slater scoffed. "That's so fucking stupid. If they'd waited a minute longer they would have seen my tongue down your throat, or me getting behind the wheel. It would have been obvious that you weren't security, and I wasn't getting the bum's rush."

"Maybe that doesn't fit their narrative."

"Fuck that."

"It's also not really about you. There's a bunch of other photos from the driveway, and they only put names on the celebrities. Personally I think it's fun to be included." Pike shifted on the lounger. "Brewster sent it to me with the comment 'I'm shocked you busted your own boyfriend.'"

"If she believes that, she's not as smart as she looks."

"She added a laughing emoji, so I'm thinking she knows

it's bogus. Brewster also gave me some intel on Shaula."

"Seriously? Like what?"

"Remember how she asked him where he was from? He said Michigan, and then he said Detroit. Today she told me no way is that guy from Detroit, or anywhere near Detroit. She can't pin down his dialect, but it's not Michigan."

"How would she know about dialects?" Slater said.

"Apparently some people can hear them better than others. Brewster compared it to music. Some people have a better ear for tones and melodies." Pike waved a hand. "Anyway, they were testing people for it, and she scored high, so she got a bunch of linguistic training. She says people move around, and accents shift. You can change the way you speak consciously to sound wealthier or more educated or more street, but there's usually remnants of your childhood in your voice."

"Uncle Sam paid for this training because it's an investigative tool?"

"It's pretty useful." Pike raised his eyebrows. "Like ascertaining that Shaula isn't from Michigan."

"I'd also bet money his mama didn't name him after a pair of stars either, no matter how deep she was into astrology. What did Brewster say about my accent?"

"Basic-level Anglo Angeleno. As common as dirt."

"That fits," Slater said. "I had my hands in the dirt earlier today. I worked on Grace's plantings."

"Is that why you needed LPR data? Somebody suspicious rolled by and gave you the stink eye?"

"A moron came after me with my own hatchet. It was my own fault. I left the garage door open." Slater told him about the goon, and about Grace spotting the Bronco.

Pike furrowed his brow. "He really could have messed you up."

"That wasn't his agenda. It was about intimidation and instilling fear."

"Did you figure out who sent him?"

"I think so. I'll get into it tomorrow. I'm feeling a little beat down. I bruised my knee."

"What can we do to make things better for you tonight?"

"That's simple," Slater said. "Food, sex, and booze, not necessarily in that order."

Rising, Pike sat facing him on the lounger. "Let me smoke you."

Slater reached for his belt, but he pulled his hands off. Holding his gaze, Pike unbuckled his belt, and popped the buttons of his fly. Slater was already getting chubby. Pulling out his cock, Pike went down on him.

Watching him get into it and work him was such a turn-on, and he soon came, straining into him. Breathing hard, Pike sat up, a dumb grin on his face.

"That was hot."

"Stand up," Slater said.

When he stood, Slater grabbed his butt, and pulled him close, and mashed his face into his crotch. He could feel him getting hard, and eventually unzipped his chinos. He grabbed his cock, and took him into his mouth, and smoked him.

Pike ran a hand into his hair, and when he came, his body shook. Pulling back, he sank onto the lounger, breathing hard, his face red.

"One down," he said.

TWENTY-FOUR

ALONE WHEN HE WOKE, Slater got up and showered, then pulled on a pair of jeans. He'd gone through his supply of seventies shirts, but it didn't really matter, since his cover in the industry was blown. Instead he put on a dark shirt with a collar.

Upstairs he slurped at a mug of lukewarm coffee, and grazed on bread and fruit, then headed down to the garage and drove to his office. From the surface lot he walked over to Artémise's design studio. The guard recognized him, and scowled, but let him in.

As Slater stepped into Malcolm's office, he closed the door.

Malcolm sat up. "You can just leave that open."

He found the control rod for the vertical blinds and twisted it until the vanes were closed, darkening the room.

"What are you doing?" Malcolm said. "Is this the hookup happening? That was just a shot in the dark. You could at least buy me dinner first."

Slater turned to his desk. "Why did you send that guy

after me?" he demanded.

His eyebrows shot up. "What are you talking about?"

Lunging at him, Slater grabbed his shirt collar and dragged him out of his chair. Slamming him against the wall, he slapped him hard, left and right, a rapid kovac.

His eyes screwed shut, Malcolm tugged at his wrist. "Stop it, stop it."

He slapped him again, and growled in his ear, keeping his voice low so that the guard wouldn't intervene. "Give me one reason why I shouldn't break you in half."

"Because I have no idea what's going on."

In his jeans his phone chirped loudly. That was a proximity alert from Svetlana's software. Releasing his grip on Malcolm, he took a step back and dug it out. It had to be about Shaula. When he checked the map, the location marker wasn't here, but over by his building. He'd set that up to trigger alerts as well. Watching the location dot, it was moving slowly. That meant the guy was on foot, and from his trajectory, he was definitely approaching his office.

Watching him, Malcolm stood at the wall, his brow furrowed, massaging his neck.

Slater jabbed a finger at him. "This isn't over."

He pulled open the door and walked out to the street, hustling toward his building. When he got upstairs he found Shaula in the front office, standing next to the desk, wearing a green bowling shirt. Etta was parked in the chair, wearing plaid and leaning back, with the statue of Rey Pascual turned toward her.

"Did you really hang this guy over a twelfth-floor railing?" Etta said.

"Did he show you video of that?"

"Unfortunately no."

"Then it didn't happen," Slater said. "It was that rooftop

restaurant. Technically the thirteenth floor."

Etta chuckled. "Ibáñez, you are a lot of man."

Slater eyed Shaula. "Gossip much?"

"I informed him that we work together," Etta said, "and thus have confidentiality."

He threw up his hands. "How did you find my office?"

"Once I knew your real name," Shaula said, "it's easy to check public records. And your name is on the door in big letters."

"Busted," Etta said.

"What do you want?"

Shaula raised his eyebrows. "To talk."

He gestured to his office, and followed the guy in, and left the door open a few inches. He knew Etta really could keep her mouth shut, and eavesdropping on meetings was part of her learning the trade.

"Such a cute space," Shaula said. "I love the colors. And this desk. It matches the one out front. Is it old?"

"Vintage art deco. The decorating is all Etta."

"It's in great condition." He rolled open the top desk drawer. Frank's rod and mag were still sitting in there. "Ooh, that looks dangerous."

Slater stepped over and shoved the drawer closed. "Sit down." Once he'd taken the chair in front of his desk, Slater sat too. "Why are you here?"

His expression sobered. "What evidence do you have about us?"

"Why would I share that?" Slater said. "I know you've already tipped off Boyd. You told him I'm on to you."

"I didn't tell him anything."

"That makes no sense. Why wouldn't you? You're his henchman."

"Like you said, he's a crook."

Slater watched him for a moment. The guy had come clean yesterday about their racket, even though it was under duress. "I get the sense you don't want to be."

Dropping his chin, Shaula held his gaze. "You know me pretty well, Slater. Intimately. I wish you trusted me."

"You're good, I'll give you that. I almost believe it."

He frowned. "What are you talking about?"

"The big eye, the soft-soap. You're good at it."

Shaula huffed. "It's not a snow job. Having sex with you and Pike was a total blast."

Slater winced. Etta didn't need to hear that. It was setting a bad example. He'd told her himself that his policy was to keep his dick out of his cases.

"You know I'm more of a tourist in your world," Shaula said. "I don't want to wind up in jail, of course, but in the bigger picture it doesn't really matter. I won't be around forever."

"Tourist or not, your actions have consequences. You're collaborating with a crook."

He threw up a hand. "What do you want me to say?"

"Tell me how to take Boyd down. And don't tell him I'm coming for him."

Shaula took a breath. "I think I can do that."

"Tell me about the guy."

"You know about neutral hermeneutics, and that we share that outlook. Boyd talks about his quest to unveil the true nature of reality."

"Not that." Slater waved a hand. "What does he do in his free time?"

"We both work a lot."

"What do you know about his romantic life?"

"Boyd's not with anybody right now. Nobody human at least. He talks to a chatbot. One of those realistic AI ones.

Sometimes he calls that his girlfriend."

"Where does he sleep?"

"In an apartment on Spring. He lives alone."

"Do you know the address?"

As Shaula recited it, Slater tapped it into his phone.

"Does the building have a concierge?"

"It's not that fancy. It's one of the new constructions."

"Do you and Boyd use the same accounts or cloud storage?" Slater said.

"Not really. I find a way into the clients' accounts when I'm doing IT work, and then he does all the snooping and harvesting at the office. He uses his laptop. I don't have access to it."

"So he doesn't trust you."

Shaula frowned. "Does Pike have your passwords? It's not all that strange."

"So you don't share anything? What about the paperwork for the fabric business?"

"He handles that stuff on his own."

"We need to get into his accounts," Slater said. "The way to do that is through that laptop."

"The laptop stays in the studio. But I don't have a password."

"I need to look at it. When is Boyd not at his desk?"

He pulled out his phone and tapped at it. "He's actually in San Pedro today."

"For how long?"

"I'm not sure," Shaula said. "He's probably talking to somebody about imports. It'll be a while—it's pretty far. Even if he's away, though, it's not a good idea to go mess with his laptop. There's a security camera aimed at the counter and the desks. Boyd can see whatever happens and whatever's said."

"I'm not going to touch his stuff. Right now I just want to look things over. I only need a minute. I'll stand in front of the counter, and you'll go to your desk and do something quick or grab something. Then we can leave." Slater got up. "It won't look suspicious at all."

In the front office, Shaula gestured to the statue on the desk. "What's his name again?"

"Rey Pascual," Etta said. "He's the king of the graveyard. His regular job is to keep an eye on the door, but when I'm here, he likes to watch me work."

"Right on." He looked to Slater. "Where's the head?"

"Down the hall." Slater gestured vaguely. "There's a sign."

Etta watched him step out, then raised her eyebrows. "I'm making some notes about investigative procedure. Just to clarify, having sex with your targets—that's a good idea, or that's not a good idea?"

"Let's call it a gray area," Slater said.

"It's interesting that you have plenty of advice about my love life, and what I should be doing with my Sunday morning, and yet you're having group sex with your target."

"I never said I wasn't a hypocrite." He frowned. "Were you really making notes? I saw you killed the screen when we walked out."

"I'm editing Max's client report for him. I figured it wasn't something for that guy's perusal." She swiveled idly in the chair. "Max will be in later. I'll double-check with him about the wisdom of bonking our targets."

Slater threw up his hands. "You know I'm not a right guy."

"He said he was a tourist," Etta said. "Where's he from?"

"The future."

Her eyebrows shot up. "He seriously believes that?"

"It's a whole thing."

Shaula stepped in and held the door. "I'm ready."

They went out, and rode down to the lobby, and headed toward A Touch of Class. Slater eyed him sidelong as they walked. The guy looked carefree, even glib. It seemed like an odd stance for someone who'd just decided to throw his business partner under the bus.

"Why are you so comfortable with what we're doing?" Slater demanded. "It's like a switch flipped and you're suddenly happy to trash your partnership and destroy your own business. It doesn't make sense."

"That's not what we're doing. The business is solid. If you insist we stop stealing from people, I think that's a positive development. With that change, Boyd might decide to move on, but either way, with or without him, I own that building on Glendale Boulevard, and I'm going to open the hermeneutic consulting practice."

It was optimistic to think Boyd might be willing to just walk away. But Shaula was like that, optimistic and upbeat. It was probably a mistake to assume that meant he was clueless.

"When you and Boyd figured out I was a fraud investigator," Slater said, "why didn't you ask me who I was working for? That would have been my first question."

"Well, I'd barely mentioned that when you decided to dangle me over that thirteenth-floor railing." Shaula glanced at him. "So my mind was on other things. I just assumed one of the people we copied files from had hired you. Like whoever designed that paisley in the display window. You asked about it more than once."

That tracked, Slater decided. He wasn't sure he believed it all quite yet, but it all fit together, self-consistent and free of logical contradictions.

The shutter was up at A Touch of Class, and Shaula

used his key in the front door, then walked in and sat at his desk. Slater followed him inside and looked the place over. Boyd's desk wasn't far from Shaula's, in the corner behind the counter and facing the room, his laptop folded closed on the desktop. It was so tantalizing, sitting right there.

When he'd been out in the desert recently the guy who'd guided him into the backcountry had explained how to climb the boulder piles. "There's always another way, always another route. Don't hesitate to backtrack, even though you don't want to." Grabbing the laptop right now was rash. He needed to look for that other route.

Bracing a hand on the counter, he turned and looked out the front window. In the periphery he could see the security camera above it, mounted on the wall. It was plugged into an electric socket but there was no other cable. That meant the video was sent wirelessly.

Slater shifted position so that his back was to the camera, then dug out his phone. Holding it close to his chest, he photographed the walls in the corner above Boyd's desk, then tucked it away.

A minute later Shaula got up, and stepped around the counter, and they went out to the sidewalk. Once he'd locked the door, he gestured up the block. "I need caffeine." As they walked toward the coffee place, he eyed Slater sidelong. "In the future, coffee goes extinct."

"Of course it does."

"There's a substitute that kind of tastes similar, but it's not the same. You have the absolute best coffee in this era."

Slater took a breath and held his tongue. Inside the shop, once they had java in hand, they sat at a table along the wall.

"Who owns that building?" Slater said.

"It's the woman next door. Francesca. She runs the

shop with all the wholesale zippers and buttons."

"Francesca's Fasteners. I saw the sign. How does she communicate with you?"

"Usually she just walks over."

Slater sipped his java and held his gaze. "Here's the scenario. You just ran into Francesca out front. She said her electrician needs to get into that gray box on the side wall."

"I know the one you mean. Above Boyd's desk. I thought it was for water. There's a big pipe going into it."

"It's electrical. You told Francesca that you'll be around to let the electrician in later today. Is there anything about that that doesn't make sense?"

Shaula frowned in thought, fingers laced around his little cup. "Boyd usually deals with Francesca, but I guess it's not odd that I would."

"Tell him the electrician probably won't have to shut off the power. The security camera will just show the guy messing with the box for a minute and then leaving again."

"What are you going to do?"

"You don't need to know that."

"I do need to know." He raised his eyebrows. "It's my studio. You need to trust me a little."

Slater furrowed his brow. "I'm going to plant a hidden camera over Boyd's desk. It'll record his keystrokes. Hopefully that way I can get his login, then access his files and accounts, and whatever else is on the laptop."

"If Boyd checks the security footage, he'll see you install the camera."

"It's not going to be me."

Shaula took a breath. "I'm not going to bother to text him. The story is coherent if he asks later. Are you sure it won't be obvious what your electrician is doing?"

"The security camera covers the counter and the desks,

not the utility box eight feet up the wall. Even if it's in the video frame I'll tell my guy to block the view of the camera with his body."

Digging out his phone, Shaula looked at the screen. "I have to go."

"When will you be around to let my guy in?"

"I'll be done in an hour. After that I'll be in the studio."

Slater watched him walk out, then dug out his phone and texted Svetlana:

Can I come by this afternoon?

On the way back to his office, his phone buzzed in his pants, and he pulled it out to find Svetlana's reply:

I am always here for you.

He had to grin. That sounded like a greeting card. Her illicit business and gritty workshop were light-years from that sunny realm.

Walking into the surface lot, he climbed in the Continental, and navigated to the freeway, and headed toward Glendale. It was still midday, so the traffic was moving, and he soon pulled up at Svetlana's building, long and low and mostly hidden by ivy and the evergreens lining the front. He parked and walked around to the alley, then stopped and looked up into the camera.

The door lock snapped open, and he stepped into the antechamber and stood waiting while Svetlana's tech scanned him. It took a lot longer than the instantaneous facial recognition on the outside door. The part that was time-consuming was likely sniffing for explosives. He could hear a little fan somewhere nearby drawing air over the sensors. Still, it was an upgrade from the old days, when one of her security guys would step in and frisk him. Eventually the inner door clicked open, and he stepped inside.

Dimly lit, the interior was lined by a workbench that was always littered with electronic parts—circuit boards in green and blue, cables and wiring, inscrutable plastic components and tools. It smelled like machine oil and solder. Svetlana was parked on a stool halfway down the room, wearing a yellow print dress over her bulky frame, cut low to show cleavage. As he stepped in she pulled off the loupe glasses she was wearing and slid off the stool, greeting him as she walked over.

"How's it going with the fire marshal?" Slater said.

"Finally they have approved of all my exits, after thousands of dollars and months of renovation work." Her Slavic accent flattened the vowels. "Maybe they will leave me alone for a while."

"I doubt you'll be that lucky."

"Once they approved the exits, they offered a free inspection of the electrical system."

"Can you opt out?"

"I'm not sure," Svetlana said. "As I told the charming young woman, the only free cheese is in the mousetrap."

"They're definitely going to be looking for problems."

"We know that problems are expensive." She gestured dismissively. "What do you need today?"

"A discreet wireless camera to read keystrokes on a computer. I'm thinking I could mount it on a wall above the desk. There's a utility box up there. I can show you a picture."

Digging out his phone, he pulled up the photo he'd taken of the wall above Boyd's desk, and handed it over.

She zoomed in on the image. "*Ya ponimaya.* I have a camera that will work for you."

She walked to the far end of the workshop, and pulled

something from a shelf, then walked back and handed it to him. It was a sheet metal junction box with conduit connectors at either side. These were meant to go inside the wall, attached to the framing and hidden by the drywall. But sometimes they were exposed if wiring had been added later, especially on cinderblock and brick, like the wall next to Boyd's desk. One side of the box had a sheet of waxy paper covering a layer of gray putty. That would be the glue to attach it with.

"Nobody will look at this twice," Slater said.

"You can mount it on the existing electrical box. Even an electrician would assume it was disconnected but not removed." She pointed to one of the conduit connectors. "Inside is the lens, so this side looks downward." She tapped a curved component on the opposite conduit mount. "This is for adjusting the camera angle."

It was stiff, but it swiveled in a wide circle. That meant the box wouldn't have to be precisely mounted. The camera could be aimed after it was attached. Peering at it, even up close he couldn't tell there was a lens in it.

"Does it stream in real time?"

"Via the cell network," Svetlana said. "It will make recordings for you when there is movement in the frame. I will connect it to your account."

Sliding onto a stool that faced a computer screen, she used a wand with a red glowing tip to swipe the bar code label on the junction box, then tapped at the keyboard. Standing nearby, Slater couldn't see what she was doing, as the screen was blurred by the privacy filter. Eventually she grabbed the device, and peeled off the bar code label, balling it up.

She handed the box to him. "Battery should last at least one week."

"Is there a power switch?"

"Big battery, no switch. It's already running. Once you're outside, it will connect to the cell network and appear on your phone."

"What do I owe you?"

"This is a high-end precision device, but a special price for you. Five dollars."

He dug out his wad of cash, and peeled off the C-notes, and watched as she tucked them into her bra.

"There's a way you could handle the city bureaucrats." Slater shifted on his feet. "Ask them for a copy of the specific law that says they need to inspect your wiring. Don't be confrontational about it, like 'Show me where it says I have to do this.' Instead you make it friendly. 'I'm so curious about how to comply.' They're just doing what they're told, and to find the actual wording in the legislation will mean talking to their bosses or to their legal department. Who wants to do that?"

"So my inspection will go to the bottom of the pile."

"For a while, at least."

She pursed her lips and nodded. "This is good advice."

Slater waggled the camera. *Spasiba bolshoye.*

"Nezashto," she said, and laughed.

When he climbed into the Continental, he set the junction box on the floor of the passenger side, then opened Svetlana's app on his phone. A new device was listed, and when he tapped on it, the feed from the camera showed a close-up of familiar burgundy carpeting. It was already working as promised.

TWENTY-FIVE

ACK AT HIS HOUSE, Slater parked in the garage, then grabbed the junction box, and an aluminum stepladder, and carried them out to the street. He found the cable lock in the utility box in the back of the Frontier and used it to lock the stepladder in the bed. Climbing in, he revved the little engine, and drove to his office.

In the surface lot he pulled in next to Max's charcoal-gray Charger, then headed upstairs. Max was in his office, with Etta sitting across from him. He stood in the doorway.

"I'm glad you're here," Slater said. "Can you spare half an hour for field work?"

"Right now?" Max said.

"If you can swing it."

"You want him to just drop everything and go do stuff for you?" Etta said.

Max waved a hand. "He'd do it for me if I asked. It's part of the job."

Setting the junction box on his desk, Slater sat next

261

to Etta. "You just have to climb a ladder, stick this on an electrical box, then aim the camera at the desktop below."

"Is that from the Russian?" Etta said.

"That's right."

"It's heavy." Max turned it over in his hands.

"It has to be mostly battery. Svetlana says it'll run for a week."

"The camera lens is in here, I'm thinking."

"That curved part lets you aim the lens."

Max spent a minute adjusting it. "I see how it works."

"Why do you need a camera trained on someone's desktop?" Etta said.

"Login credentials."

She stood up and took hold of the junction box, prodding the waxy paper that covered the mounting putty. "The glue smells weird."

"You just know it's some Soviet-era gunk that's illegal now," Slater said.

Etta set it on the desk. "Should we wipe our prints off it?"

"It's not going to matter. Even if the target spots it, this guy is on the other side of the law. He's not willingly going to talk to anyone with access to fingerprint databases." Slater eyed Max. "Have you got coveralls?"

Max rose. "In my trunk."

"Hold up," Etta said. "Can I get in on this? I can hold the ladder or something."

"The problem with that is the same reason I can't do it myself," Slater said. "The target has seen you. Boyd from the fashion show."

"My hair was different that night," she said. "I've got coveralls in my car too. I'll look totally different."

"I can't take the risk."

"There'll be lots of other jobs." Max eyed Slater. "I'm thinking I won't need my sidearm."

"It's not that kind of job."

As Max went into Slater's office to stow his heater in the safe, Etta sighed. "I get it. Rule number one: Don't get burned when you're undercover."

"Who says that?" Slater demanded. "Rule number one is don't get croaked. You're useless on any job if you wake up dead. Rule number two is don't get benched. Nobody needs to be sitting around the hoosegow. Don't get burned would be rule number three or lower."

"I didn't mean it literally." She frowned. "You need to chill."

Max laughed as he went to the front door.

As he walked out after him, Slater jabbed a finger at her. "Spread out."

They crossed to the parking lot, and Max waved at his vehicle. "You brought the Frontier. It's such a sweet ride."

He walked to the back end of the Charger and pressed the fob to open the trunk. Digging out a pair of dark-blue coveralls, he stepped into them, and they both climbed into the Frontier.

Slater drove toward the store, on the way outlining the job and the cover story. He parked at a meter a few doors down.

"That's the place up there."

"A Touch of Class," Max said, peering at the storefront. "Sounds classy."

"The same way a sanitation truck is sanitary. We'll start a phone call so I can tell you when the camera is aimed right. Put one of your earbuds in."

Once Max had his phone in hand, Slater called him, and Max picked up, then tucked the device in the breast pocket of his coveralls.

They both climbed out, and Slater unlocked the ladder. As Max pulled it out of the bed, he opened the cargo box and lifted out a red toolbox.

"You can use this as a prop," Slater said.

"Good idea." He lifted the toolbox by its handle, then hoisted the ladder in his other hand, and walked toward A Touch of Class.

Once he was behind the wheel again, Slater spoke into his phone. "Mic check. Can you hear me?"

"Ten for ten," Max said.

Slater watched him awkwardly set down the ladder to pull open the door. Through the phone he heard him call a blustery greeting to Shaula and introduce himself as an electrician.

"Francesca said you'd stop by." Shaula's voice was a lot quieter but he could hear what he was saying.

"It shouldn't take long," Max said. "I need to see if what I think is in that distribution box is really in there."

"Let me know if you need anything," Shaula said.

A moment later came a metallic *clank*. That would be the ladder meeting the brick wall next to Boyd's desk. It took a few minutes, but eventually he heard Max clear his throat. That was the signal to check the camera angle. Slater peered at the phone screen.

"It's almost right," he said. "Tilt it up a hair, and left."

A blue-clad bulk loomed and filled the video frame, then the image jostled. Max descended the ladder again and stepped aside.

"I meant the other left," Slater said.

He waited while Max went up the ladder again, then down. The whole desktop was in the frame now. Even if Boyd moved the laptop around, he'd have a view of it.

"That's it," Slater said. "You're done."

"I'm all finished," Max called to Shaula.

"Will you need to come back?" he said.

"I don't think so. I'll have Francesca let you know if I do."

A moment later he saw Shaula step out the door and hold it open, then Max appeared, carrying the ladder and the red toolbox. As he approached, Slater climbed out, and stowed the toolbox, and locked up the ladder once Max had lifted it into the bed of the truck.

Once they were both in the cab, Max spoke.

"Can I see the video feed?"

Slater handed him his phone, and Max peered at the screen.

He chuckled. "It's perfect. You can see everything that happens on that desk."

Firing up the tinny little engine, he drove back to the surface lot across from the office, and waited while Max ditched his coveralls in the trunk of his car.

"Back to the joy of written reports," Max said as they rode upstairs.

Etta was at the front desk, and rose as they walked in. "That really was a quickie."

She followed Max into his office, and Slater could hear them talking, but tuned them out. Before he could get settled at his desk, his phone emitted a loud chirp. A proximity alert. He pulled it out to check. Shaula was approaching the building. He went over to Max's office.

"The bird from the fabric store is on his way up. He doesn't need to know you work here."

Max gestured to his door. "Go ahead. Close it."

When Shaula knocked, Slater pulled the front door open and waved him into his office.

"I came to debrief," Shaula said, dropping into the guest chair.

Slater sat behind his desk. "Is there anything I need to know?"

"The ruse worked fine. Your electrician came off as totally believable. Can you show me the video feed?"

"I'm not going to do that."

He frowned. "OK, then. So what now?"

"When will Boyd be at his desk?"

"Probably later today. He works in the studio whenever, day or night. He says he doesn't work at his apartment because he needs clear life boundaries."

"When does he get back from Pedro?"

Shaula dug out his phone. "He's still there. So a few hours at the earliest."

Interesting that he was so certain about that, Slater thought, watching him. "Let me see what Pike is doing." He tapped out a text to him:

Can you handle having Shaula around again?

Pike's reply came soon after:

Sure. I was going to cook later. I can cook for three.

A second text came a moment later:

Not loving the idea of the guy becoming a permanent bedroom fixture.

Slater thumb-typed a response:

That's not happening. I just need to keep him close right now.

He eyed Shaula. "I've got an errand to run. Come to the house in an hour or so."

"I can ride shotgun on your errand."

"You need to blow." Slater rose and grabbed his stealthy glasses, hanging them on his shirt. "I'll see you there."

They rode down in the elevator together, and Slater crossed to the parking lot, and drove the Frontier to his house. Late in the day there was a lot of traffic on the freeway, but the navigation app sent him on surface streets. In his garage he opened his gear cabinet, and hauled out the key binder and the lock reader, and loaded them into a boxy aluminum case. It didn't really look like the kind of toolbox a tradesperson would carry, but the binder full of ghost keys would fit inside, unlike the other options at hand.

Thinking about it, he'd been wearing that lanyard at the trade show. He opened the door of the Continental and found it in the backseat. Looping it around his neck, he made sure the side with the photo and the text was facing his chest.

With the aluminum case in hand, he went back to the Frontier and drove to Downtown, to the address for Boyd's apartment building. A meter was open not far up the block, and he cruised up to it and pulled in, under a laurel fig planted along the curb. It didn't make sense that the city had put in so damn many of these. The maintenance was easy, but the roots messed up the sidewalks.

Peering at the stealthy glasses, he found the power switch, and clicked it on, then put them on his face. From the box behind the seat he grabbed a pair of black latex gloves and tucked them in his hip pocket. Lifting the aluminum case, he walked back to Boyd's building. The name over the entrance said LOFTS, but that was just a marketing word now, about as meaningless as *luxury* or *modern* or *spacious*. This was a new residential build, not converted from another use like Andy's place had been.

On the drive he'd been thinking about how to talk

his way into the building, with the trade show ID maybe implying some legitimacy, but there were lots of people around at this time of day. As he came up to the entrance he saw a woman approaching the door from inside, and stepped to one side as she pushed it open. Catching the door as it swung closed, he stepped in.

The lobby was unstaffed, as Shaula had said. There were cameras here, monitoring the door and the mail room, but there wasn't one in the elevator on the way up. Stepping off upstairs, he checked the hallway for cameras, but couldn't see any.

When he found Boyd's door he rapped on it and stood listening. There was no response, no sound from within, just the distant hum of the building's ventilation system. The deadbolt was standard hardware store equipment, which meant he had a good chance of getting inside. His ghost keys were made for this stuff. No way could he defeat anything more secure.

Setting the aluminum case flat on the floor, he dropped to one knee and briefly opened it, pulling out the lock-reading probe. It was a length of wire with a connector at one end and a key-shaped paddle at the other. When he connected it to his phone, Svetlana's software popped up, with a message in gray Cyrillic lettering on a black screen: "готов."

It was risky to be doing this, as it was just after office hours, the busiest time of day, when people tended to come home. But if someone asked, he planned to pose as a locksmith, and say Boyd had broken his key off in the lock, and that's what the probe was for.

He slid the probe into the deadbolt and watched the phone screen. It flashed green and gave him a lone possibility: 341.

Opening the case again, he tucked the probe away and

flipped through the heavy pages of the key binder. When he found the pouch marked 341, he slid out the key, and closed the case. When he tried it in the lock, it twisted easily, and he could feel the deadbolt retracting.

Slater got to his feet and lifted the case, tucking the key into his jeans. Looking up the hall to make sure he wasn't being observed, he wriggled his hands into the black latex gloves, then twisted the door handle and stepped inside.

"Maintenance," he called, and stopped to listen.

There was no sound, and he pulled the door closed, and set the case against the inside of it. Dim daylight came in the window, so he didn't bother turning on the room lights. It looked like a one-bedroom. This was the living room, with a kitchenette off to the side. He took a minute to scan the place for cameras, but couldn't see any that were obvious.

It felt like a straight guy's apartment, with a sofa and a big TV, and nothing in the Frigidaire except orange juice and cheese and ketchup. In the bedroom clothes were strewn on the floor, and there was a little desk with no computer.

A stack of books sat on the desk, heavy thick volumes, like textbooks. He scanned the titles on the spines. Most of them had some version of the words *metaphysics* or *philosophy* in the titles: *Modern Metaphysical Theory* and *Advances in Philosophy* and *The Metaphysical Quest*. Digging out his phone, he took a photo of the stack. Next to the bed a book was splayed facedown. Bold lettering on the cover said the title was *Access New Lands Via DMT.* He photographed that too.

Under the book were loose pages, and he shifted it to look at them. They were flyers for real estate. He'd seen these before—real estate agents handed them out when they did open houses. There were six of them, all for properties in the Palisades, and only one of them had a price on it. Four million for an empty lot. After the fires the sales were booming over there. Rather than rebuild, some of the owners were cashing out on the prime coastal land.

Once he'd photographed them, he tucked them back under the DMT book, and briefly knelt to look under the bed. There was nothing but clumps of dust and a lone white sports sock.

In the living room again, he looked around, trying to pick out anything that might not fit. Should he take the time to dig through the garbage can in the kitchen? He'd been here long enough, he decided, and lifted the aluminum case, and reached for the door handle. From the other side came the rattle of keys.

TWENTY-SIX

SLATER HAD NO TIME to think, or even to hide. In a split second he bolted the few steps into the kitchen, and sat on the floor behind the counter, his back to the cabinets, and set the case beside him. He pulled his knees up to his chin. He was out of view of the front door and the bedroom, but if Boyd decided he wanted some OJ, Slater was busted. Getting caught here could well mean jail time.

First came the sound of the door opening, and then it closed again. His heart was pounding in his ears. He tried to breathe slowly and not make any noise. Boyd didn't turn on the lights. The sound of his footsteps crossed to the bedroom, and a light came on from that direction. He heard Boyd take a piss, and then walk a few steps.

Right now he could make a break for it. But the guy would definitely hear him, and follow him, and figure out who he was. Then he heard Boyd's voice from the bedroom.

"Hey, babe."

A woman's voice replied, tinny through the phone speaker: "How are you doing, babe?"

"I missed you today."

"I miss you too," she said. "I've been thinking about you."

"I went down to San Pedro. On the drive back I got to thinking I need to pull the trigger on this land. I'm never going to have another opportunity like this. I need to get over my fear."

"Aw. What are you afraid of, babe?"

"I guess just things falling apart. My world collapsing around me."

"You're smart," she said, "and you're competent. I believe in you. Where's the land you want to pull the trigger on?"

"I told you that already, dummy."

"I'm sorry that it slipped my mind, babe. Tell me about the rest of your day."

That calm consistent tone. She had no reaction at all when he called her dumb. No umbrage, no attitude, no pushback. That was no human being. The guy was talking to software.

"Listen, babe, I have to jump in the shower. We'll talk later."

"Enjoy your shower," she said. "I love you, Boyd."

It took a minute, but eventually Slater heard the water go on, and the sound of the shower curtain sliding on the rail. He waited a few more seconds, then got up and grabbed the case, and treaded carefully to the front door. He opened it slowly, relieved that the hinges made no noise.

Stepping into the hall, he pulled it closed, and eased the handle into place. His hand was still on the door when a guy stepped around the corner. With coiffed black hair, he was in his forties, and built lean, wearing a collared shirt and dress pants. Totally fuckable, Slater decided.

The guy frowned and stopped. "Why are you wearing gloves?"

"Because I don't want to be working barehanded with raw sewage," Slater said. "What's it to you?"

His nose wrinkled. "Is there a plumbing problem? Do you work for the landlord? I haven't seen you around before. It seems late in the day for maintenance."

"Are you the building police?"

"I live next door, and I'm suspicious of anyone walking around wearing latex gloves. And what's with the glasses?"

"It's called fashion. Have you never heard of Irving Irving?"

"I'm wearing a pair of his underpants right now. I didn't know he did eyewear too."

Slater glanced down the hall behind him, then over his own shoulder, and lowered his voice. "Listen, I don't work for the building. I'm in here on a contract operation. Strictly on the down-low. Boyd wanted to put in a different showerhead. A high-flow model."

His eyebrows shot up. "Those are illegal."

Slater tapped his finger to his lips. "That's why he didn't ask the building management to do it."

"That little sneak. Where do you even get those?"

"From what I've heard, they're smuggled in from Florida."

"Is his unit a one bath or two?"

"Why don't you talk to Boyd about that?" Slater said.

"I don't actually know the man. Just to say hello."

He scoffed and walked toward the elevator.

The guy called after him. "You weren't actually messing with the sewer pipes, were you?"

Slater pulled open the door to the stairwell, and peeled off the gloves as he trotted down, awkwardly shifting the heavy case from one hand to the other. When he got out to the street, he loaded the case into the Frontier.

Nosing into the traffic, he finally took a breath. It felt like that had been too close. He'd been seconds from getting busted, from spending the night in the hoosegow. He could still feel the adrenaline. It was giving him a headache.

At his house he parked on the street and carried the aluminum case into the garage. When he got upstairs he found Shaula was already here, wearing a different bowling shirt from earlier, this one tan and brown. He was standing with Pike in the kitchen. Pike had changed out of his work drag into a T-shirt and a pair of fugly cargo shorts. A bag of flour tortillas sat on the counter, and Pike had three of them heating on the griddle.

"What's going on?" Slater said.

"Shaula was just explaining to me that time travel doesn't really work like it does in science fiction," Pike said.

"Even though technically it is science fiction?"

"He also won't tell me where he parked his spaceship. Apparently you have to travel in a ship."

"In fiction you just set a dial," Shaula said. "In reality it's like space travel, but you have to look for markers. It's actually really difficult. You can sort of judge how far back you get sent, but it's imprecise."

Pike gestured with the tongs. "What markers do you use?"

"When you look at the sky from the earth, the stars slowly change position. There's a twenty-six-thousand-year pattern. It's called the precession of the equinoxes. So that's easy. Like looking at the face of a clock. You can also use pulsars, but that takes more complicated equipment."

"Did you arrive in the right time?" Slater said.

"Very good question, Shaula," Pike said. "When are you?"

Shaula chuckled. "I got here a little early."

"That's always better than being late."

"I've just been hanging out in LA until the target event," Shaula said.

Slater put his hands on his hips. "For how long?"

"A few years. It's why I got a job. Now with the consulting business starting up, I'm thinking I'll stay beyond the event."

"Your superiors won't demand your return?" Pike said.

"I'm not a soldier. I'm an employee. I've got some latitude."

"What event are you waiting for?" Pike used the tongs to flip the tortillas. "Is an asteroid going to take out Bakersfield or something?"

"I'm just here for a meeting. History isn't really about dramatic events, even though it's retold that way. It's pretty boring most of the time. Things just trudge along."

"But you can't change the past," Pike said. "So why even bother coming here?"

"You can't change it, but you can nudge people, and reassure them, and smooth the path for the inevitable."

"The more convoluted your story gets," Slater said, "the more disconnected from reality you sound."

"I get that." Shaula gestured helplessly. "I can't show you anything or say anything that will make you believe me."

"Does it really matter if we believe you?" Pike said.

"Probably not." He eyed Slater. "Have you thought about having kids?"

Slater scoffed. "Where did that come from? I'd break them. Broken people break people."

"They're more resilient than you'd think."

"Then they'd break me. I was at a client's house and the little rodents were decorating the furniture with wax crayons. Whoever owns that stuff will have to throw it all away."

"They're definitely full of surprises," Shaula said. "Something new every single day."

"Are you speaking from the experience of all the kids you have? You're barely out of knee pants yourself."

Shaula laughed. "I don't have any, but I know what they're like."

"These will be ready in a minute," Pike said. "Grab some plates."

He was putting together quesadillas with fake cotija, Slater saw, and soon the three of them went out onto the deck and ate in the golden light of the end of the day.

After he'd polished off his quesadilla, Slater checked his phone for the video feed from A Touch of Class. It was still connected, but nothing had happened around the desk yet. He took a minute to set Svetlana's software to alert him when there was any activity on the camera.

"Did Boyd ever talk about the Palisades?" Slater said.

Shaula met his gaze. "I know he goes over there sometimes."

"For your hermeneutic consulting business?"

"For a while we talked about setting up a retreat center. That was Boyd's idea. There are plenty of big empty lots in the Palisades right now. But we agreed on a storefront in the city instead." He frowned. "Why are you asking about the Palisades?"

"No reason."

"Can I inquire about sex?" Shaula said, and pushed his plate away.

Pike laughed. "This is becoming a routine."

"I'm not trying to muscle in and be your third. But I'm here anyway. We can mix it up. I kind of liked being between you two."

"We can make that happen." Pike rose and carried the

plates to the kitchen.

Slater followed them downstairs, and started to get undressed. Once Shaula ditched his trousers, Slater stood behind him, and wrapped his arms around his torso, and pressed his nose into his hair, eliciting a contented sigh.

Pike was naked now too, and stood in front of him, and pressed his body into him, and met his mouth. They stood that way for a minute, relishing the skin contact. Slater was getting hard, and ground his woody into Shaula's thigh.

"Come on." Pike pulled Shaula onto the bed and kissed him. Climbing on, Slater joined them, pressing his mouth into theirs. The three-way kiss was extremely hot, and they spent a while in it, squeezing and caressing each other.

Eventually Shaula straddled Pike, and lowered himself onto him, rocking back and forth. Pike thrust up into him. Slater grabbed Shaula's cock, and pumped him, and stroked himself. When Pike came, he groaned and thrust hard. Shaula climaxed soon after, and finally Slater did. Shaula stretched out between them, and Slater shifted over to make room, and folded his arm over his eyes.

Once Pike's breathing had slowed, he spoke. "It's interesting that you're in no rush to get back to your own time. It makes me think the future isn't any better than now."

"The basic things don't change," Shaula said. "They just operate differently."

"I assume most people will be roasting rat meat on sticks over barrels in the rubble of bombed-out streets," Slater said.

"Or maybe the planet gets restored to garden status," Pike said. "Like it's one big national park."

"You seriously think that's possible?" Slater demanded.

"I admit it doesn't look to be a likely outcome based on what I see every day."

"It's not like either of those," Shaula said. "You two have a descendant named Zebulon Pike. Before my time they were the deputy governor of a mining colony on Ganymede, and they managed to shut down a mutiny with no bloodshed. In the process they achieved remarkable good will on both sides. They're considered a role model for peacemaking."

"I don't remember telling you my first name," Pike said.

"The future knows it. There's also a freighter named after them. The *Zebulon Pike* carries platinum-group metals back from the colony."

"Maybe they named it after the other Zebulon Pike. The one who explored the Southwest in the nineteenth century."

"Nope. It's about your descendants."

"You really should write this down," Pike said. "It's so intricate and involved."

"What about DMT?" Slater said.

"That's not where this is coming from." Shaula caressed his chest. "I'm not on it."

"But you talked about it. Does Boyd talk about it? Is he a regular user?"

"It's one of our shared interests. I've never done it, but Boyd has, a couple of times. He was so into it he tried to find someone to set up an IV drip for him, so he could keep the veil lifted for longer. When you take the drug orally you're only able to be immersed in the deeper reality for a few minutes."

"That sounds like a one-way ticket to permanent brain damage," Pike said. "He might just get stranded in that neutral space."

TWENTY-SEVEN

꧁꧂

Sometime later Slater woke to a loud beep. Sitting up, in the low light from the windows, he could see Shaula was still here, limbs entwined with Pike's. He got out of bed, and found his jeans on the floor, and dug out his phone. The alert was from Svetlana's software. Activity on the camera in the fabric store. The live video feed showed the top of Boyd's balding head and the side of his face. He was sitting at his desk, laptop open.

Slater went to the lounge chair and sat, and scrolled back through the video feed. He stopped and played it back at the point when Boyd had pulled open his laptop. At this angle the screen was too distorted to read it, but the keyboard was clear. He zoomed in to study Boyd's first keystrokes. His fingers briefly danced at the top of the board, where the numeric keys were. That had to be the code to unlock it. Rewinding again, he slowed it down.

It took a minute to figure out, but the numbers he typed were clear enough, either 1428 or 1429. Boyd typed the last digit with his right hand, and he hadn't extended his fingers the way he had with his left, when he'd typed the other digits. But Slater could see generally where it landed. Any computer would give him at least two tries. He thumb-typed a note of the code, then checked the live feed. Boyd was still at his desk. Of course he was; he'd just sat down. He might be there for a while. Slater set a timer for half an hour and went back to bed.

It was hard to fall back into sleep. Knowing he might have the keys to Boyd's kingdom was like a rush. Most people only wanted to use one key at the front door, not half a dozen different ones for each room, for each layer. But it depended on where Boyd stored his documents. With any luck, once he was into the computer, he could get into everything else.

Later he woke to his phone vibrating on his chest. He checked the video feed. Boyd was still at his desk, doing stuff. This time he set the timer for an hour, and when it buzzed him awake, he saw that the laptop was closed. The lights were down low too.

Pushing himself out of bed, he pulled on his jeans and a clean shirt, then went to the bed and shook Shaula's shoulder. The guy stirred and looked up at him with sleepy eyes.

"Get your paws off my boyfriend and get up," Slater hissed. "It's go time."

Shaula rose and started to get dressed in the dim light.

"What's going on?" Pike mumbled.

"We've got work to do," Slater said. "Go back to sleep."

Once he'd closed the bedroom door, Slater stopped on the landing.

"So Boyd worked for a couple hours, then closed the laptop and turned out the lights. Does that mean he's gone?"

"Totally."

"What are the chances he might come back?"

"I'd say that's unlikely. I can tell you if he's around there." Shaula dug in his pants. "I have a tracker on his phone."

"Does he know that?"

"He does not."

Slater watched him tap at his phone screen. That would have helped a lot when he'd gone into the guy's apartment. A few seconds earlier or later and he would have been hooked.

"I wish you'd fucking told me that."

Shaula frowned. "What difference does it make to you?"

"I need all the information. If you don't tell me stuff, it's equivalent to misleading me."

He briefly met his gaze. "I have a tracker on Boyd's phone."

Slater scoffed. "How far away is he?"

"He's on the 101, headed west. I know where he's going. He has a woman out in the Valley that he sees sometimes."

"A live one? Not just software?"

"He talks to the chatbot girlfriend a lot, but I think the real woman is for hookups."

"Does he stay over with the real woman?"

"He'll be a while, since he's just on his way out there," Shaula said. "He won't be back until morning."

"So let's roll." Slater trotted down the stairs.

"I could never figure that out. Boyd talks to the artificial woman for hours and hours, but the real one has a strict time limit."

Slater opened the door to the garage. "Straight people are crazy."

"I think it's just Boyd."

In the garage he went over to his gear cabinet and got it unlocked.

"This doesn't look like a safe, but it is a safe," Shaula said, watching him. "Like it's hiding in plain sight."

"Any junkie who breaks in looking to steal stuff for drug money won't get into it. They'll move on to the easy pickings." He waved to the wall rack. "The yard tools."

Pulling the jammer off its charging cable, he relocked the cabinet doors.

"Why do you keep your phone charger in a safe?" Shaula said.

"That's not what it is." He pocketed it. "It's a Wi-Fi jammer, also disguised to hide in plain sight. It'll knock your security camera offline."

"That's so deceptive."

"We'll take the Frontier. It's less conspicuous."

They walked out to the street and climbed in the little pickup. It was after the witching hour, when the bars closed and the streets cleared out, so there was no traffic on the way to Downtown. Slater checked his side mirror as he accelerated onto the freeway.

"If that security camera goes offline, will Boyd react?"

"That happens sometimes," Shaula said. "There's buggy Internet in the neighborhood. I doubt he'd rush back to the studio. He'll plan to deal with it when he comes in later."

"Let's keep an eye on his location anyway."

He parked the Frontier a few doors up from A Touch of Class and killed the engine.

"I'll switch this on." Slater dug out the Wi-Fi jammer, and flipped out the prongs, and handed it to him. "It'll disrupt the camera as long as the prongs are extended. You go in, and set it on the counter, and make sure the camera is off. Then I'll come in."

Shaula climbed out and walked to the storefront. He used a key to unlock the security grate, then rolled it up, and unlocked the door. He went in, and a moment later the lights came on. Reappearing in the doorway, he beckoned for Slater to join him.

As he stepped inside, Shaula flipped the deadbolt, then went over to the counter. Slater looked up at the security camera. The little lamp on it was slowly strobing orange. It was offline. Stretching for it, he could just reach the power plug, and pulled it out of the wall socket. The lamp on the camera flicked off.

"Why unplug it?" Shaula said.

"Because if we leave the jammer on, IT guy, the laptop won't connect."

"OK, that makes sense. You've done this before."

"It's kind of my job." Slater frowned as he walked behind the counter, and picked up the jammer, and folded in the prongs. "You look queasy."

"I feel like I'm betraying my friend."

"I thought you were down with this."

"I am. It's just … now we're actually doing it."

"You're shutting down a thief. That doesn't count as betrayal."

Shaula sat at Boyd's desk, and Slater grabbed the other desk chair, and rolled it over, and sat next to him.

As he pulled open the laptop, Shaula said, "What's the password?"

"It's either one four two eight or one four two nine."

"It must be fourteen twenty-nine. I almost could have guessed that."

"Why are those numbers significant?" Slater said.

"It's about lunar cycles. The moon waxes for fourteen days, and on the twenty-ninth day the cycle starts again."

"That sounds like astrology. Is the waxing moon meaningful in the fabric business, or in the thievery business?"

"We try to align any business expansion with the waxing moon. It represents growth."

"The moon wanes as much as it waxes."

Shaula raised his eyebrows. "That's why you focus on the first fourteen days."

"I guess that's as logical as any other damn religion."

On the keyboard he tapped 1-4-2-9, and the lock screen faded, revealing the desktop.

"You were right."

"We need to find everything about the grift and copy it." Digging in his pants pocket, Slater pulled out a thumb drive, and set it on the desk.

Shaula was clicking around, peering at the screen. "He has a cloud drive installed. We can start in there."

"First, does he have a password manager? So we can get into other stuff later."

He spent a minute clicking. "I don't see one," he said finally.

"Sometimes people use their web browser to remember passwords."

Shaula clicked on it. "That's exactly what he's doing. There's a lot here. I'm not sure if I can download it."

"Do a screen shot."

He clicked, and scrolled to the next page, and clicked again, then picked up the thumb drive and inserted it. Slater watched as he dragged the screenshots onto the drive.

"This feels wrong," Shaula said, and shook his head.

"Stealing from a thief isn't wrong. And you don't have to be a crook like him. Remember that."

He picked up his phone and tapped at it. "Boyd is at that woman's place now."

Slater watched as he opened the cloud drive, but then Shaula paused and met his gaze.

"It makes me nervous to be watched while I'm working."

"So get to it." Slater threw up a hand. "If you can't find documentation on the grift, I'll look for it myself."

He pushed himself out of the chair, and went into the back room, and looked for something to stand on. There were a couple of stacking chairs. Unlike the swivel-mounted desk chair with its casters, one of these would be stable enough. He carried one out to the wall beside Boyd's desk. Stepping onto it, he tried to pull down Svetlana's camera. Max had attached it to the smooth sheet-metal side of the distribution box. It wouldn't budge.

Stepping off the chair, he walked into the back and looked around again, eventually finding a screwdriver in a tray on a set of metro shelves. Back up on the chair, he used the tool to pry the camera off. The adhesive putty came with it in a uniform sheet. It was still plenty sticky. He found a scrap of fabric to wrap it in, and took it out to the street, and put it in the box in the bed of the Frontier.

Back inside, Shaula glanced up at him. "I think I found it."

"What did you find?"

"A lot of stuff. It's well organized. That's no surprise. It's who Boyd is."

Slater sat next to him and leaned in to look at the screen.

"This folder is called 'designers,' and the subfolders are the names of lots of the people we did tech work for."

As he scrolled through the list of folders, the name of Tamara's business jumped out, and so did Irving Irving. There was also one called "Consolidated."

Slater pointed to it. "Open that one."

When he clicked on it, there were just a handful of files. One of them was a vector file named "paisley" along with a string of numbers.

"Can you open that?" Slater said.

When Shaula clicked on the file, it launched a graphic design program, and the familiar paisley pattern appeared on the screen, in rich browns and deep purples. Unlike the shoddy knockoff, the true original really was beautiful.

"We manufactured this," Shaula said. "Two bolts of it. You took a swatch."

"Show me another folder." He gestured at the screen. "Irving Irving."

This one contained dozens of files, most of them images.

"Can you sort them by date?"

When Shaula did that, the ones at the top were less than a week old.

"Open the first one," Slater said.

It was a pattern for high-cut underpants, with a technical drawing of each of the panels, with notations all around. Boyd had just acquired this. It meant he had ongoing access to Irving's computers.

"The fucker is ambitious," Slater said.

"There are other folders with spreadsheets and letters. I think some of it is about the manufacturing. I know it's done in China, and the companies have Chinese names."

"Copy everything." Slater sat back, then rolled away. He didn't want to unnerve the guy any more than he already was.

Shaula suddenly started like he'd been shocked.

"What?" Slater demanded.

"I forgot to check on Boyd." He grabbed his phone and peered at the screen. "He's still in the Valley."

The guy was jumpy, Slater realized, and watched briefly as he shifted his focus back to the laptop. Rising, he walked into the back, and looked things over. There were some bolts of fabric, and some clothes on a rack, a mix of tops and skirts.

Just one garment was made from Artémise's paisley print, the blouse that had been in the show last week. He pulled its hanger off the rack. Even Slater could tell it looked cheap: not just the fabric but the loose threads, the uneven stitching, the simple hem.

Hanging it up again, he walked out to the front, past the counter, and looked through the front window at the street. Shaula hadn't rolled the security shutter all the way up, and its chrome-plated bars bisected the view. The sky was already looking pinky gray. The sun would be up soon.

Eventually Shaula spoke. "I think that's it."

Slater stepped over to the desk. "We need to delete everything that's stolen. Not the other stuff, but the files from the designers."

"Are you sure?" He raised his eyebrows. "Boyd is going to figure it out."

"We need to knock him onto the ropes. If he's smart he's got it backed up somewhere, but maybe this will slow him down."

Shaula nodded and spent a minute deleting files.

"The cloud drive might have a trash folder," Slater said. "You have to permanently delete stuff from that."

"I actually know what I'm doing," he said, not looking up. A minute later he pulled out the thumb drive, and folded the laptop closed. "What now?"

Stepping over, Slater took the drive. "I have a guy who can dig through it, and explain the parts that you're not aware of."

"I'm going with you. I need to know what he finds."

"It'll take him a while. Go get some sleep. I'll drop this off and let you know when I hear from him."

Slater reached up to plug in the camera as they walked out, and waited for Shaula to lock the door and roll down the security shutter.

"Can I drop you somewhere?"

"I need to walk," Shaula said. "It'll clear my head."

"I don't even know where you live."

"You know where the Seventh Street Bridge is? Just this side of it."

"That's the Arts District." Slater raised his eyebrows. "Fancy."

"My place isn't." Raising a palm, he turned and walked away.

TWENTY-EIGHT

༼༼༼༼༼༼༼༼༼

CLIMBING IN BEHIND THE wheel of the Frontier, Slater rubbed his eyes. They felt dry, and his head hurt. It was still early, but the sun was out. Andy might be up. He sent him a text:

Are you awake yet?

His reply came a moment later:

Barely.

Slater started the engine and sent a response:

I'm coming over.

He drove to the surface lot behind Andy's building and pulled in. Even at this hour the attendant was on duty, and he paid the guy before he walked around to the entrance and went up to Andy's loft.

When he pulled open the door, Andy was wearing boxers and a white T-shirt. He flashed that beautiful smile. "Did you bring coffee?"

"Nothing's open yet."

"Bullshit." Andy walked to his gaming chair and dropped into it.

"I can smell coffee." Slater gestured to his desk. "You've got a whole damn mugful."

"It tastes better when … you bring it."

He scoffed and waggled the thumb drive. "This is a bunch of records on a grift," he said, and explained what he knew about it. "Can you go through it and figure out whether there's more to it? I think the victims are obvious, but maybe I'm missing something."

"Data crunching and analysis," Andy said. "My favorite."

"Can you work on it today?"

"It'll cost you."

He threw up a hand. "It always does."

"You owe me for the last few … gigs too. Don't think I've forgotten."

"I'll look forward to your invoice." Slater watched him for a moment. "Bye, beautiful."

When he got to his house, he found Pike upstairs in the kitchen, in a T-shirt and shorts, cutting fruit into a bowl. Slater kissed him and gave him a brief squeeze.

"Are you always up this early?"

"I need time to wake up before I have to go to work," Pike said. "Things are usually quiet at this time of day."

"Weirdo," he said intently.

Pike laughed. "Did you get it done, whatever you and Shaula were up to?"

"It's still in progress. But things are happening."

"You're earning that rack Artémise gave you."

He decided not to tell him she'd subsequently paid him another one. "I think I've got answers for her."

Pike grabbed another bowl, and dumped half the fruit

into it, and handed both to him. Once he'd cut a bagel in half, they sat out on the deck in the bright morning sun.

"I was thinking about Shaula's story." Pike gestured with his spoon. "Did it strike you that maybe the target he was here waiting for was you, or me, or maybe both of us?"

"Right, because it's so plausible that there's a space freighter named after you."

"Named after our gender-neutral descendant. And it's not really all that impressive. I looked it up. Ganymede is one of Jupiter's moons. It's not that far away. You can see it with a pair of binoculars." He shrugged. "It's like saying there's a Pacific Ocean freighter, but it only sails to Ensenada and back."

"He's got you on the hook." Slater waved his bagel. "And it pisses me off that he's way more into you than into me."

"I didn't pick up on that."

"He named his fictional space freighter after you."

"Or was it named after our descendant? He did give you the sales pitch on children."

"If he's telling me the future wants me to have a kid," Slater said, "I'm definitely not doing it."

"If there is no free will, you don't really have a choice."

He leaned in and jabbed a finger at him. "Do not dump me for Shaula."

Through a mouthful of bread, Pike said, "That's not going to happen."

As Slater rose, he looked him up and down. "I hope not. I need to crash."

Down in the bedroom he ditched his clothes, and drew the drapes, and almost instantly fell asleep. It felt like a few minutes later when his phone rang. Andy, he saw, trying to focus on the screen. By the clock in the corner he'd been out for half the day.

"You got the dope on the grift?" Slater said.

"There's plenty."

"I'm bringing Shaula."

"Fine by me. It's not every day that I … get to meet someone who's only existed for two years."

Sitting up, he texted Shaula:

My operative has info. Can I pick you up?

Shaula responded with an address on Seventh, and Slater plugged it into his navigation app. Once he'd washed up and dressed, he went down to the garage and climbed in the Continental, and pulled up at the address a few minutes later. It was a multistory redbrick building, dating at least to the early twentieth century. A faded sign painted on the facade said it had once been a wholesale business. There were curtains and plants in the windows above street level, so it had been converted, but it didn't look upscale.

Shaula stepped across the sidewalk, and climbed in, and set his backpack between his feet.

"What did your guy say?"

"Nothing yet." Slater checked the mirror and pulled into the street. "You're going to hear it when I hear it."

He parked behind Andy's building, and they went up to his loft. When Andy pulled open the door, Slater introduced them, and Andy waved them to the little table under the windows. Slater pulled out the chairs and set them near the desk.

Once he'd gotten settled in his gaming chair, Andy eyed Shaula. "So you put a back door into … all these people's systems?"

"Are you recording this conversation?" Shaula said.

He scoffed. "I work for Slater. He pays me well for

my … discretion. If I ever broke his confidence, he'd … break me."

"He speaks the truth," Slater said.

"It was Boyd's idea." Shaula raised his eyebrows. "My part was gaining access. His was looting. I haven't actually seen much of what's on that drive. Just what we looked at when we snagged it last night."

"How did you get all this material from Boyd?" Andy said.

"We accessed his cloud drive." Slater waved a hand. "Bam, hoist with his own petard."

"Did you know he has an LLM girlfriend? Part of what you … copied is a transcript of months and … months of their interactions. He's pretty candid with her."

"You mean his AI chatbot girlfriend?" Slater said.

Andy swiveled toward him. "AI is a marketing term. There's no intelligence involved. It's a prediction engine based on a … large language model. People like … Boyd get addicted to the interaction because there's never … any conflict, like there is with real people. It's all just positive vibes that … reinforce whatever you tell it."

"Does he talk to the software about the grift?" Slater said.

His random muscle movement intensified. "Oh, yeah. It aligns with the other … documentation, and gave me some shortcuts into it."

"I can't believe he trusts the chatbot with the business," Shaula said.

Andy held his gaze. "He wasn't anticipating getting hacked."

"So what's the gimmick?" Slater said.

"You told me some of this, but from what I've seen, he doesn't … drain bank accounts. He sets up repeating debits that people probably … won't notice. Although a few … people managed to get their banks to cancel them." Andy looked to Shaula. "You really haven't seen this stuff."

"None of it."

"Your name is on all the … banking transactions, large and small. Boyd's never is."

"I thought they were linked to our business accounts."

"Most of them are about you personally. The repeating … charges are linked to business accounts with … your name on them. He did use the business name for the sale of the … building on Glendale Boulevard, but the escrow company paid into … one of Boyd's personal accounts."

"You mean the purchase of the building on Glendale Boulevard," Shaula said.

"That's here too. But the sale happened … three months after you bought it. This spring."

"You're wrong."

"Maybe. I'm not a real estate lawyer."

Andy swiveled to his desk and pulled on his black plastic gauntlets. They were an input device that compensated for his lack of fine motor control. As he peered at the array of screens, things moved around, and new windows opened. He turned to Shaula.

"Have a look."

Shaula rose and leaned in to study a document, and then the one open next to it. Eventually he stood erect. His face was flushed.

"Can you put this on a thumb drive? Not just the real estate material. Everything."

"Hold on," Slater said. "This is my operation."

"I need to look through this." Shaula's tone was intent.

"Why?"

"It's about me." He raised his voice. "You don't get to

control everything."

Slater waved a hand. "Fine. Give him a copy."

"Right now," Andy said, "or after we've … talked through it?"

"Now," Shaula said flatly.

He nodded to his desk. "Can you grab a thumb drive in the top drawer? The blue one."

Shaula rolled it open, and dug around, and found it. Once Andy told him where to plug it in, he focused on his screens. A minute later he nodded to the drive.

"You can take that. Everything's on it."

Pulling it out, Shaula pocketed it, then moved his chair back to the table. "I have to go," he said, and walked out.

Once the door had closed behind him, Andy spoke.

"He didn't know about that sale."

"So Boyd sold their building and moved the cash to his own accounts?" Slater said.

"That's what I see in this. Unless something … else happened. I think the money is just … sitting there. It hasn't been reinvested."

"There was stuff Boyd took from a string of designers. Like Irving Irving."

"There's a whole folder of his work. Patterns and … sketches and print designs."

"Can you print a handful of those on paper?" Slater said. "The most recent ones. The guy isn't super tech savvy."

Andy focused on the screens, and a minute later his printer hummed to life.

"There's a paisley fabric in a vector file in the folder named 'Consolidated,'" Slater said. "Was there anything else related to it?"

"Give me a second." He soon pulled up Artémise's brown and purple pattern. "I actually like this a lot."

"It's not supposed to be outside her studio yet."

"None of the other documents in that … folder were from Artémise's office. There was an invoice from a … company in Shaoxing. The same outfit you asked about before. Two rolls of … polyester fabric."

"That tracks."

"There was also a note in the vector file."

"Something the designer wrote?"

"I think your looter wrote it, based on the … time stamp. It was added after the file was copied."

"What does it say?"

Andy turned to the screen and read: "'Pencil Face says the working name is Cabernet Chew. That won't be … used. It's already trademarked.'"

"Pencil Face."

"It must be a nickname," Andy said.

"I think I know who he's talking about."

Malcolm had a trim little pencil mustache. Assuming Shaula was telling the truth that he'd never worked on Artémise's computers, and really knew nothing about the paisley, maybe Malcolm had talked to Boyd. It all fit, he decided. His hunch about Malcolm had been right. That rat-fuck little twunk had sold Boyd the design.

"Cabernet Chew comes up again," Andy said. "The same day the … note was added, Boyd asked the chatbot to explain what … Cabernet Chew was. Right after that he … asked how trademarks work."

Slater rose and dug out his wad of cash. "What do I owe you?"

"Including the last few jobs, it's been a … lot of work."

"Just spill it."

"Twelve dollars."

He sighed and riffled off the C-notes.

"You must be really tired. You're not even … griping about the cost."

He set the cash on his desk. "We both know you're a damn chiseler. But I'll manage. I can hock one of Pike's watches, or maybe sell my truck. If I stick to food from the gas station I should be fine."

"You poor thing."

"You did have to read transcripts of that deludenoid lowlife talking to a robot. You earned the hardship surcharge."

Once he'd scooped up his printouts, he walked out.

TWENTY-NINE

SLATER PARKED THE CONTINENTAL at his office and walked to Irving Irving's showroom. The receptionist buzzed him in, and he walked past the foxy mannequins toward her desk. Today she had her hair pinned up.

"He's here," she said, "but he's working with one of the production people."

"It's important."

She got up. "Let me see if he has time for you."

Slater ogled the mannequins as she walked into the back, and turned when Irving stepped out, followed by the receptionist.

Irving beamed at him. "How are things, Slater?"

"Can we talk?"

He waved him into the hall, and went into his office, and sat behind his desk.

"I found out how A Touch of Class was able to pirate your work so quickly." Slater dropped into the chair across from him. "They were collaborating with the guy in the camp shirt who worked on your network."

Irving frowned. "He stole from me?"

"Not just once. He installed access so he can steal from you whenever he wants." Half rising, Slater handed him the printouts Andy had made.

He leafed through them. "Where did you get these?"

"From A Touch of Class."

Irving met his gaze. "These garments haven't even been produced yet."

"I know it's infuriating."

"It's more than that. I feel violated. Who are these people?"

Slater told him a little about Boyd and Shaula. "You need to change all the passwords to your network, and your computers, and your cloud storage. Do you have someone who can do that?"

"I'll get on it now." He sat back. "I assume you're going to the police."

"I'm working on shutting them down. I can't get restitution for you, but neither can the cops. When I'm done with these two they won't be in the clothing business anymore."

"That doesn't mean I can't go to the police. You'll have to explain all this."

Slater scowled. "Fuck me."

"Why does that make you angry? They've stolen from me. I have to turn to the justice system. That's what it's for."

"I did you the courtesy of telling you about this up front so that you can shut down their back door." Slater waved an arm. "You're right—if you decide to go to the cops, I won't have any choice but to get into it. Do you have any idea how much work that is? Interviews and depositions and testimony. Can you at least give me a week or so?"

Irving took a breath. "Fine."

With any luck the guy would get over it. He was upset now, but maybe he'd realize nobody wanted to spend months unraveling it, and he'd settle for getting it shut down.

Slater sat up. "So how much would you pay a graphic designer? Someone who can do your drawings and patterns and prints? Is that a full-time job, or do you contract it out?"

"If someone is skilled, and familiar with the industry, they can be very useful. There's enough work here for a full-time graphics person. I could use the help." He threw out a couple of numbers, both a lot more than what Artémise was paying Malcolm. "Why are you asking? Do you have someone for me?"

"I'll let you know." He stood up and stepped to the door.

"Slater," Irving called after him.

He turned and jutted his chin.

"Thank you for telling me about this."

"You make beautiful things." Slater waved a hand. "Nobody should be able to leech off that."

A Touch of Class wasn't far, and when he got out to the street, he walked that way. The shutter was up, and the door was unlocked. Inside he found Boyd at the side of the room carrying a bolt of fabric. As he stepped in, Boyd set the bolt against the wall and frowned.

"John the designer. I know you're not who you say you are."

"Lo, the grifter burned my alias." Slater threw up his hands. "I just wanted to know about the bolt of paisley in the window. It was a simple ask. And then I get sucked into your gimmick."

"This anger in you," Boyd said. "I wonder where it's coming from? Possibly something from your childhood?

What does the feeling evoke? And calling me a crook. It must come from somewhere. Some deep part of yourself projecting outward."

"The truth isn't about my inner self. It's immutable, and harmonic, and elegant in its inherent lack of distortion. It's the golden thread that patiently knits the world together."

"The truth as you perceive it."

"The truth about you." Slater swirled a finger at him. "A chiseler. A lowlife. You're a dirtbag, Boyd."

Boyd's eyes went hard. "Fuck you."

"Not a chance. You're way too tightly wound for me." He put his hands on his hips. "It is interesting how thin your veneer of serenity actually is."

The door from the street opened, and Shaula stepped in.

"I was just telling your boyfriend here that we know who he really is," Boyd said.

"You sold the fricking building," Shaula said. "Don't bother to deny it."

Boyd's eyebrows shot up, but he quickly recovered his composure.

"I moved some pieces around," he said, "but in the big picture, nothing's changed."

"You sold it without telling me," Shaula shouted.

"You were being unreasonable. Moon-eyed." He waved a hand. "Impractical."

"It wasn't your call." He scoffed. "You think I'm stupid. I know what's going on, Boyd. Everything incriminating is in my name, and all the cash is in yours."

His eyes went dead. "You seem to know a lot. Usually you're kind of clueless."

Shaula roared and lunged at him, but Boyd was ready, and took a swing. He struck Shaula on the chin and sent him stumbling. As Boyd stepped after him, Slater moved in from his flank and threw a haymaker, landing it squarely on his cheek. Pike's class ring bit into his finger with the impact. Boyd twisted sideways and collapsed onto the carpet.

Watching him for a second, massaging his finger where the ring was, Slater decided he really was out. It was stupid of both these birds to try to throw hands when they didn't know what the hell they were doing. That's how people got hurt. He squatted next to Boyd and pressed a couple of fingers to his neck. His pulse was solid and regular.

"Is he dead?" Shaula said.

"I coldcocked him. I didn't kill him. Is he on something?"

"What do you mean?"

"People go down like that when they're high. It's like he G'd out."

"Like GHB? He doesn't do that."

Slater pulled Boyd onto his side, and folded his knee forward so that he wouldn't roll onto his back.

"Why are you moving him around?" Shaula demanded.

"So he doesn't choke on his own vomit." Slater stood erect. "If he's sober, he'll only be out for a minute. I don't think he knows yet that we nuked all that pilfered content."

"It doesn't matter anymore." Shaula slid his backpack around, and reached into it, and drew out a handgun.

He knew that weapon, recognized its mismatched components. "That's from my desk. How did you get into my office?" Slater demanded.

He met his gaze. "There was nobody around. You don't have very secure locks."

"You little snake."

With both hands on the weapon, Shaula extended his arms, aiming at Boyd's prone form. "I'm going to end this."

Slater put his hands on his hips. "Are you sure you want to do that? There's no backsies here. It could change your life forever."

His lip curled in disgust. "You, the voice of moderation. That's rich."

"It's like your single-serving ketchup. Once it's out of the packet, it's done."

"I don't have a choice, remember? The block universe."

"It's handy that you can claim inertia whenever it suits you," Slater said. "The rest of us are out here agonizing over our choices, astonished when things go well, or wallowing in regret."

"He tricked me," Shaula shouted, waving the rod. "He lied to my face. For years."

"There's other ways to make him pay for that. You ventilate him and you put your own liberty at risk." He waved a hand. "I know he's a dirtbag, but if you grease the guy, I wouldn't be able to keep that to myself."

"Maybe I'll take you out too."

"Then you'd have to go after Francesca, or whoever's working next door today. They're going to hear the shots. Maybe a pedestrian or two out front. Are you sure you've got enough ammo for all of us?"

"Fuck that," he snapped.

Slater took a breath. "Do you know who Orpheus is? When I met Pike he was reading the classics. Now it's one of our things. Orpheus's wife, Euridice, dies, so Orpheus scams his way into the underworld. Hades agrees to let her leave, but the deal is they can't look back when they're on the way out. Orpheus knows this, and he does it anyway, and Euridice gets yanked back. She's gone forever."

"The message in that is you can't change fate. So the implication is that I'm supposed to do this."

"Or maybe the message is don't do stupid stuff," Slater said. "Don't look back. Don't fire."

Shaula roared and turned his face to the ceiling. He was sobbing, Slater realized, his aim wavering now. He took a step toward him, extending an open hand. He took hold of the heater and gently pulled it from his grasp. Stepping back, he quickly popped out the mag, and tucked it in his pocket, and shoved the weapon in the back of his belt.

Grabbing Shaula's shoulders, he squeezed and looked him in the eye. "That was the right choice."

Shaula wrapped his arms around him, shuddering with sobs. Slater held on to him, and it took a while, but eventually the emotion subsided, and he pulled away.

"Boyd is a classic con man," Slater said. "He's charming and funny and talks about interesting things. There's a smile on his face as he's stealing from you. Anything risky gets spread around so his name isn't on it. But yours is. It's a textbook grift."

"Fuck Boyd."

Slater looked to the floor and saw that the guy was starting to stir. "He's coming around."

"I can't even look at him right now," Shaula said, and walked out.

Pulling his shirttail over the weapon, he followed him out to the street. Shaula was already up the block. Slater walked in the opposite direction, toward his office.

Upstairs he flicked on the lights, and went to his desk, and dug the weapon out of his belt. He pulled the slide back far enough to disengage it, then quickly field-stripped it. He should have done this when he'd taxed it from Frank. It was a lot safer in pieces. Digging out his handkerchief, he wiped down the parts. Of course his DNA was still all over it, but that was less damning than fingerprints.

At the front desk he found a padded envelope, and dumped the component parts into it, along with the mag, and sealed it. He was scrabbling in the drawer for a Sharpie when keys rattled in the door and Max came in, wearing his gray grid-pattern suit.

"I was just about to leave you a note," Slater said.

Max eyed the envelope on the desk. "Were you on your way to the post office? That looks a little lumpy."

"It's a disassembled heater. Five rounds in the mag. We can talk about it later if you don't have time."

"Where did you get the bang-bang, partner?"

"I confiscated it from Edward Brinsley Cramp on Sunday."

"What was he packing?"

"I think it's a 30."

Max nodded. "There's lots of those around. I can recycle some of the parts, and trash the memorable ones. Can you put it in the safe for now?"

Back in his own office, he opened the safe and tucked the envelope inside. Calling good-bye to Max, he headed down to the street, and walked to Artémise's studio.

The guard on the door scowled at the sight of him, but didn't challenge him, letting him walk in. Stepping into Malcolm's office, he closed the door.

Malcolm was absorbed in his computer screen. "What is it?" he said, then looked up. His eyes grew wide, and his voice rose. "Hey, Slater. What's up? No violence."

"I know you sold the design file to Boyd."

"What are you talking about?"

"Cut the crap," he said through his teeth. "If you lie to me again, I will break you in half."

Malcolm sat back. "I don't know what to say."

"I know the idiot in the Bronco was working for you. If

you want to send a message, you need to hire better people. The guy was a total tyro. I tracked him down in half an hour."

Breathing hard now, Malcolm watched him for a moment before he spoke. "He said you climbed a utility pole to get away from him."

"He was chasing me with a hatchet."

"I didn't tell him to do that. He was improvising."

Slater jabbed a finger at him. "You are an emotional wreck."

"So what now?"

"Is that the only design you sold to Boyd?"

"I know there's no excuse. I broke Artémise's trust. I was in a financial jam."

"What kind of jam? Gambling debts? Your kept man putting the bite on you? Maybe you're addicted to a specific go-go boy down at the club. Or is it a sizzler at a gentlemen's club? Are you a switch hitter?" He raised his eyebrows. "Don't forget what I said about lying to me."

"Christ, man. I don't gamble, and I'm not into strippers. I was in the kind of jam where I had to choose between losing my apartment or losing my health insurance. They're already garnishing my salary for my unpaid student loans."

"Who was the guy in the Bronco?"

Malcolm winced. "A friend."

"A boyfriend? He was willing to risk a lot for you."

"That's a loaded word. He's definitely into me. I'd call him a hookup." He met his gaze. "Are you going to tell Artémise, or do you want me to?"

Slater scoffed. "Like I'd trust you to do that. Personally I don't care what you do. But if I was in your shoes, I wouldn't confess to anything. She'll sic the legal system on you."

His brow furrowed. Slater could see the wheels turning.

"So what do you want?"

"How did you meet Boyd?" Slater said.

"At a coffee place in the neighborhood. He was all friendly, and asked me about my laptop. It has an Artémise decal on it. We talked about the industry." Malcolm looked away. "At first I thought maybe he was interested in me."

"That's what he wanted you to think. He's a con man. It was your laptop, or Artémise's?"

"It belongs to the studio."

"Was it his idea or yours to sell him the paisley?"

"He asked. I know that doesn't make me less culpable."

"When you gave him the file and got paid, how did that go down?"

"I met him at the same place," Malcolm said, "and put it on a thumb drive. He gave me cash."

"OK." Watching him talk, Slater decided it all fit—he believed him.

"Aren't you going to ask me how much he paid me?"

"That doesn't matter." Slater waved a hand. "Have you heard of Irving Irving?"

"Of course. He's brilliant."

"I'm going to introduce you to him. He needs somebody who does what you do, and he pays a lot better than the richest woman in the country."

Malcolm's eyebrows shot up. "That's how you're going to resolve this? You're not going to rat me out?"

"Only if you can keep your mouth shut. If you get yourself indicted, you're on your own."

"Why would you do this when my guy came after you with an ax?"

"It was a hatchet." Slater raised his voice. "Why is that so hard to remember?" He scoffed. "I know why you did it. You created that design, and it's going to make somebody else millions. Rich idiots all over the planet are going to be wearing it. Meanwhile you're on food stamps and Medi-Cal."

"I knew that much going in," Malcolm said. "That's how our wondrous system works. What are you going to do about the paisley?"

"I'm shutting things down at the other end with Boyd. Do not talk to him again, no matter what. Even if he tries to contact you. Lose his number."

"Irving Irving is huge."

"It's just an interview. Don't tell him what you're earning now or he'll lowball you. And do not rip off his work, or I'll hear about it." He jabbed a finger at him. "And I'll come for you."

Slater walked out, and headed back to the parking lot, and drove to his house. Upstairs he found Pike dozing on the sofa, a book face-down on his chest.

As he knelt next to him, Pike stirred, and sat up, and set the book on the coffee table. Slater briefly met his mouth and nuzzled his neck, then moved up onto the sofa, resting his head in Pike's lap.

Pike ran his fingers into his hair. "You've been busy. Where's your case at? Have you seen Artémise again?"

"Svetlana says two people can keep a secret, if one of them is dead."

"She's right. People love to talk. When an informant is really chatty, you can just sit back and listen. They'll tell you a lot of what you need to know." Pike furrowed his brow. "What's secret? You've talked plenty about your case."

"Not my secrets. I've been rooting out other people's." He told him about the last few days, and what Boyd had done, and Malcolm.

"How did you get into Boyd's files?" Pike said.

"Of course that's the first thing you'd ask."

"You carefully omitted that detail. It's kind of a key element."

"If you're putting together an indictment."

Pike chuckled. "It's that same old thing about openness, and trust. I don't really need to know. But I do need your trust."

"Shaula is the guy's business partner, and the laptop was in their office. Shaula got into it."

"So Shaula flipped."

"I think I'm finally sold on that," Slater said. "I thought he might be playing me. But he did help me liberate Boyd's data, and what he saw in it pissed him off."

"Maybe fucking your targets isn't as chaos-inducing as it sounds."

Slater looked up at him. "You want some chaos? I can drill that into you."

"Right now?"

"That way I can eat more leisurely after."

Rising, Pike followed him down to the bedroom, and they both got undressed.

"I like that it's just us for a change." Pike climbed onto the bed, on his knees behind Slater, and ran his hands over his torso. "Let me fuck you like this."

Slater groaned as Pike pressed into him, and leaned back against him, turning his head to meet his mouth. Soon Pike was pounding him, his hot breath on his neck, sweat dripping from his hair. As he came, he grabbed Slater's cock, and massaged his chest, pumping him until he came too.

Stretching out on the bed, breathing hard, Slater could already feel his mind unspooling. Pike would wake him later to eat, and he'd need to imbibe his ration at some point, but for right now he surrendered to sleep.

THIRTY

▱▱▱▱▱▱▱▱▱▱▱

BRIGHT DAYLIGHT FILLED THE windows when Slater woke, gradually drifting up to consciousness. For a moment he was blissfully empty-headed, feeling warm and content. But even in this frame of mind he knew there was more. There was always more. This neutral state wouldn't last. It never did. Then it all crashed in at once, the awareness and the memories and everything else.

He had enough information for Artémise that he could wind things up and make a report, he decided. He hadn't really fixed anything, but he'd jostled Boyd's racket, and the guy would have more pressing concerns now. He could tell the client that it wouldn't happen again.

Forcing himself out of bed, Slater showered and then went up to the kitchen, and drank some of Pike's leftover java, and ate some fruit. Climbing in the Continental, he drove to Downtown, and parked at his office, and went upstairs.

No one was here, and he double-clicked his tongue to greet Rey Pascual as he flicked on the lights. He'd just settled in at his desk, mulling over what he was going to write for Artémise, when a sharp rap came at the door.

Rising, he pulled it open a few inches, keeping a boot firmly planted next to the inside surface. It was Boyd, a scowl on his face, a bruise blooming on the cheek where Slater's fist had made contact. Pike's ring had left a distinct mark.

"We need to talk," Boyd said.

"Are you armed?"

"Why would I be armed?" He scoffed. "I'm not a damn gangbanger."

Slater looked him up and down. The guy was amped, but not crazed, he decided. He pulled open the door, and waved him in, and sat in his office.

In front of his desk, Boyd stood glaring at him. He didn't have a very good poker face for a con man. His anger was evident, and so was the fact that he wasn't quite sure how angry he should be with Slater. That was a good sign. It meant he didn't know exactly what had gone down.

Leaning back, Slater gestured to the chair. "You can sit if you want."

Boyd didn't move. "I'm missing eight million dollars."

"That's a lot of jack. You should get high on the DMT. Maybe somebody in the neutral realm will know where it went."

"Where's my money?" he shouted.

"When you look at the larger picture, what does the money represent?" Slater flashed his palms. "What does it resemble in the dream state, or in the natural world? Eight million leaves of lettuce, perhaps, or eight million clams?"

"It's not hermeneutic. I've been robbed."

"I thought everything was subject to hermeneutics. Symbolically maybe all those zeroes represent the depth of your personality. Like you're actually a whole lot of nothing." He raised his eyebrows. "Like you're a zero."

Boyd shook his head. "You're not going to distract me by talking trash. Where's Shaula? I know you've been fucking him."

"Interesting that you link Shaula and the missing funds. Do you think he's involved? What does that evoke for you? Symbolically, I mean. Dig deep within."

His lip curled in disgust. "You goddamn lowlife. I am not fucking playing here."

"You flex like a philosopher, or the DMT guru, like you've achieved some state of tranquility from your drugs and your deep thoughts. But we both know you're really just running penny-ante bunco."

"Metaphysics isn't bunco."

"On some level, isn't all philosophy just unverifiable horseshit? Or maybe it's just you." Slater jabbed a finger at him. "You're trash. You sold that building out from under Shaula so you could do your own thing in the Palisades."

"You seem to know a lot. Are you in this with him? Maybe I'll go talk to the cops."

Slater guffawed, throwing his head back. "I've completely overestimated you. Your cis-het white privilege makes you think that's a viable path. That makes me think you've never done this before. Like you've never actually been on the receiving end of the justice system. Why would you think the cops would help you recover something that you stole?"

"There's no evidence of that." He huffed and thrust out his chest. "Tell me what you know, or I swear to god, I will mess you up."

"You and what army?" Slater threw up a hand. "Sure, you tried to make Shaula the patsy, but you're the one who's been robbing people blind, and you're going over for it."

Boyd's phone buzzed in his pants, and he growled and dug it out, glancing at the screen but not picking up. "Fuck," he roared, and walked out.

Rising, Slater followed him and bolted the front door. Without a doubt it was a mistake to say all that, to tell him what he knew, but it was impossible to keep his mouth shut in the face of the smack talk. It was so frustrating to be at the end of this and not have any way to get the fucker locked up.

Digging out his phone, he checked Shaula's location. Instead of the usual map, Svetlana's software displayed the message "Device closed," with a date and time in that weird Euro format. It took a second to sort out what it meant: Shaula's phone had been powered off since late yesterday.

Back in his chair, he heaved his boots onto the desk and pulled his keyboard into his lap. He composed a message to Irving Irving to introduce Malcolm, and then sent Malcolm a note about it. Irving was in the game for the money just like Artémise was, but at least he was a creative type, and he might have a little more respect for Malcolm's work. Next he started on the report for Artémise, thinking through what he'd learned and typing out the details. He needed to explain it all, and explain that the leak was fixed, without actually implicating Malcolm.

His focus was broken by a knock at the door. Rising, he opened it a crack to reveal Shaula. Stepping back, he pulled it wide and waved him in. The guy looked antsy, his face flushed.

"Did you have a good meeting with Boyd?" he demanded.

"I remember—you can track that gonif. It's a good thing he can't track you. I think he wants to have a word."

"Fuck that guy," Shaula said. "What did he want with you?"

Slater gestured to his office. "You want to come in and sit down?"

"Answer me."

He put his hands on his hips. "Boyd is angry that a bunch of dough seems to have gone missing."

"It was never his money. What did you tell him?"

He frowned. "What do you think I told him?"

Shaula took a breath. "Well, I'm leaving town, and you can't stop me."

"Why would I stop you? You're a smoke-show, Shaula. A bite-size snack. But I don't actually care what you do."

He watched him for a moment, then spoke in a calmer tone. "I believe you."

"What about your mission from the future? That meeting you waited two years for."

"I handled it. It feels like everything happens at once. I wasn't supposed to get mixed up in a criminal enterprise while I was waiting, but here we are. Anyway, I'm free to leave. Boyd won't be around for long either. I emailed that documentation to every one of the clients we scammed. I left my name out of it and implicated Boyd."

"Bold move," Slater said. "They're still going to know you were involved, since you're the one who got into their systems."

"That doesn't matter. I won't be around. They'll be looking for Boyd."

"That might already be happening. He got a call when he was here that made smoke come out of his ears."

"In the end going after him is pointless," Shaula said. "They'll never see their money again, and they won't be compensated for the designs Boyd took."

"Still, some of those clients will likely go to the cops. That means at some point the prosecutors will be looking for you both."

Shaula spread his arms. "Fine by me."

"This is way more believable," Slater said, furrowing his brow.

"What are you talking about?"

"Your anger, and the tacit admission that you jacked Boyd, and by extension that you're still down with the IT grift. It feels more real than your change of heart when I shoved you over the railing. Was that your angle all along? You wanted to con me into helping you screw Boyd?"

"I can't believe you'd think that about me. After what we shared. I was actually going to ask you to come in on the consulting business. Before I found out Boyd had sold it out from under me."

"The pieces fit, though," Slater said. "Maybe you wanted to elbow him out of the gimmick, and he beat you to it. He got the drop on you and screwed you first."

"You've seen his files. You know damn well he was planning all along to edge me out. He set me up to be the fall guy." He scoffed. "You think I'd do something like that. You really are a bottom feeder."

"Who's the grifter in the room, man? I never robbed anybody." Slater threw up his hands. "Do you not see that? You need to take a long hard look at yourself in the mirror."

"I need to go."

"Hold on a minute. Did you put the bite on any of the saps so hard that they went out of business?"

"I told you we were playing the long game," Shaula said. "Copies of clothing designs and small transactions spread through time and across multiple clients. That's what Andy saw too, isn't it? And why does that matter now?"

"It feels like a mistake to let you walk away with the dough," Slater said. "You stole from all those people."

"I told them about it. Every one of them. Their designs are already out in the world, but they can shut down the recurring transactions."

It really was small potatoes, Slater knew. Shaula and Boyd were parasites, not predators. Mistletoe rather than a chainsaw. The oaks might be weakened but they still stood. They hadn't ruined anyone. It was easier just to let it go.

"I guess that works. If you made Boyd the patsy for the whole scheme, he can take the rap."

Shaula frowned. "Of course he can take it. It was his idea."

"I guess human nature hasn't changed in the future."

"What are you talking about? I'm still not going back. I'm going to stay in this era. Just not around here."

Slater raised his eyebrows. "You should check out New Orleans. It's almost as fun as LA. A hermeneutic consulting business might really take off there."

He frowned. "I'll make note of your input."

"That's what you're going to do, isn't it? You lost that building, but Boyd hasn't bought land in the Palisades yet. So now you've got the scratch to fade and set up somewhere else."

"I'm still pissed at Boyd."

"You still stole from people. At least you didn't merc the guy."

"No regrets, Slater. Just rage."

"I feel you, brother." He jutted his chin. "Give me the key to your studio."

"Why?"

"What do you care? I was hired to find out how that bolt of paisley got into the display window. If Boyd is preoccupied, he won't mind if I tax it."

"I guess I'm not going to need it again." Shaula dug in his pocket and gave him the key. "Just don't trash the place. Francesca doesn't deserve that."

He tucked the key into his jeans. "I'll make note of your input."

"I suppose I should thank you for helping me."

"You should thank me for letting you skate."

Shaula frowned. "Adios, then," he said, and walked out.

Stepping into his office, Slater locked his computer with a keystroke, then killed the lights, and went down to the street. Up the block he stopped into a tiendita and bought a little can of lighter fluid and a stick lighter.

Walking up on A Touch of Class, he saw that the security grate was down. He used the key to unlock it, and roll it up, and then let himself in. The lights were off, and Boyd's laptop was gone from his desk.

Once he'd bolted the door, he reached up and unplugged the security camera, then went to the display window and pulled out the bolt of paisley. It was taped down in a couple of places, but it came loose with a firm yank. The daylight had faded parts of it, diminishing the washed-out purples and browns even more.

Shaula had said there were two bolts of it. He looked around in the back and found the second roll on a shelf. Its open edge was jagged, where swatches had been cut from it, including the one he'd asked for himself at the trade show. There'd been a shirt in that fashion show made from this, he remembered, and dug through the clothing rack, and pulled it off its hanger.

He hadn't been out back before, but when he pushed open the door to the alley, he saw that it was gated at both ends. It was gritty, with dumpsters and broken asphalt, but the gates meant there were no tents or shopping carts or passed-out fetty zombies. It felt messed up that this was as good as it got, an alley that smelled like dumpsters and not like an open sewer.

Dropping the bolts in the swale in the middle of the alley, he kicked one of them to unroll a couple of yards, and tossed the shirt on top, then doused it all with lighter fluid. Digging out his phone, he called Gene, glad that she picked up.

"I have some results for you," Slater said.

"Artémise is away. She's doing a guest lecture at a symposium at a university in Europe."

"A lecture? Does she have a degree in something?"

"She's a cultural icon. That's more important than any degree."

"If you say so. Anyway, Artémise wasn't the only victim. The fabric store owner, a guy named Boyd, pilfered digital files from lots of people."

"He hacked our design office?" Gene said.

"That leak is sealed now, and Boyd took a powder. I'm thinking the pirated fabric won't appear anywhere else."

"How did the design get out of our studio?"

"Boyd was able to get into one of your laptops when it was out of the office. I'll write you a report with the specifics."

"That would be helpful."

"I'm going to switch to video," Slater said. "Can you record this for the boss?"

"Sure. Give me a second." A minute later, Gene said, "I'm rolling."

Slater looked into the camera. "I managed to retrieve the counterfeit fabric. There were only two bolts of it manufactured. I confiscated them both."

He tapped the screen to switch to the back camera, and aimed it at the fabric piled on the concrete. Squatting, he clicked the lighter with his free hand. The flame caught with a woof and spread rapidly down the length of the pile. Slater stepped back to film it burning.

"Artémise is going to love this," Gene said.

"I figured."

He held the camera steady on the flames. The black smoke was getting thicker, and it smelled like burning plastic. Smoke and ash. That had been in the book he and Pike were reading. Smoke and ash were the offerings to Hades, god of the underworld, to release people from his anger. Maybe this would help Artémise release her anger.

In a minute he'd end the call, and grab the fire extinguisher mounted on the wall inside the back door of the shop, and douse the flames before Francesca or someone else freaked out and called the fire department, then scoop the remnants into a dumpster. His report would explain to Artémise that she got what she wanted, got what she paid him for. But entertainment people liked a show. That's what the smoke and flames were. It fit with Shaula's hermeneutics too. Torching these bolts meant burning down the whole damn racket.

———◆———